UNKNOWN THREAT

Marshal Series
Book 1

Robin Lyons

COPYRIGHT

ACKNOWLEDGMENTS

To my husband, Jon, because of your continued support and understanding, I am able to fulfill my dream to write books. To my biggest fans, my son, Chris, daughter, Jessica, and sister, Gwen, your love, encouragement, and excitement have fueled my passion to write.

After twenty years of service, my son-in-law, Alex recently retired from the U.S. Air Force. I'm so proud of him. His assistance with the military content was and continues to be extremely helpful.

My extended family and friends have been patient and encouraging while I've written and rewritten and rewritten. I appreciate all of you so much.

CREDITS:

EDITING & PROOFREADING: Write Divas, Editing Service; Affordable Proofreading & Editing Service; Word Refiner, Proofreading Service

LAW ENFORCEMENT: El Dorado County Sheriff Jeff Neves, retired; El Dorado County Sheriff Captain Craig Therkildsen, retired

SECRET DOOR: Steve Humble, president of Creative Home Engineering

INTRODUCTION

Dear Reader,

This famous quote by Andre Malraux describes several of the characters in Unknown Threat, "Man is not what he thinks he is; he is what he hides."

Sergeant Mac MacKenna retires after 20 years as a pararescueman in an elite special ops unit in the U.S. Air Force and returns to his hometown. Aiding others at all costs is what the air force trained Mac to do—it's all he's known for his entire adult life.

Mac admittedly knows nothing about children or school other than he remembers being a child and attending school.

When the police chief asks Mac to pose as a marshal at Brookfield Academy to rid the school of crime—he accepts the mission. Soon enough, Mac's former life of loaded weapons and death-defying rescues is replaced with tangled webs of deceit, twisted wealthy and powerful people, murder, and a dangerous den of corruption disguised as a prestigious academy.

Unfortunately for Mac, meddling with the rich can have deadly consequences.

Best regards,

Robin Lyons

ROBIN'S READER CLUB

Learn more about Mac MacKenna in **MAC: A prequel Novella**. The ebook is a FREE gift when you join Robin's Reader Club.

Reader Club Members are automatically included in FREE curated, member's only bookish giveaways. Because of sweepstakes laws and shipping cost, most giveaways (not all) are only available to USA residents. Robin's family members are not eligible for drawings.

Email addresses are never shared. Robin values your privacy as much as hers.

Join on the website at: www.robinlyons.com

UNKNOWN
THREAT

CHAPTER 1

The morning began with a hike in Desolation Wilderness. Mac MacKenna, and his dog Roxy, a long-haired black and tan German Shepherd rescue, hiked at 7,000 feet above sea level.

Twin Lakes trail head begins and ends just after the Chappell Crossing Bridge. Mac had enjoyed going to the peaceful and quiet mountaintop escape since he could drive. On this day, a Tuesday, he and Roxy had the trail all to themselves. As a form of therapy, Mac often rose early to hike up the mountain and catch the sunrise. Roxy tagged along sniffing trace scents from everyone and everything that had come before them.

Sometime around noon, they arrived back at Mac's truck feeling refreshed. For several years the area had experienced severe drought making it possible to hike in April.

Mac gave Roxy some water and let her sniff around while he stripped off his flannel jacket and tossed it onto the passenger seat. After ample time to cool down, he hoisted Roxy up onto the backseat, mindful of her breed's tendency for hip issues. Besides, he was in no hurry. Since his retirement from the U.S. Air Force, he took life one day at a time.

Mac found retirement a bit boring compared to the military. He'd torn down the wall between the kitchen and living room to open up the space and install hardwood floors in an old Victorian house he'd purchased in his hometown of Brookfield, California. Remodeling his home gave him something to do.

As he headed west on the highway, Mac's cell phone rang. It was his long-time buddy, Jason. They'd both joined the air force while in their senior year of high school. Jason stayed in eight years and then returned home to become a police officer.

Mac pressed the call button on his steering wheel, "Hey, Jason, how's it going?"

"Can't complain. Do you have a few minutes to talk?" he asked.

"Sure. Roxy and I just finished hiking up at Wright's Lake. We're headed back to town. I'm about to pull into Handley's to pick up cinnamon rolls for Maggie and the girls. What'd you need?"

Mac's older sister Maggie and her two daughters lived on the other side of town in the home where she and Mac grew up.

"Did you see any snow up there? Feel free to drop off some cinnamon rolls here at the office; they're the best."

"I just might. No snow, not even in the shady spots."

Mac waited in his lane to turn left into Handley's parking lot.

"It's gonna be a bad fire season. Do you have plans to leave the area anytime soon or are you sticking around?" he asked.

"That's pretty vague. What's up?" Mac was intrigued.

"I have a job for you if you're interested. To tell the truth, I need your help."

"Keep talking," Mac said as pulled straight into a parking spot near the front door.

"Blackstone Academy has a serious drug problem. In fact, over the weekend, the mayor's fourteen-year-old son overdosed and almost died. He's in the hospital recovering. Heroin, we think. Lucky for him, his older brother found him and called 911 shortly after he went unconscious. The police chief and the school board president want someone on the inside to help identify the source of the drugs. Somebody's getting rich over there and the next time there's an overdose the kid might not be so lucky."

Jason paused, took a drink of something.

"I'm not sure how I can help." Mac watched the lunch crowd pile into the coffee shop.

"They want someone outside of law enforcement so that nobody will tag him or her as an undercover cop. I suggested you. Everyone in town knows you're ex-Air Force. The Chief thinks you're the right guy for the assignment."

"He doesn't know me. Am I supposed to pretend to be a teacher or something?"

Mac glanced in the rearview mirror and saw Roxy was still asleep.

"He knows of you. Small town chitchat. No, the board wants to hire a marshal to watch over the students and staff because of the increase in school violence across the nation. The Chief thinks it's the perfect cover. The superintendent and other school board members won't be privy to your real purpose. But they're in agreement it's time to hire a marshal."

"I don't know shit about kids, or about schools. I don't see how

I could be the right man for the job."

"Your military experience with air force special ops trumps your lack of experience with kids."

"Is there some training?"

"As a matter of fact, California recently began a marshal program like the one Texas has had in place for many years. The Chief thought you could do it over the summer and be ready to roll when school starts."

"What about training on how to deal with kids? What age kids are we talking about?"

"Kindergarten through twelfth grade. The young ones are on one side of the school and the older students on the other."

"So, I'd need to deal with all ages is what you're saying? And what about the parents? I'm not the best people person." Mac paused. "How long will the job last?"

"You'll mostly deal with the older students. On occasion, the younger ones. But they aren't bringing drugs and weapons into schools. At least not yet, anyway. It's a public school, but some parents act like they own the place, they can be a little territorial at times. Not sure if they'll like that you're there or not. I can't sugarcoat any part of this for you. How long depends on how long it takes you to figure out who's dealing the drugs."

Mac fell silent.

"Mac, are you still having nightmares about the sandbox?"

"I know where you're going with that, Jason. The kids playing near the car when the bomb went off. We wanted to help, but weren't allowed to."

"That's it," Jason said, "It haunted me for a few years. The time I've spent giving back to the community has helped me feel like a better person. I seldom have nightmares anymore. Maybe the marshal gig will help you push past it. Another thing to consider, Maggie might shift the girls to Blackstone for high school. Better to clean up the drugs before they get there."

"That's hitting below the belt."

"I'm just throwing it out there for you to consider." Jason continued his pitch, "And, it's a paid position."

"You do know I receive a pension from the air force, right?"

"We all know the retirement pay is shitty. You could pay for the remodeling of your house, pay off your truck, and travel when school isn't in session."

Mac exhaled loud enough to cause Roxy to open her eyes and

glance up to be certain all was well. "I'll give it some thought and get back to you."

"That works. You'll see this will be a good assignment for you. You may not know it yet, but you're the perfect guy for this job."

"I haven't said yes yet."

"The school board will approve your hiring at their June meeting. You should plan to attend and get a feel for how it works. Remember, nobody must know what you're doing there. Trust no one other than me, my partner Dan Ruiz, Chief Contee, and the school board president Michael Stromberg. Also, the Chief spoke to the school board about hiring a marshal. And whether or not he or she should carry a weapon. They agreed to amend their policy that prohibits weapons on campus by excluding the marshal."

"Jason, I haven't said yes yet."

CHAPTER 2

As Jason had suggested, Mac went to the June school board meeting to see how things worked. He wasn't sure if he was ready for more bureaucracy.

"Psst, mister," the small brunette seated to Mac's right patted his thigh, "would you like a sign?" She smelled of too much perfume which failed to hide the hint of booze on her breath.

Expecting him to accept, she pushed a cardboard sign at him, the homemade poster board kind with a tongue depressor-style handle. It resembled the ones seen at high school sports events that say 'Go Team Go.' Except this one had a photo of a pistol inside a circle with a dark line through its center. Written above the crossed-out handgun photo was 'NO GUNS,' and beneath it, 'At Blackstone Academy.' Moms and dads, but mostly moms, held similar signs face down on their laps.

"No, thanks," Mac said.

She gave him a puzzled look and waited for him to change his mind.

The meeting room had theater seating with ten rows of forty seats and an aisle down the middle leading to the podium. Each row sat higher than the one in front, giving everyone an unobstructed view.

Of the two hundred or so people in the audience about half held protest signs. Only a few of the brave, well-dressed men and women ventured to the podium. They spoke into the microphone with quivering voices. None had been happy, but all were polite and courteous. Unlike the man currently at the podium. This guy was one smug son of a bitch. He looked about Mac's age, short by anyone's standards, he had dark hair and was clean shaven. And if Mac were to wager a guess, the man's suit cost more than his first airman's paycheck.

The crowd was amped up, feeding off the speaker's hostility. A man in the audience yelled, "No guns at school." Heads turned toward him.

"Order. Order." Michael Stromberg, president of Blackstone

Academy's school board, banged his gavel on the square of wood. "Order in the boardroom." He continued to pound his gavel until all voices quieted.

President Stromberg leaned closer to the microphone. His posture stiffened. He said in a booming voice, "Randall, if you cannot refrain from using profanity while addressing this board, you'll need to leave the room."

President Stromberg was a large man, not so much in size as in presence. He was older than Mac by a good ten years; his skin appeared weathered from too much time in the sun. A tall man, he spoke with a deep baritone voice and gave off a Hollywood mobster, kingpin vibe. Not someone Mac intended to cross. His signature cowboy hat hung alone on the coat rack in the corner. He'd worn a similar one two weeks prior when he'd offered Mac the marshal job. The silver and turquoise collar tips on his fancy white shirt matched his bolo tie.

Marlene, the superintendent's administrative assistant, told Mac, President Stromberg was a modern-day cowboy, a local cattle rancher who'd done quite well. That explained his deep tan and premature wrinkles. Marlene, a sweet, older lady, gossiped a bit too much for Mac's taste.

No sound from the other board members. The three men and one woman's nameplates all included the title 'Doctor' in front of their names.

Mac's phone was on silent. He typed a text to his sister.

Mac: Are you still up?

Maggie: Yes. How's the meeting?

Mac: A jackass is speaking at the podium. Parents are waving signs that read, NO GUNS.

Maggie: Not feeling the love?

While President Stromberg continued to admonish the speaker for his use of profanity, the fragrant woman to Mac's right patted his thigh again. She leaned his way and whispered, "Do you have kids at Blackstone?"

He stared at her for a long moment. She was about his age, wore too much makeup, had fake fingernails, and an unnatural looking tan. "No," he said.

"Are you from the newspaper? Why are you here?"

"To observe."

"Observe what?"

He returned his attention to the front of the room. In his

peripheral vision, he saw the woman lean over to the lady on her right and whisper.

In the front of the room, each board member had a microphone and a laptop that sat lower than the table giving them a clear view of the audience. The blue hue from the screens in front of them illuminated their faces. At the far right, Marlene took notes. With lightning speed, she clicked on her keyboard.

"Randall, California's schools, are beginning to employ marshals, or resource officers on their campuses whether you like it or not. We received a grant to participate in a state-run marshal pilot program like the one in Texas. It's a done deal. On behalf of the board, we thank you for sharing your thoughts and opinions. Now sit down." President Stromberg dismissed the speaker with a flip of his hand.

The man didn't budge. He leaned in so his mouth almost kissed the microphone. "That's it? That's all you have to say?" He pounded his fist on the podium. "Not acceptable. You need to explain to all of us why you morons think we need a guard with a loaded gun on our campus. To hell with the state program. To hell with the program in Texas. I want answers, and I'm not sitting down until I get them."

A rumble rippled through the audience members. Several people waved their signs in the air. The inquisitive woman on Mac's right waved hers with great enthusiasm.

President Stromberg banged his gavel in rapid succession until the audience quieted down and signs landed on laps.

The speaker gripped the sides of the podium, as though he were about to go for a bobsled ride. His elbows extended out from his body. "Our school hasn't had problems. We don't have gangs, the kids don't do drugs, and they come from good homes. An armed guard standing sentry like they're entering a prison sends the wrong message to our kids. We pay a lot of money for our kids to attend school here. Excuse me; we donate a lot of money. So unless you want a serious hit to your pocketbook, you better reconsider." His voice cracked and squeaked like a thirteen-year-old boy's.

"You don't intimidate me with your threats, Randall." President Stromberg jabbed his gavel toward the speaker. "Listen up folks. A committee made up of parents and staff decided we needed a marshal. They developed the job responsibilities for the position. The committee also screened the applications and narrowed their selection to three candidates. Superintendent

Sawyer and I made the final decision."

The speaker waited his turn to speak. "Gosh, Michael, that sounds so professional. Thanks for sharing, but I doubt the parents on your damn committee knew you planned to allow the person to carry a loaded gun."

President Stromberg motioned with his gavel to include the four other board members. "We discussed the final candidate at length before offering the job. And for the record, we are fortunate and honored to have someone as experienced as our finalist. He's a decorated Chief Master Sergeant retired from the U.S. Air Force Special Operations. He's undergone emergency medical training and is a weapons specialist. He fought in Iraq during Operation Desert Thunder and Desert Fox. His unit also helped rescue and treat victims of Hurricane Katrina. I could go on, but you look as if I were boring you, Randall. One last point, he's already scheduled to attend an 80-hour Marshal training course during the summer. 'We'…" again he motioned to include the board as a whole, "approved the marshal to carry a loaded handgun." A collective gasp rippled through the audience. "Police Chief Contee supports our decision. The marshal won't be prancing around the campus waving a gun. If there were a real threat, I'd want him to protect your kids and the staff. Should a threat present itself, we expect him to use his weapon only when necessary."

Like zombies, the four other board members lowered their heads and shifted their attention downward to their laptop monitors. A loud rumble spread through the quiet room. Signs bobbed up and down.

The speaker opened his mouth to respond. Before he said anything, President Stromberg held up his hand to stop him.

President Stromberg waited for the room to quiet again before he continued. "I'm not going to engage in further conversation with you about our new marshal's employment. Furthermore, Randall, if you or the other parents have a problem with our decisions on how to keep your children safe while they're on campus, then I suggest you run for office in the November election. Your three minutes were up ten minutes ago. Step away from the podium and either leave the room or take a seat and be quiet."

The harsh, overhead fluorescent lighting, spotlighted President Stromberg's red face. His jaw jutted out, and a vein bulged across his forehead. He looked like he needed to loosen the slider on his bolo tie.

The speaker left the podium in a huff and went to a small woman sitting in the front row. He pulled her to her feet by her arm and yanked her along as he stormed out of the room.

"If anyone has a comment we haven't already heard, please step up to the podium," offered President Stromberg.

The audience sat frozen. Heads turned right then left. Nobody stood. No signs waved in the air.

The woman seated to Mac's right whispered too loud to the lean, athletic-looking woman on her right, "My kids have never seen a real gun. I don't like this. At all."

"My son hasn't seen a real gun, either. I'm undecided how I feel about it. I want to see how it plays out once school starts."

"Well, we'll see about the ridiculous notion that a glorified security guard should carry a loaded gun. I know people," the alcohol-fueled woman said, as she crossed her arms and straightened her posture.

Mac was like the proverbial fly on the wall. The hot topic of hiring a marshal had lasted about an hour. Of the parents who'd spoken on record, there'd been a common theme of dissension concerning him carrying a loaded gun. The school board understood disallowing him to carry a weapon would nullify his acceptance of their job offer.

President Stromberg banged the gavel hard, twice. His face glowed red. "Is there a motion to approve hiring Mac MacKenna as our new marshal?" he asked, through his teeth into the microphone.

"I move to approve the new marshal," Dr. Littleton said, a small, meek-looking man with gray hair combed over a balding head.

Another man leaned in and seconded the motion. President Stromberg banged the gavel again. "All those in favor?"

The three male board members plus President Stromberg leaned in and said, "Aye." Stromberg stared at the lone female board member, Dr. Ward, who'd said nothing.

"Those opposed?" asked President Stromberg glaring at the woman.

Dr. Ward leaned into her microphone without looking at the school board president and said, "Nay." Most of the audience jumped to their feet and applauded.

"Are you serious, Wanda?" He continued to look at her, as he banged his gavel and said, "Motion carries."

Wanda ignored him.

President Stromberg banged his gavel hard and bellowed into his microphone, "Order. Order. Order in the boardroom."

CHAPTER 3

Mac woke early on the first day of school. Even though the job was more a favor for Jason, he felt a bit excited and maybe a little nervous. Not that he'd admit either to anyone.

He checked himself in the mirror. He'd visited the barber on Sunday for a haircut and shave. He asked for his hair to be left a little shaggy and to leave some stubble on his face. He'd had his last buzz cut a month before he retired. It felt liberating to no longer have rules to follow, dictating his appearance and behavior.

Since his weapon was a heated discussion at the June board meeting, he decided to use a concealed waistband holster attached to the belt on his jeans. Leaving his t-shirt untucked should help hide his controversial handgun.

Roxy knew something was up. An anxious habit, she paced in the kitchen while Mac made his lunch. When Mac looked at her, she tilted her head one way and then the other trying to understand what was happening.

"No girl, you stay here," he said.

She flopped down with a thud onto her cushioned dog bed in the corner of the alcove off the kitchen.

"Roxy, it's okay."

On his way out the door, he scratched her big hairy neck to ease her nerves. When the back door shut, she followed by way of her giant-sized dog door. She stood in the fenced backyard and watched him drive away.

Anticipating a hot day, Mac rode his motorcycle to his new job. He had arrived an hour before school started. There were a few other early-risers parked in the staff parking lot across from the school's main entrance.

Mac flashed his ID badge at the scanner, and the main door slid open. He stepped inside and paused. The school was quiet. On the way to his office, the third door on the right, the one with the large bold word 'SECURITY' written on it, sat Marlene, sentry to the boss.

"Good morning, Marlene."

"Right back at you," she said, as she popped her gum. "Are you ready for the kiddos and their parents?"

"I'm as ready as I can be, never having dealt with kids before."

"If you have questions or concerns, come see me. And, you let me know if anyone bothers you." She winked and returned her attention to her computer screen.

Dismissed by Marlene, Mac swallowed hard and went outside to the front of the school. Part of his job required him to watch the kids as they arrived.

The clasp on the flag clanged against the metal flagpole. Reality washed over Mac. He was about to enter a foreign world. Kids. Busybody parents. Politics.

Parents started to park across the street and walk their kids to the school.

"You must be Mac?" Someone said from behind him.

He turned to see a tall young lady with a bouncy ponytail walking toward him.

Mac thought she might be a student. She was at least twenty years younger than him.

"I'm Roni," she said, thrusting her hand out to shake. "I'm your partner in crime. Just kidding. I have monitor duty before and after school too, sort of like your assistant. Is it true you were…"

"You." a woman screeched from the direction neither Mac nor Roni faced. They both spun around to see who made the fuss.

"Good morning, Mrs. Ross," Roni said with a cheerful voice.

The woman ignored Roni.

Mac recognized the woman he'd sat next to at the board meeting in June.

The mother held her little girl's hand tight. Mom on a mission, she stormed straight toward Mac and Roni. Her son followed. She was quick to send her son and daughter into the school. She stood before Mac with a hands-on-hips, feet-planted stance.

"You. You're the new marshal. Why did you pretend to be from the newspaper at the board meeting in June?" Her bare chest was crimson and blotchy; the redness spread up her neck.

Roni looked confused.

Mac's hand went up to stop her in her tracks. "Whoa, wait a minute, lady. I didn't pretend to be from the newspaper," he replied. "I said I was there to observe and that was the truth."

She squared her shoulders and planted her high heels. Again, she wore too much perfume, and maybe a possible faint hint of booze.

"Do not speak to my daughter," she said waving her index finger in his face.

"Okay," he said.

"I don't want you anywhere near her. Do you understand?" she said.

"Okay."

"I mean it," she said.

"Okay."

She turned and stomped back to her Jaguar.

Mac shrugged at Roni.

The front of the school buzzed with kids and parents. Moms, dads, nannies, and chauffeurs dropped off their darlings on the sidewalk before speeding off to do whatever they did while their kids were in school.

Family cars of the rich looked the same on the inside as everyone else's. Strewn about were candy wrappers, fast food remnants, and empty water bottles. Animated movies played on six-inch screens nestled into the backs of headrests. Stained car seats, toys, and other kid stuff cluttered the interior.

The younger boys scanned Mac up and down. The girls looked and giggled. All students wore blue and white uniforms and approached at a brisk pace from all directions. The older kids, boys, and girls alike, didn't pay much attention to the new marshal. Almost all said hello to Roni.

The young kids also said good morning to Mac, and more parents than expected introduced themselves. Ten or so even thanked him for his service to the country.

By lunchtime, those who ignored Mac on the way into school asked him questions. Did he wear a gun? Where was it? Where did he learn how to be a marshal? Why did the school need a marshal? What was a marshal? Would he be at the school every day? The standard interrogation.

Savannah Ross even said hello to Mac. Her demeanor was much more calm and polite than her mother's. She asked him if he was married and if he had kids or pets. She squealed when he told her about Roxy. She said they had a dog and a cat.

Nothing could have prepared Mac for the auditory assault brought on by hundreds of kids confined to one area.

Teddy Ross stopped Mac as he left the cafeteria. "Mr. Mac, what types of markets do dogs avoid?" His face looked serious as he peered over the top of his glasses.

"I'm not sure Teddy. What types of markets do dogs avoid?"

"Flea markets. Hahahaha." He chuckled and then laughed so hard he bent over slapping his leg. It took him a minute to pull himself together. "Get it? Flea markets."

"I got it. That's funny Teddy. You're quite the jokester." He couldn't help but smile because of his vivacious personality and a mass of brown curls that went every which way. Teddy also differed from his mother. His eyeglasses seemed to spend more time on the tip of his nose than on the bridge. Parts of his shirt hung out of his shorts, and he had a big Band-Aid on one knee.

"What'd you do to your knee?" Mac pointed.

Teddy looked down at his leg. "Oh, that. I rode my bike too fast downhill. My bike got the high-speed wobbles. When I tried to round a curve, I crashed into a bush. It's nothing." He shrugged.

By early afternoon, the noise level had given Mac a headache. He was more than ready for the day to end. Roni stood next to him in front of the calm school while they waited for the dismissal bell to sound.

"Is it true you were in Special Ops in the Air Force?" Roni said.

"I was."

"The single teachers are already talking about how handsome you are, wait until they hear that."

Across the street in the visitor parking lot, fathers waiting for their kids exchanged head nods with Mac. Mothers smiled. Mrs. Ross slammed the door of her Jaguar and marched toward them. The perfume assault arrived before she did.

"Did you speak to my daughter today?" she said with the same hint of booze on her breath. Sweat beads formed on her nose.

"Your daughter spoke to me."

"I told you not to talk to her."

"She approached me."

The bell rang, and kids exploded through the main door.

Other parents observed the confrontation unfold as they hustled their kids past Mrs. Ross and Mac. Roni stood her ground next to Mac in a show of solidarity.

Mrs. Ross jabbed her index claw toward Mac's chest. "I'm serious when I say you aren't to converse with my daughter. You're the adult."

"Mrs. Ross, have I offended you? You seem angry with me."

She poked her finger at him again. "Stay away from my daughter. I mean it."

"Look, Mrs. Ross. We're going to have to figure out a way to get along. I was…"

Savannah bounced out of the building toward her mother. "Hi, baby. How was your first day?" She knelt down and hugged her daughter.

Dr. Jekyll and Mrs. Ross.

Mac stayed at the front of the school waiting for stragglers to leave. He received a text from his sister.

Maggie: How was your first day?

Mac: Remember the woman at the board meeting? With the protest sign?

Maggie: Yes.

Mac: She forbade me from speaking to her daughter.

Maggie: Because?

Mac: Unhappy they hired me. She accused me of posing as a reporter at the meeting in June.

CHAPTER 4

School had been in session for one week. Every morning Mac heard fifteen-second snippets of conversations about homework, or lunch or going to practice or piano lessons after school. Most parents said 'I love you' as their offspring hustled away from them. A few moms planted a kiss, their sentiment filled with sweetness.

There were a handful of parents who appeared loveless, at least in public, anyway. Then there were a few parents who seemed downright mean to their kids. Kevin Jackson's father, the parent who'd asked the school board members at the June board meeting, which moron thought they needed a guard with a loaded gun, was one of those parents.

Mr. Jackson stopped his fancy red sports car at the curb. Kevin flung open the passenger door and hit the sidewalk running. Mr. Jackson slammed the transmission into park and thrust himself out of the driver's seat with the speed of a tiger. Not a single strand of his perfect hair style fell out of place. He yelled to his son, "Kevin, come back here." He smoothed the seatbelt creases from his suit jacket. Kevin had almost made it to the school entrance when he turned and walked back to where his father's car sat idling at the curb.

Mac took in a slow, deep breath and watched the parent-kid interaction before glancing at his wrist watch. Time was ticking, and the disturbance was holding up the drop-off routine.

Roni leaned toward Mac. "He's such a jerk. He does this almost every day. What's his problem?" she whispered, as she bobbed her head toward the Jacksons. "And Kevin creeps me out."

In Mac's peripheral vision he saw someone headed his way, he knew by the fragrance in the air Mrs. Ross was about to stage another attack. She shooed Teddy and Savannah toward the school entrance.

"Well, Mr. Marshal, start marshaling and make Mr. Jackson stop bullying his son. Why do the rest of us have to hear their family squabbles every morning?"

Mr. Jackson appeared to have overhead Mrs. Ross and changed his focus from Kevin to her. "Anna Beth, our 'family squabbles' are none of your business. Shut the fuck up."

Mrs. Ross gasp and put her hand to her chest as if she were to have said, 'Who, me?' His brashness stunned her. She turned and retreated to the safety of her car.

Mr. Jackson returned his attention back to his son.

There was a tug on Mac's pant leg. "Mr. Mac?"

Without looking, he knew by the distinctive sing-song style with just enough nasal whine that it was Jillian, his little first-grade gal pal.

"Good morning, Miss Jillian. How are you this morning?" he replied without shifting his gaze.

She tugged on his pant leg again and dismissed his inquiry. "Did that big boy do something bad?" she asked.

"I don't think so, Jillian. Go on inside before the bell rings."

She held her ground, her concern evident by her stubbornness. Mac looked down into her golden-brown eyes and turned her shoulders in the direction of the school entrance.

"Please go inside before the bell rings."

Jillian turned back toward Mac and then looked at the scene the Jacksons were making.

Roni placed her hands gently on Jillian's shoulders and turned her toward the school entrance. "Go inside Jillian," Roni said.

Jillian did as Roni told her to do. When she crossed the threshold of the school, the first bell sounded signaling school would begin in five minutes.

Kevin's father clenched his jaw. His face reddened. He wasn't much taller than Kevin. An inch, maybe.

Kevin stood an arm's length from his father.

Mr. Jackson took hold of his son by the lapels of his shirt and yanked him close.

"I hate that he yells at…" Roni started to say.

"Hey," Mac pushed off from the brick wall and yelled at Mr. Jackson in an authoritative voice that made stragglers stop and look.

Mr. Jackson looked at Mac. Kevin looked also.

At this exact moment all around the world, parents were abusing their kids. At this time and place, it wasn't happening on Mac's watch.

Mr. Jackson pushed Kevin away like he'd launched a boat

from a dock. Kevin's slight body stumbled head first, but his over-sized feet caught up with him after a step or two. He hurried toward the school.

While pretending not to look at the Jacksons, parents scurried along the sidewalk with their kids in tow. Kids gawked at the Jacksons. Parents turned their sons and daughters away from the confrontation and told them to hurry along.

The chatter from kid to parent and vice versa had gone quiet.

As Mac walked to the fancy red sports car, he said, "You don't need to get physical with your boy. You're upsetting the other kids. It's time to move on."

Mr. Jackson walked toward Mac.

"Mind your own fucking business," Mr. Jackson said.

"Move your car. You're holding up the other parents."

"I'll move my fucking car when I'm ready to move it." He stood like a statue.

"Your son has gone inside. You have no further business here. It's time to leave," Mac said, as he turned around to walk away.

"You've made a big mistake," Mr. Jackson said.

The next thing Mac heard was the slam of his car door. Then his car sped away from the curb and almost hit a parent and kid in the crosswalk.

"Wow, Mac, that was excellent and long overdue," said Roni. "I've never seen anyone stand up to that jerk."

"Talking like a dick's one thing when he got physical with Kevin, he crossed a line," Mac said.

Across the street, in the visitor parking lot, fathers who'd been standing guard gave Mac an approving nod before they drove out of the lot.

As Roni walked inside the school, Chuck Andrews walked out. Chuck taught physical education and coached most of the sports offered at Blackstone. He didn't look like a hardcore athlete. He looked more like a teacher who fell into a cushy gig. Everyone called him Coach. So far, he'd been welcoming and cordial.

Mac had spent a good amount of time perusing through the Blackstone Academy archives, yearbooks, and remembrances. Years ago, Coach fit the profile of an athletic coach. Stress and time had not served him well.

"Mac. Mac. Mac. What's this I hear about Mr. Jackson giving you a hard time?" Coach said.

"It's all good for now. What can you tell me about Kevin and his father?"

Coach and Mac talked for a few more minutes. Mac wanted to learn more about Kevin.

Coach and Mac walked into the school together. Coach asked Mac if he played golf. He needed a fourth for a round at the Country Club after school.

Mac accepted Coach's invitation. When they were inside, Coach went toward the gymnasium and Mac to his office. While he watched the security feeds fade in and out showing the many views of the campus, he texted Maggie.

Mac: WTF. The crazy woman came at me again this morning demanding I break up a father-son conflict. The father went off on the crazy woman who ran to her car like a scalded dog.

Maggie: Sounds like she now sees that the school needed a marshal after all.

Mac: I think that revelation may have fallen short with her.

Maggie: LOL. Come for dinner tonight.

Mac: Can't. Playing golf with one of the teachers. Tomorrow?

Maggie: Golfing with a teacher? Ooh la la. Tomorrow's good. See you then.

CHAPTER 5

After school ended, Stuart Collins, Stu for short, walked out of the school with Coach. The afternoon heat smacked them in the face the moment the main door slid open.

Stu was an average looking kid with tan skin from sitting poolside all summer. He was a little skittish most of the time, showing more machismo when he was with his friend Kevin Jackson. He made short fast strides to keep up with Coach who was hustling to his car carrying golf clubs.

"How's it going Stu," Coach said, not expected to get a genuine response.

"It's going," Stu said, "Have you heard anything about the marshal guy?"

"Like what?" Coach said.

"I don't know. Like, is the dude a Narc?"

"Why would you think that?" Coach asked.

Coach and Stu stood at the back of Coach's old lady Cadillac with the trunk open. The bag of clubs leaned against the bumper while he rearranged things so the clubs would fit. Once he created a void, he heaved the clubs in and slammed the trunk shut. Coach could see Mac was across the street trying not to be obvious about watching him and Stu.

"It just seems like they went to a lot of trouble to have a cop dude at the school. And my dad said they spent a lot of money for the security system too."

"Ehh," Coach said with a shrug. "Don't make more out of it than it needs to be. A lot of schools are hiring marshals or resource officers. Big districts have a police department."

"My dad told me I have rights. Even if I don't do something wrong. If that guy tries to search me or my stuff I can say no," Stu said.

"Sounds like something an attorney would tell his kid," Coach said, "Mac seems like a good guy. Why don't you try getting to know him before you decide to hate him?"

"Hey, it's not just me. All the kids are skeptical of why he's here," Stu said.

Small groups of teachers exited the school for the day. Coach made sure to wave at each one as they drove past him and Stu. More and more parking spaces became available as the two talked.

"You kids need to stop being conspiracy theorists and stick to kid's stuff," Coach said.

"So, you're not concerned about his ulterior motive for being here?"

"Nope. In fact, he's going golfing with me this afternoon."

It startled Coach and Stu when Mac said, "Do you need some help, Coach?"

"Geez. Man. You scared the shit out of me," Stu said.

Mac looked at Stu for an extra second before he said, "Sorry about that."

"I'm good, Mac," Coach said, "How about we meet at the Pro Shop about four o'clock?"

"That works, I'll see you then," Mac said.

Coach watched Mac walk back to the school. He stopped to talk with Rita Cortez, a 7th-grade Science Teacher. It was no secret Coach had the hots for Rita.

Stu rambled on as Coach watched Mac and Rita. They talked for several minutes. Rita laughed and threw her long hair back in a flirty fashion. Coach wasn't listening to Stu talk about his paranoia. He watched the body language and conversation he wished he could hear.

He saw Rita touch Mac's arm in a familiar way as she turned to walk away from the school.

Kevin blew past Mac and Rita when he came out of the school and walked straight to Coach and Stu.

"What?" Kevin said when he was close.

"What's going on with you and your dad?" Coach said, "Anything I should know about?"

"No." Kevin shrugged.

"You brought a lot of attention to yourself fighting with him like you did this morning," Coach said.

"So," Kevin said.

Coach looked Kevin in his eyes.

"What?" His hands were deep in his pants pockets.

"That's what I want to know. What? What's going on with you," Coach said, "Why are you trying so hard to make your father angry?"

"Why do you care?" Kevin said.

"I care about you, Kevin."

"I can take care of myself. I don't need your help," Kevin said as he flipped off a boy who looked at him and Coach for a second too long.

"Your father has always had a flash temper. You and he have gotten along before. What's different this year?" Coach probed.

"Nothing's different. My dad's a dick. He always has been. I like pushing his buttons. He's pissed off about the new marshal, so it's fun to watch my dad get riled."

"Did you know Marshal MacKenna is a war veteran and he was on a special ops team in the air force?"

"So."

"If your father were to get into a physical altercation with him, your father would lose," Coach said.

Kevin said, "That'd be awesome."

"What's behind your anger with your father? There's something more going on here," Coach said, "Drop the tough guy act. And stop fighting with your dad."

"Or what?" Kevin asked.

The three stopped talking altogether when Roni walked by them.

"Hi, guys," she said.

Coach returned her greeting.

Kevin's cell phone rang with a dark and dreadful tone, something like you'd hear in a horror movie when death was on the other side of the door. He turned and walked away. He flipped his middle finger up at Coach as he walked toward the sidewalk.

"What's his problem?" Coach asked Stu.

"I'm telling you all the kids are jammed up about this marshal dude being here, they're watching us like we're lab rats."

CHAPTER 6

Mac and Roni waited for students to arrive at their usual place near the front of the school. Roni's cheeks were red, and she was fanning her face with her hand.

"You think this is hot? This heat's nothing compared to Kuwait," Mac said.

"Is it super-hot there?"

"Super-hot." He nodded. "In more ways than just temperature."

"How'd your golf date with Coach go last night?" She pretended to swing a golf club.

"How'd you know about that?" Mac raised one of his brows.

"People talk," Roni said with a smirk on her face.

Mac didn't respond.

Roni added, "I'm working on a Criminal Justice degree with the dream to become a cop like my dad. I'm listening to conversations I'm not a part of and watching how people behave."

"Yesterday, Stu Collins was looking sketchy, let me know if you hear or see anything involving him that sends up a warning flag for you."

"Okay." Roni said with enthusiasm. "Did you see the tweets on Twitter last night about the scene yesterday with Kevin and his father?"

"I don't do Twitter," Mac said.

"OMG, dude, get with the times. Twitter was abuzz. Some kids posted a video of you and Kevin's father going at it before school, and it was re-tweeted like a billion times."

"I didn't see anyone recording us."

"Seriously? It's not hard to do with a cell phone. Please tell me you know what a cell phone is."

"Funny."

"Anyway, kids were saying mean stuff like 'what a loser,' and 'psycho dad strikes again.'"

"I'd agree with the last sentiment," Mac said.

"Uh-oh, here comes Kevin and psycho dad. I'm outta here. See you later." Roni was inside before Mac had time to reply.

Mr. Jackson was stomping down the sidewalk like a raging bull headed straight toward Mac. Kevin followed. An invisible tether attached him to his father, keeping him close. Kevin stared at his feet while he walked. Jackson stared at Mac.

Being mindful of the politics, unlike himself, Mac initiated pleasantries. "Morning, Mr. Jackson. Morning Kevin," he said.

Neither said anything in return. Jackson gave Mac a menacing glare.

Something was up; Mac could smell it as Mr. Jackson stomped by him wearing a cologne of sorts. *Vengeance.* Mac had twenty years of sniffing out bad guys. Enemies who thought they had the upper hand had a bounce in their step. Mac thought, *This battle's going to be interesting.*

After the tardy bell, Mac took his time to go inside. He stayed at his post and watched the late comers. When the front of the school was calm, and the only other living creatures were the scrub jays scratching under oak trees for their breakfast, he moseyed inside.

Before Mac saw her, Marlene called out to him. She sounded serious. "Dr. Sawyer would like a word with you." She gave him a half-smile as he walked into her office area.

"Sure thing." He smiled back at her.

The boss' door was open. Mac could see Mr. Jackson sat on one of the floral print chairs facing Dr. Sawyer. His left leg crossed over his right in a way that made Mac wonder if he had balls. Before he reached the threshold, he smelled it again. Vengeance. Mr. Jackson's cologne choice for the day.

"Yes, Dr. Sawyer?" Mac poked his head into her office.

Dr. Sawyer looked sophisticated in her tan colored power suit with soft brown ruffles billowing around her neck. To most men she had an alluring look with her jet-black hair and piercing blues. She didn't fool Mac. He hadn't seen her friendly side yet. Most of the time they'd spent together so far, she always seemed agitated with him.

"Come in, come in." She waved him into her office. "Please, shut the door and take a seat."

He followed directions most of the time. Although he'd left the military, the military hadn't left him. Mac pulled the vacant chair away from Mr. Jackson and took a seat. He hoisted his boot up onto his knee and leaned back.

"Marshal MacKenna, I believe you've met Mr. Jackson." She indicated the asshole seated next to him, knowing full well they'd met.

"Not formally, but we've talked."

She continued, "Mr. Jackson has asked to file a harassment report against you because of an altercation that took place yesterday before school." She looked at Mr. Jackson. "Is that correct, Mr. Jackson?"

"Yes."

Mac said nothing.

Jackson couldn't stand the silence. He turned toward Mac. "You all, but accused me of abusing my son. That's a serious accusation and a bald-faced lie." The volume of his voice rose with each word until he finished his spiel.

Mac's attention never wavered. He waited for Dr. Sawyer to say what she needed to say. She looked at him, and then she looked at Mr. Jackson.

Ah, the uncomfortable silence. Mac thought. It didn't bother Mac one bit. In fact, he excelled at it. For twenty years, he participated in drills to remain silent for extended periods of time to be prepared for capture. *Stay resolute, give the enemy nothing.* He believed that was also applicable here as it appeared to him Mr. Jackson was the enemy and Dr. Sawyer might be one as well.

They stared at each other for a few seconds before Dr. Sawyer broke the tension. "Marshal MacKenna, please describe what you believe happened between you and Mr. Jackson yesterday."

Mac was a straight shooter, he told her word for word, yank for yank, shove for shove what he'd observed. While he spoke, he kept his focus on Dr. Sawyer. He could see Mr. Jackson in his peripheral vision shaking his head, and he'd uttered, "Not true, not true."

Mac stopped talking to look at Mr. Jackson for a second and then continued. "I told him he was upsetting the other kids and since his son was in school, it was time for him to leave." He thrust his thumb toward Mr. Jackson. "Should I have allowed him to bully his son? My job is to protect the kids from harm, right?"

Dr. Sawyer turned her attention to Kevin's father. "Mr. Jackson, if you disagree with Marshal MacKenna's description of the conversation, feel free to share your version."

"On the way to school, Kevin and I talked about his school

work. I told him he needed to push himself. His mother and I believe in tough love. Is that against the law? When we arrived at school, Kevin jumped out before our conversation was over. I told him to come back so we could finish when he interrupted us." He pointed at Mac.

Mac stared out the French door leading to the patio outside Dr. Sawyer's office. There were a couple of evergreens, a mature oak tree and a few shrubs with a table and four chairs to use during warm weather. The door to the patio was open allowing the fresh morning air inside before the air conditioning kicked on. Under the oak tree, two scrub jays squawked and fluttered about, scratching their beaks in the dry leaves. He thought the birds were more interesting than the psycho dad next to him.

Mr. Jackson stopped talking. Mac used the moment to see if his hunch was correct. "Dr. Sawyer, is this the first time Mr. Jackson has made a claim against anyone here?" he asked.

That caught her off guard. Before she could answer, Mr. Jackson huffed and puffed. Must've struck a nerve Mac thought.

"We're here to talk about yesterday," Mr. Jackson said. He turned his attention to Mac. "Was your daddy mean to you or something? Now you need to save all the children? Listen up, Military Man, kids need discipline. And how I discipline my kid is none of your fucking business."

Dr. Sawyer's head jerked and her eyes bulged a little bit. "Randy, please don't use that kind of language at the school."

Randy? He'd had enough of the jerk. "Dr. Sawyer, is there anything more you need from me?"

"Mr. Jackson has a valid point. How he and his wife discipline their child is none of your business." She turned her attention to Mr. Jackson. "I don't believe what happened warrants a harassment report against Marshal MacKenna. How about we agree to disagree and stay in neutral corners from now on?"

"If that's how you want it to be." Mac stood and walked out before Mr. Jackson responded.

Marlene whipped her head around when she saw Mac. She spun her chair around.

"So, what's going on? Is Mr. Jackson filing another harassment report?" Marlene asked while she popped her gum.

"Another harassment report?" he asked

CHAPTER 7

Mac was still infuriated with the boss for placating Mr. Jackson. He watched the various camera views scroll by on the many video screens mounted on the wall across from his desk. Almost everywhere on the campus was under surveillance, except Dr. Sawyer's office, restrooms, utility closets, and the changing area in the locker rooms. He watched the daytime custodian go into a utility closet. Mac stopped the scroll on the hallway feed to see what he was doing. He'd left the door open while he was doing whatever he was doing in there. Mac sent his sister a text.

Mac: I just had my ass chewed from the boss because I stopped that father yesterday who was pushing his son around.

Maggie: Serious?

Mac: Serious. She told me to stay in neutral corners from now on and mind my own business.

Maggie: That's messed up.

On day one, Mac made a list of potential drug dealers—all employees started out on the list. One by one he had been moving employee names from potential to doubtful and student's names from doubtful to potential. So far, the daytime custodian had remained on the potential list.

Mac watched a young student, third-grade maybe, go into the utility closet for a few seconds and then come back out. The custodian came out a minute or so later pushing a rolling mop bucket. *Someone must have thrown up.* Mac guessed.

Mac: The boss doesn't seem to like me or like that I'm here. I'm not sure which it is.

Maggie: What's not to like about you?

Mac: Says his sister.

The teacher's lounge camera caught Mac's attention. Coach and Rita were in the midst of what appeared to be a heated conversation. Mac and Rita met in June when President Stromberg gave him a tour of the campus. They had an instant attraction to each other and began dating shortly after. So far, they'd kept their relationship private.

Mac: Gotta go.

Maggie: Bye.

Mac was unable to hear the conversation between Coach and Rita. He focused on their body language. It almost looked like Coach was scolding Rita. She kept shaking her head denying something. When another teacher entered the room, Coach moved in closer to Rita. His nose was almost touching hers. The other teacher paid no attention to the conversation in the far corner of the room. Rita turned and looked at the teacher who'd come into the room; she looked uncomfortable.

Mac had seen enough. The teacher's lounge was at the end of the hall from the security office. When Mac yanked open the heavy door, the three people in the room stopped doing what they were doing to see who was at the door. Mac walked straight to Coach and Rita.

"What's going on?" Mac said.

Rita shrugged.

Coach said with the friendliest tone, "Not much. We were talking about a few of the students who need some help with their studies. What's going on with you?"

Mac waited for Rita to look at him. She didn't.

"Not much," Mac said, "I'm making my rounds."

"Well, nice chatting with you Rita, I should get back to the gym. Great game last night Mac," Coach said, as he gave Mac a pat on the arm when he walked past him.

Rita didn't respond to Coach.

Mac waited for Coach to leave the lounge. "Is everything okay, Rita?"

"Yes, we were talking about students," she said.

"You looked nervous when I came in. Why would talking about students make you feel that way?" Mac said, "Did Coach say something to upset you?"

"No, not at all. We were talking about students. Sometimes he gets a little too close when he's talking to you. Maybe it was that, him getting too close, that made me appear to be uncomfortable."

"Maybe," Mac said, "You'd tell me if there was a problem, wouldn't you?"

"Yes."

CHAPTER 8

Scramble, scramble, scramble," blasted through the communications system. They had a mission. They were out of their bunks in seconds. The team grabbed the gear and were off the ground in under three minutes.

The radio blared static in his ears, quick bits and pieces of information came through. Not enough to form a clear directive. Both doors on the Pave Hawk helicopter were open. Jefferson's legs dangled from one side; Marten's from the other. Both soldiers aimed machine guns toward the ground.

Even with the headset on, the whomp—whomp—whomp from the rotor wash was deafening. It was eight in the morning and already over a hundred degrees. Heat waves radiated upward on the horizon of the desert. The landscape was colorless. You could see flat rooftops for miles. Sand, light brown homes, and beige business facades that had long since closed.

The team headed toward a hot spot where an explosion had occurred. Their mission was a 'Cat Alpha' Category A for life-threatening injuries. Two local kids were playing around some vehicles and encountered a Vehicle Borne Improvised Explosive Device VB-IED. One female, approximately nine years of age, had a partial amputation of the right leg. One male, approximately six years of age, had a partial amputation of the left arm.

The radio squawked to life in Mac's ear. "Stand down, stand down." He watched Manny, the pilot, for instruction. He was in charge while they were in the air.

Manny circled and waited for further direction. Mac could see small explosions going off in a residential area a few miles away. The sun was bright and hot on his face. Below was chaos. Adults and kids waved their arms in the air.

The radio came to life again. "The landing zone's hot. Stand down. I repeat the LZ's hot. Stand down."

Whomp—whomp—whomp. They circled and waited. The crowd below grew; the chaos continued.

In his peripheral vision, he saw Jefferson sweep back and forth with his machine gun. Marten did the same.

"Jefferson, see anything?"

"It's a fucking ant farm down there. It ain't good. They look pissed."

The radio crackled in his ear. "Do you copy? Stand down; negative injured. Not our IED. Not our injured. Rules of Engagement apply. Return to base."

"Ten-four," Manny replied.

As the Pave Hawk turned away, Mac saw the group gathered around the injured kids. There was a lot of blood. Their mouths were all open. They screamed at us. We couldn't hear anything going on below. Mothers cloaked in burkas raised their hands to beg for help.

Shots pinged off Jefferson's side of the helicopter. He pulled up his legs and lunged inside. Mac looked out where he'd heard a ping on the metal exterior, but didn't see any damage. The landscape was barren. There were no houses. No people. Nothing. Where had the people gone? Where were the houses and shops?

When Mac turned back around, a woman wearing a hijab covering her hair had replaced Jefferson and Marten. She sat on a jump seat with a machine gun slung over her shoulder and held a handgun pointed at Mac's head.

His father was there too, kneeling in front of the woman. She held him by the neck of his white button-down shirt. She twisted the collar so tight the top button was cutting into the flesh of his neck and the red skin around it started to ooze blood. The blood from his wound saturated the shirt collar.

Most of what the woman screamed was inaudible. His headset muffled his hearing. He understood her body language. She thought she had leverage. She'd kill Mac's father if he didn't do what she wanted. Her movements were in slow motion. She shifted the gun to his father's ear and pointed it toward his brain.

"It's okay," his father mouthed to him.

Mac willed his eyes to open in the darkness of his bedroom. He flung the wet sheets off and sat on the side of the bed. The stillness was a relief. It was quiet except for the jangle of the tags on Roxy's collar as she shook her big head. She lumbered to his side of the bed and bumped her wet nose against his bare knee. Her breath was warm and atrocious. There was no helicopter, and there were no screaming people, no woman pointing a weapon at him or his father. It took a minute for him to get his bearings; it always did. His sweat-drenched the sheets. He thought to himself, *When will the nightmares stop?*

"Are you okay, Mac? Did you have a bad dream?" Rita asked, in a hushed voice. Her gentle hand was on his back.

"Mmhmm." The bright green glow of the clock showed it was four forty. "I can't sleep. It's Saturday, you sleep in."

"Okay, baby. Thank you. You sure you're all right?"

"I'm good."

Roxy followed Mac and into the kitchen. He made a cup of coffee and then booted up his laptop to catch up on current events. Roxy plopped onto her dog pad in the corner. He pulled up his list with probable drug dealers on one side, and the least likely to be involved on the other. Mac's cursor settled on Stu and Kevin.

CHAPTER 9

Mac was already sweating. The forecast predicted a high of 95 and poor air quality. The smog from the Sacramento region had a tendency to blow up the hill to Brookfield. There was an advisory to limit outdoor physical activities to before noon.

Two weeks of school had passed, and Mr. Jackson was the same jerk. He had the convertible top down on his sports car. As he drove away, he gave Mac the middle finger.

Roni said, "That was nice. A one finger salute to start your week."

"Whatever," Mac said. He was more intent on watching Kevin who'd made a beeline to Stu. The two boys fell into step with one another and began a lively discussion about something. Because of their body language, Mac's intuition waved a cautionary yellow flag.

"Those two are up to something," Mac said to Roni, as he jabbed his thumb toward the boys.

"You think so? Based on what?" Roni asked. She turned everything that hinted at law enforcement into a case study.

"My gut," Mac replied.

"But what did they do that made your gut feel they were looking for trouble?"

Student traffic had increased in the last five minutes. The bell was soon to ring.

"I don't know. The way Stu hung back and waited for Kevin to get here. And then Kevin, who doesn't hustle anywhere hurried to Stu. Then the moment they were side by side, they talked and laughed like school girls discussing a boy."

"Hmmm," Roni said.

The bell sounded and a new day had begun. Mac and Roni followed the last few habitually tardy students inside.

The entrance door slid shut, and Mac entered the code to secure the exterior doors of the school. Anyone wishing to leave the building must scan their photo ID badge first. Every time a door opened, there was a date, time, and I.D. stamp on the daily log.

After he parted ways with Roni and said good morning to Marlene, Mac sat at his desk with a fresh cup of coffee.

He watched kids cover their hearts and mouth the Pledge of Allegiance. The security feed didn't have audio capability. The morning announcement crackled to life on the PA system. Mac tried to tune it out while he checked his emails.

"Good morning, Blackstone Bulldogs and happy Monday. Today, in the cafeteria during all lunch periods the student body will be selling…"

His attention was drawn back to the announcement when he heard the teenage female stop talking, but the microphone remained live.

He heard papers rustling and then giggling. He shook his head and refocused on the security feeds. When the announcement ended, Coach moved the boys in PE outside to the track.

Mac's attention bounced back and forth from the security screens and the daily logs from last week. He made sure there wasn't anything out of place with regard to door usage and after-hours presence. He highlighted anything irregular.

Movement on the security screen caught Mac's attention. A fight broke out as a PE class was ending, and the kids were walking back to the building from the field.

On the way out of his office, Mac grabbed his two-way radio.

"Hey," he said to Marlene, as he ran past her office. "Fight on the blacktop at the rear gymnasium door."

Mac pushed the door open and ran out to where there was a huddle of kids. Coach stood near the altercation and yelled at the kids to stop. The wind carried his words away from the crowd.

Mac pushed through the kids to the center where he found Kevin pummeling another boy. He grabbed Kevin by the scruff of his collar and yanked him off the kid.

Kevin was like a feral cat. He clawed at the handgun secured at Mac's hip. Mac zipped around behind him. Before Kevin could process what had happened, Mac had his skinny neck wedged in the crook of his right elbow. He grasped his left bicep and held him in a classic jiu jitsu rear-naked choke hold. It wasn't tight enough to make Kevin pass out, just enough to slow the blood flow and control his actions.

The kids around them were recording the moment with their cell phones.

"Coach," Mac yelled. "Take your class inside. Tell Marlene what happened and send that kid to the nurse."

Coach herded the kids to the same door Mac had run through a few moments earlier. It was now Mac and Kevin alone on the blacktop.

"Stop fighting me," Mac said in a controlled voice.

"Fuck you," Kevin croaked.

Mac moved faster than Kevin could counter and switched his control from the choke hold to an arrest control hold with Kevin's bent arm behind his back. Mac forced Kevin to walk ahead of him.

"My dad wants you fired. You just gave him all he needs. You fucked up now," Kevin said.

Mac ignored the boy's talk. He'd met many a big-mouth in the air force. The ones who thought they were in control because they were the loudest. In Mac's experience, those were the ones who were the most insecure.

When Mac and Kevin entered the administration offices, Marlene was standing with an angry mother look on her face.

She pointed to the chairs lined along the wall facing her desk. "Kevin, I called your father, he's on his way to pick you up. Can you sit down and behave while you wait or does Marshal MacKenna need to babysit you?"

Kevin said nothing.

Mac released Kevin's arm. Kevin sat down with a thud. He stared at Mac, never shifting his focus.

Marlene broke the silence. "I'm disappointed in you Kevin. You're not the kind of boy who bullies and fights."

Kevin remained silent.

Mac sat in a chair across from Kevin. "I'm going to wait here until Kevin and his father have left," he said to Marlene.

The three sat and said little for the next ten minutes or so until Mr. Jackson arrived.

Marlene saw Mr. Jackson approach the entrance door on her security monitor. She buzzed the door lock to allow him to enter.

Mr. Jackson looked at his son, then at Mac. Without saying a word Kevin stood up and exited the school behind his father.

CHAPTER 10

M ac left his office for afternoon duty at the front of the school and almost collided with Roni. He put his arm around her and pretended to give her head a rub with his knuckles like he used to do with his sister.

"Hey, I heard about Kevin getting into trouble this morning. Your gut was right. Is it true, you put him in a choke hold?"

"Yes, he was out of control. That was just to subdue him. Kevin wasn't going to stop hitting the kid."

They walked together to the front of the school. It was the quiet before the storm. Parents packed the visitor parking lot across the street and parallel parked for as far as you could see before the road curved out of view.

The parents were conversing in clusters. Fathers, for the most part, talked with fathers and mothers, for the most part, talked with mothers. Except for Mrs. Ross, who arrived thirty minutes early to secure the same parking space every day and then waited in her Jag without socializing.

"That's awesome. Did you learn that in the Air Force?" Roni said.

"Learning how to use non-lethal combat's standard training in special ops. I've also been active in Brazilian Jiu Jitsu for quite a few years. If you want to be a cop, then you should sign-up for a class at the Training Center on Rock Street by the theater. It would give you an advantage during arrest control and help you take a man down. Marco Moreno owns it. He's an excellent instructor. Be forewarned, his Brazilian-English is a little hard to understand at times."

"I'm going to do it. Do you wear a kimono like in karate?"

"You mean a Gi. Some do. I don't wear one. I practice no-Gi," he said.

"Hey, I also heard about last week's board meeting." Roni said, "I heard Mr. Jackson went off on the board about you and your mistreatment of him and Kevin. Is that true?"

"That's right. You weren't here Friday. Where were you?"

Mac said.

"My mom had a medical procedure on Friday, so I drove her and stayed with her at the hospital. She's good. It's nothing serious. So, did psycho dad make a scene at the board meeting?"

"In my opinion, he made a scene. Screaming and intimidating people seems to be his standard operating procedure."

"More details, come on spill it," she coaxed.

"Not much to spill, he told the board members he was sure they didn't know what was happening with the new marshal. He said I accused him of abusing his son and other parents have said I'm too gruff with the kids." Mac shrugged.

"I don't think so."

"If it's true, it's the first I've heard of it. I'm pretty sure if Dr. Sawyer had a reason to scold me she would have," he said, "So who knows. He wanted to give his complaint more oomph."

Roni nodded, and then the bell rang. Conversation time was over.

Kids of all ages stormed out the main door of the school. Mac wondered how the older students were able to reach the front of the school from the farthest point before the younger students whose classes were closer.

Stu was in the front of the pack looking lost without his friend, Kevin, by his side. He stopped just outside the door to talk with another kid. Jillian, a first-grade student Stu babysat after school, skipped out the entrance. They passed by Mac. Stu gave him a stare that all but said, 'fuck you'.

"Goodbye, Mr. Mac," said Jillian with a big smile revealing a missing front tooth.

"Goodbye, Jillian," Mac said.

Stu and Jillian walked down the sidewalk as they always did, but instead of turning the corner at the end of the block to walk in the direction of Jillian's home they crossed the street and got into a small older car.

Stu buckled Jillian's seatbelt in the backseat before getting into the front. They drove by; Jillian sat alone in the backseat. She waved to Mac with much gusto. Mac waved back. Stu sat in the front next to the driver who looked older, maybe mid-20s. He was a big guy with long wild hair. The driver had an image of a gun tattooed on his neck and a full sleeve on the left arm sitting on the window frame. The driver was smoking a cigarette. Mac made a mental note of the license plate until he could enter it in a note on his phone.

Whatever Stu was up to, gave Mac a bad feeling. He also didn't like that Stu took Jillian with him. As soon as the front of the school was quiet, the students were either gone or lingering with a parent, Mac hightailed it to close his office for the night. Since he had no idea where the trio had gone, he decided to wait for Jillian's safe arrival home. He jotted down the home address listed in her student file.

Mac's wait lasted about forty minutes parked near Jillian's home. The same older car sputtered to a stop in front of Jillian's. Stu bounced out of the front seat and then unbuckled Jillian's seatbelt. She skipped up the walkway to her house and waited on the front porch for Stu. Stu hung back and leaned into the car to talk to the driver.

Less than a minute later Mac was following the tattooed man. Mac called Jason. The call went straight to Jason's voicemail. He left the license plate info of the car and asked Jason to run it and get back to him.

The tattooed man drove through town to the east side and stopped at a smoke shop. Mac waited.

Mac's phone rang. It was his sister, Maggie.

"Hey, bro. What're you doing? Are you home?" she asked.

"No. I'm still at the school," he lied. "What'd you need?"

"Some bro time. The girls want Uncle Mac to come over for dinner," she said.

Back on the road, the tattooed man drove farther east to a residential neighborhood unfamiliar to Mac. Based on the gang tags on just about everything, Mac surmised gang members were living in the neighborhood. He wondered if this was where Stu and Jillian had gone to after school. The tattooed man parked in a driveway. Mac parked down the street.

"Can't. I'm going to jiu jitsu tonight. How about tomorrow?" Mac said.

"I'm disappointed, but happy I'll see you tomorrow. Stay out of trouble," she said before disconnecting.

Mac waited fifteen or so minutes. He jotted down the address and then called Jason. The call went straight to his voicemail again. "Hey buddy, run this address while you're looking into the car plate I gave you," Mac explained about the license plate and the address. He also told Jason he feared Stu played a role in the drug scene and that he'd speak with Coach to see what he might know about Stu.

CHAPTER 11

I s that you Chucky?" Coach's mother bellowed on the intercom from her upstairs bedroom as Coach entered the kitchen from the garage.

Coach slumped and walked to the intercom panel nearest the door between the kitchen and the garage. "Yes, mother."

"You're late. I'm going to miss my appointment." she scolded her son.

Coach shook his head as he climbed the stairs to her bedroom.

His mother sat near the French door that led out to a balcony. The door was closed to keep out the afternoon heat. She sat at her table ready for her regular dialysis treatment.

"Are you ready to go?" Coach said.

"I've been ready for thirty minutes. Where the hell have you been? You know I can't be late. They have other patients to see after me and if one person's late it messes everything up."

"I hit all the lights red, Mother. I wasn't late on purpose," Coach said, "I need to pack your cooler."

"For God's sake, next time leave earlier," she demanded. "I don't ask much of you, and you know my life depends on my treatment."

"I can't leave before school's over. I leave as soon as I can."

"Why can't you leave before school's out? I remember when I worked, I was able to take time off to take you boys to a doctor appointment. Schools must see the importance of people needing time off to tend to family matters," she said, "Oh, forget it. Go pack my cooler, and I'll be down in a minute."

He heard the elevator start its descent. He hustled to be at the door when it slid open.

"Let's go, let's go." She pushed her ornate walker toward the door to the garage. Her dutiful son followed with a small cooler filled with bottled water and snacks.

"Sweet Jesus it's like an oven in here." his mother said when she opened the door to the garage.

It was even hotter for Coach after he'd struggled to help his two hundred plus pound mother into her low sitting Cadillac. He slammed her door, loaded her walker into the trunk, and they were on their way.

"Crank up the AC. I'm melting."

Coach watched Brookfield get smaller and smaller in the rearview mirror of his mother's caddy. Her treatment clinic was about thirty minutes away, a straight shot west on the highway. He turned the radio on and settled into the seat. He wanted to listen to anything besides his mother complaining about everything.

"Madeline called me this morning," she said over the music. "I don't know what's wrong with the woman. She complains about her achy knees. If she lost fifty pounds, her knees wouldn't ache so much. You don't dare tell her that because she has an excuse for everything. She wanted to come by for a visit this afternoon. Thank goodness I had an appointment."

Coach lowered his sun visor to block the bright sun in his eyes. He reached over and lowered his mother's as well.

She said, "You're a good boy, Chucky. You're nothing like your brother."

They finally arrived at the clinic. Coach helped his mother out of the car and into the clinic. She went on and on about why they were late. Told the staff how terrible the school is her son worked for because they won't let him off a little early to take his sick mother to an appointment. Not even when her life depended on it.

Late to his mother was arriving five minutes before her appointment instead of fifteen minutes before her appointment.

The staff at the facility waited for his mother to stop talking so they could take her to a chair.

He made himself comfortable in the waiting area provided for family and began grading papers. In the background, he could hear his mother rambling on about this and that. She didn't socialize much so she was like a locomotive once she was able to converse with someone besides her son.

About ten minutes into her treatment, she bellowed out, "Chucky. Bring me some water." He wanted to ignore her but knew she'd continue until he followed her orders. He heard a staff member offer to get a bottle of water for her which she declined explaining she was particular about the water she drank.

"Chucky. Oh, there you are," she said when he turned the corner in front of her, "I thought you left."

"I was grading papers, mother. It took me a minute to set

everything down. Here's your water," he said, handing her a bottle.

"Open it for me. And start the tablet thing so I can watch my soap opera."

He showed her how to touch the screen so her show would begin to play the same as he'd done almost every time they'd been at the dialysis center. He placed the earphones in her ears, so she didn't disturb the other patients any more than she already had. Once she seemed content, he returned to his cocoon in the waiting area.

Forty minutes later, which felt like ten minutes, he heard, "Chucky. It's over. Chucky."

Embarrassed as always, he hurried to her. He gave the patient care tech assigned to his mother an apologetic look; she gave him an understanding half-smile.

"I'm tired, turn on my music, I want to close my eyes and listen," she said.

He did as she requested, made sure she was content before he walked away. She didn't say thank you. She seldom did. Why would he expect her to start now?

After thirty more minutes he heard her snoring—it was music to his ears. He finished grading his papers and worked on his sports schedule.

Coach looked at his watch. She'd been asleep for a little more than one hour. He was sure everyone in the clinic appreciated her nap as much as he did.

Coach heard whispered conversation and the rustling of fabric. "Chucky." her booming voice penetrated the serene atmosphere. "I'm done, Chucky."

Before she could holler again, he arrived at her chair with her walker. She gave him a critical look. "Let's go. I'm done."

He assisted his mother onto her seat in the car, loaded her walker in the trunk and plopped himself onto the driver's seat.

"I'm hungry. Get me a banana," Coach's mother said to him.

"You know you're not supposed to eat bananas." He was frustrated that they hadn't left the parking lot yet.

"It's a banana for God's sake, not a bacon cheeseburger," she said. Her look told him to shut-up and do as she asked.

Along with the regular commuters, they were finally on the highway headed toward home. The sun sat low in his rearview mirror.

His mother gobbled her banana down and grabbed a bag of

potato chips. While she crunched, she talked nonstop during the thirty-minute drive that took forty because of traffic.

Before they made it to Brookfield, his mother said, "I'm hungry. Let's stop at the Grill for dinner."

Coach turned off the highway and went straight rather than turning toward the Grill.

"Where are we going?" his mother asked.

"I wanted to see something," he replied.

"What?" she asked.

"A training center." He'd been curious since learning Mac taught jiu jitsu there.

"Why?" she probed.

"I just want to see it. My God, it'll only take a minute."

He made a loop around the block and drove past the gym. As he prepared to go right on Washington Street, he saw Mac exiting the parking lot. He waved to Mac and Mac waved back.

"Who was that?" his mother said.

"Just a guy I work with," he said.

"They probably haven't given him time off to take his mother to an appointment either."

CHAPTER 12

Mac had been too busy during the week to get to the Training Center for a workout. He hadn't been since Monday. He'd had a good two hours with the jiu jitsu class he taught. He headed home from his Sunday class feeling exhausted and invigorated.

The temperature had dropped twenty-three degrees overnight and the first rain of the season was coming down with a fury. His wipers were on fast speed.

His home sat on a quiet cul-de-sac at the top of a hill. It was an old Victorian style home the previous owner had started to renovate. He wanted it when he saw how quiet the street was and the property backed up to a greenbelt with a year-round creek. The secret room behind the master closet was a bonus.

Mr. Jenkins, who lived across the street, rarely came out at night. His house was across from Mac's. He was the self-appointed neighborhood watch captain and quite a character. The day Mac's furniture arrived, Mr. Jenkins shuffled over to his place with his dog, Mimi, a miniature white poodle, and introduced himself. The first thing he told Mac was he had been a navy mechanic, and spent most of his time stateside, except for the few years he served overseas in World War II. When Mac told him he'd retired from the air force, Mr. Jenkins saluted him.

Through the water-streaked windshield, Mac saw a Brookfield Police Department cruiser parked in front of his home. No lights on. Parked and idling. Mr. Jenkins was peering out his living room window. Mac pushed the button on his rearview mirror to open the black iron security gate at the end of his driveway. He pulled in and parked.

"Roxy, stay." He gave her the visual command as well. The last thing he needed was for Roxy to sense she needed to protect him and attack a cop. Two uniformed officers wearing rain gear walked toward him. They met on the sidewalk halfway between their patrol car and his truck.

"Something I can help you officers with?" he asked.

The taller of the two officers pointed to Roxy. "Will the dog stay in the truck?" he asked.

"Yes."

"Are you Mac MacKenna?" the same officer asked him.

The shorter officer shined his flashlight in Mac's eyes.

Roxy watched from his vacated seat.

"I'm Mac MacKenna," he said as he lifted his collar to keep the rain from streaming down his neck.

"You go by Mac?" the officer asked.

"Yes," he said.

"We know you have a concealed weapons permit. Where's your gun?" The taller officer asked.

"In the glove box," he pointed over his shoulder with his thumb.

They looked around him at Roxy.

"Where are you coming from?"

"Why do you ask?" He wasn't sure what happened or what was going on, but he was certain this had Mr. Jackson written all over it.

"We'd like to ask you a few questions."

"Go for it," he said.

"Do you know a man named Randall Jackson?"

"No, I don't know him. I know who he is. He's a parent of a student at the school where I work."

"Someone assaulted Mr. Jackson at his home this evening. They jumped him when he took out the trash. He claims you were the assailant," the taller officer said.

"Well, that's not possible. I was teaching a class at the Training Center," he said.

"What time was the class?"

"I opened the building at half past six and closed it at half past nine. You can check with the alarm company. In fact, I bet if I looked over the sign-in log, I'd see the names of some of your co-workers who can attest to my whereabouts."

"Can you give us those names?"

"Yes, but not tonight. I'll need to get the names from the sign-in log and get the contact information from the owner, Marco Moreno. Will tomorrow work?"

"Sure, that's fine." The taller officer continued to do all the talking.

He handed Mac his business card with his contact info. "Give me a call."

"Is Mr. Jackson, okay?" Mac asked. Seemed like the right thing to say.

"He suffered a few contusions, has a nice shiner on his left eye. The assailant did a choke-hold maneuver on him until he passed out. When he came to, his wife was shaking him and saying his name. She didn't see anything. She thought he'd fallen. His pride took a hit."

"Is there anything else, officers?" he asked.

He could hear Roxy whimpering. She was ready to get out of the truck.

"That's it for now."

Mac couldn't call Marco. It was after ten. It was too late to call Jason also.

He wasn't going to worry about Mr. Jackson.

Mac had a solid alibi. Since the assailant used a jiu jitsu move, Mac hoped Marco's guys did too.

Mac was too amped up to go to sleep. When he picked up her tennis ball, Roxy's thick tail wagged with excitement. He grabbed a beer and sat on the back porch, listening to the rain.

Mac: Hey, are you up?

Maggie: Yes, I'm reading.

Mac: I taught the jiu jitsu class tonight. When I got home, a cop car was waiting for me.

Maggie: What happened?

Mac: Someone assaulted Mr. Jackson, the jackass parent. I was at class (solid alibi), but he blamed me anyway.

Maggie: Was he hurt?

Mac: Roughed up.

Maggie: Do you know who did it?

Mac: No. I hope it wasn't one of Marco's boys from the training center. I told Marco what was going on.

Maggie: They wouldn't do that, right?

Mac: I don't think so. This parent drama sucks. It's not how I pictured retirement.

CHAPTER 13

D ang, I'm already sweating," Roni said as she approached Mac for morning duty, "I think I'm going to melt."

It was also either too hot for Teddy and Savannah's crazy mom to get out of her car or she'd started drinking earlier than usual. Mrs. Ross dropped the kids off at the sidewalk and allowed them to walk by the scary marshal and into the school all by themselves.

"Good morning, Savannah," Mac said, "Teddy." He bobbed his head.

Teddy stopped in front of Roni and Mac. "Hello, Mr. Mac. Miss Darling. It's a good morning. What do you call a paleontologist who sleeps too much?" he asked.

"Whoa, Teddy that's a big word for this early in the morning," Roni said.

"I'm not sure Teddy, what do you call a paleontologist who sleeps too much?" Mac asked.

"Lazy bones. Hahaha." Teddy started to laugh before he finished the punch line. He held his stomach for an extra animated laugh. He let out a snort and laughed even harder.

"That's funny, Teddy." Roni patted his back.

"Good one, Teddy. I liked that joke. I'll have to tell my nieces next time I see them," Mac said.

Teddy and Roni said in unison. "You have nieces?"

"I have two nieces. Now get to class." He turned Teddy around and pointed him toward the entrance.

"Uh-oh." Roni elbowed him in the side. "Look whose driving creepy Kevin to school today." She shifted her eyes in the direction he should look.

Mrs. Jackson had driven Kevin to school. It was rare; in fact, Mac hadn't seen Kevin's mother since Mr. Jackson dragged her out of the school board meeting in June. Roni hustled in the opposite direction the second Kevin hopped out of his mom's car, a black sedan with tinted windows. From behind his sunglasses, he watched as Kevin approached the school entrance.

"Good morning, Kevin," he said.

"Mac," Kevin replied without looking at him.

Stu was waiting for Kevin inside the front door. The two joined up, and two walked off together.

The moment the entrance door slid shut, Roni resumed her position next to Mac. "O-M-G," she said, "His mom never brings him to school. What do you think's going on?"

"I heard somebody assaulted Kevin's father last night. Rumor has it he's got some scrapes and a black eye. Maybe he didn't want people to see his shiner."

"Are you serious? Where? Why?" Roni asked. Her bright blue eyes were large with wonder.

"I don't know the details. That's what I heard." Roni turned away from him to go inside. "Hey, if you hear something different, let me know."

"Okay, I will," she said. Roni stopped to talk with one of the moms.

A heavyset, middle-aged man in jeans and a t-shirt, wearing a black and orange baseball cap rounded the corner and walked straight to Mac.

"Are you Mac MacKenna?"

"I am. And you are?"

The man handed Mac an envelope, which he accepted.

"Doesn't matter who I am. You've been served," the man said before turning and walking away.

Several parents and kids stopped what they were doing and looked at the man walking away from Mac. Roni hustled back to his side.

"What'd that man give you?" she asked.

"Hell if I know," he said, as he tore open the envelope. "A restraining order."

Roni gasped.

"He was a process server," Mac said.

"What the heck?" Roni said.

"Looks like I have to stay at least twenty-five feet away from Mr. Jackson."

The bell rang, and the stragglers ran inside. Mac and Roni followed. They parted ways inside. Mac went straight to Marlene.

Marlene was in the midst of taking a bite out of a piece of toast when Mac walked into her area. The printer on Marlene's credenza whizzed and spat out papers at rapid speed. She swallowed fast when she saw him. "Hey, Mac. How're you doing?"

"I've been better. Mr. Jackass Jackson just had me served with a restraining order.

Marlene let his cursing slide. "What a jerk. Why would he do that?" Her forehead wrinkled, and her eyes squinted. She said in a whisper, "You haven't done anything to him, have you?"

Mac leaned over Marlene's desk to be closer and looked in her eyes. "Of course, I haven't done anything to him."

For a moment, he weighed the pros and cons of sharing what little information he had with his main ally who also happened to be the biggest gossip he knew.

He repeated what he'd told Roni.

Her hand covered her mouth. "Oh my gosh."

"Mr. Jackson told the cops he thought it was me," he continued. "And no, I did not assault him, nor would I. I was teaching a jiu jitsu class at the Training Center at the time."

"You teach a jiu jitsu class?" Marlene batted her eyelashes at him and popped her gum. From the look on her face, you would've thought he said he was fighting crime in a red cape at the time of the assault.

"Yes, every Sunday evening from seven to nine. If you're interested, it's a great way to equip yourself with self-defense skills, and it's a good workout too."

"Oh, I'm too old for that kind of stuff." Marlene blushed.

"You're never too old for exercise," he said.

"Back to Mr. Jackson. How will you handle this twenty-five-foot limitation?" Marlene asked.

"My guess is it's about twenty-five feet from where I stand in the morning to the curb where Jackson drops Kevin off."

"That's still ludicrous. You work at his kid's school."

"What's ludicrous? What kid?" Dr. Sawyer asked as she rounded the corner into Marlene's area. In one hand, she held her briefcase while the other squeezed a stack of papers to her chest and held a latte.

Marlene looked at Mac to answer Dr. Sawyer's question.

"More Jackson sh… stuff. Some guy handed me a restraining order about five minutes ago instructing me to stay at least twenty-five feet away from Mr. Jackson."

Dr. Sawyer heaved her briefcase onto one of the chairs across from Marlene's desk.

"Are you serious?"

"See for yourself." He handed her the document. She placed her latte on Marlene's desk and gave him her stack of papers to hold.

"We've had restraining orders when parents are going through a nasty divorce, but this is a first for a parent to file one against an employee," Dr. Sawyer said, "Let's go into my office so we can talk about this."

Mac told her about the assault or as much as he knew. "It looks bad for me in one way. I have a brown belt in Brazilian Jiu Jitsu and Jackson's attacker used a choke hold to make him pass out. That's a classic jiu jitsu move, but it's also something a criminal might use. My alibi's solid. I was teaching a jiu jitsu class. There were even cops there. I've already sent the roster to the officer who was at my house," he said.

"Mr. Jackson must believe you assaulted him regardless of what you or the Brookfield P.D. say," Dr. Sawyer said with her brow furrowed.

"Should I worry about my job?" he asked.

She hesitated before answering. "I'll need to inform the school board members about the RO. After I've spoken to them, I can give you a more definitive answer." Her manner was curt.

"I like my job. I like most of the staff. And don't tell anyone, I've even grown fond of most of the kids," he said.

"Mmhmm," she said.

"Business as usual then. Twenty-five feet from Mr. Jackson at all times," he said.

"And try to stay out of Kevin's business while you're at it."

He closed Dr. Sawyer's door and went to whisper to Marlene, "I'm going to be out front measuring twenty-five feet from the curb. After that, I'll be in my office if you need me." He winked at her.

She whispered back. "Okay. Hang in there. Mr. Jackson's a jerk." She also winked, smiled, and popped her gum.

He turned the corner leaving Marlene's office and ran into Coach.

"Sorry, man," Mac said.

"Where you headed so fast?"

"I need to get a measuring tape to measure the distance from the curb in front of the school to the entrance. Kevin Jackson's father had me served with a restraining order to stay twenty-five feet away from him," Mac said.

"What's that all about?"

"Who knows? It's complicated."

"I'm intrigued. You up for another round of golf this afternoon and you can fill me in then?"

"That'd be great. I also want to pick your brain about Stu Collins," Mac said.

"Meet me in the parking lot at four o'clock," Coach said.

"I'll be there. I better measure the sidewalk before the boss blows a gasket."

Mac found the custodian and borrowed his measuring tape.

Surprise, surprise. The distance from the brick wall at the school entrance to the curb was twenty-seven feet. Mac thought, *What a weasel thing to do. A restraining order. Does he think I have some type of vendetta against him because I don't like the way he bullies his son?*

CHAPTER 14

The lower grades were eating lunch. It was the first lunch period of the day. Kids were around the playground, the blacktop, the ball field, the picnic area, the library, and the cafeteria.

Mac ventured outside to get some fresh air. Still dumbfounded as to how Mr. Jackson was able to pull off a restraining order against him when he had provided evidence that he couldn't have been the person who assaulted him.

Kids huddled in cliques. Boys played dodge ball and tether ball. Girls snickered and pointed.

At the far corner of the blacktop, Nate Collins stood with his back to the building. He leaned forward, his hands on his hips and his face too close to Teddy's face.

As Mac approached the group of boys, he overheard Nate say to Teddy, "What're you going to do about it, four-eyes?

"Nate," Mac said to the pack leader, "What's going on?"

Nate was Stu's little brother, the youngest son of Fred and Vanessa Collins. Fred Collins was 'the' criminal attorney in town. He'd built quite a name for himself, representing some notable cases in California. Nate must have gotten his moxie from his Daddy.

"Nothing that concerns you, Mr. Mac," Nate replied smartly.

His pals snickered at his boldness.

Mac looked at them for a long moment. The snickering stopped. "Boys, I'd like to speak with Nate. Leave," Mac said. Teddy ran off first.

The pack leader looked at Mac with a blank expression.

"Guys, you don't have to go anywhere," Nate hollered after his friends. They stopped and looked at Mac.

"Leave. Now," Mac said.

They scampered off.

"Nate, what were you saying to Teddy?"

"Nothing."

"You don't seem to understand that bullying isn't cool and it's prohibited at school," Mac said.

Nate stepped to his right to walk around Mac. Mac stepped to his left and blocked him. They danced a few steps right and left.

"Did you understand what I said?" Mac asked.

"Yes, I understood what you said. I'm not a moron. I wasn't bullying anyone. And you better let me go, or I'll tell my father, and he'll get a restraining order against you. Do you know who my father is?"

Mac thought, *News travels fast. The kids already know about Mr. Jackson's restraining order.*

"Does your father endorse bullying?" Mac said. Nate gave Mac a look the kids called a 'death stare.' "Last warning. If I see or even hear of you bullying anyone again, I'm going to talk with your father about your behavior," Mac said.

Nate glared at him. His lips were tight and pooched out, arms crossed at his chubby chest.

"Did you understand what I said?" Mac said.

"May I go now?" he asked.

"I mean it. That's your one and only warning. You don't want to be on my bad side, Nate," Mac sighed with exasperation. "Yes, you may leave."

From the blacktop area, Mac went into the cafeteria and made an appearance.

It smelled like pizza was on the menu today. He checked in on the lunch ladies to see what was happening. Elsie handed him his daily apple—Fuji.

His cell phone vibrated in his pocket. It was Jason. There was too much clanging and banging in the cafeteria. He talked while he walked into the hallway so he could hear better.

"I believe your pal Randall Jackson's in tight with a small network of good ole' boys a couple of attorneys who have a lot more clout than Jackson. You know he's been here since he graduated college, right? These guys may have met in college. They're tight," Jason said.

"Wow, that's great." The sarcasm shot from his lips.

"Don't despair, my friend. This guy sounds like a loose cannon ready to blow. One thing about the good ol' boy network, I've learned through observation and experience, is that when a member of the network goes rogue, the network cronies drop the loose cannon fast. If it gets out that Jackson abused his kid — they'll kick Jackson to the curb," Jason said.

Mac walked around the campus until the last lunch period ended.

He ate lunch at his desk while he watched the security feeds on the monitors. The kid's behavior fascinated Mac. The little ones were squirrelly. The middle grades were defiant. The high schoolers were sneaky and rude.

Paperwork consumed Mac's afternoon. Before he knew it, the last period was about to end. He met up with Roni as she was exiting the building.

He slid into step with her. "Hello," he said.

"Hi. How's it going?"

"Can't complain," he replied.

"I heard Nate Collins was in a bit of trouble at lunchtime," she said.

"Is there anything you don't hear?" Mac smiled at her.

She giggled.

"He was bullying Teddy," Mac offered.

"Not sweet Teddy." she said, "Woo-wee, it's hot." She began to fan her face. "It was hot, and then it rained, and now it's hot again. Crazy weather."

Mac noticed Mrs. Jackson's black sedan idled at the far end of the parking lot. Through the windshield, he saw it was Kevin's mother behind the wheel.

The bell rang. Kids poured out the school entrance.

Parents waited in idling cars parked along the curb on both sides of the street and in the visitor parking lot.

Roni stood in the center of the crosswalk holding a stop sign while the younger kids crossed the street. The older kids crossed wherever they wanted.

Kevin and Stu strolled out the door. Kevin hurried to his waiting mother. When he opened the passenger door and climbed inside, it shocked Mac to see mother and son hug. Mac had a brief thought about his mother.

Most of the kids had left by the time Coach exited the school.

Mac nodded. "Hey, Chuck, I have a question for you," he said.

"What's up?"

"Kevin Jackson, how's he doing?" Mac asked.

"Did well today." Chuck shrugged. Mac could see Chuck was trying to look calm but wasn't.

"What's the deal with him and his father?" Mac asked.

"Some parents talk like babies to their kids. Other folks use 'tough love.' I've heard it all," Chuck said, "Are we still on for golf?"

CHAPTER 15

The week was settling down after the restraining order issue on Monday. Mac played a fairly decent golf game with Coach earlier that afternoon. He was still rusty, but showing improvement.

After dinner, Roxy and Mac headed to the front porch. Something was calming about the squeak of his old rickety wooden porch swing. It was another treasure left behind by the previous owner. He didn't partake too often, but it had been a hell of a day, so it seemed like a good enough excuse for a Partagás-Habana Serie-D No. 4 cigar. Roxy sprawled out on the small patch of grass that was their front yard. She appeared to be enjoying her occasional guilty pleasure as well, a raw beef bone from the local butcher.

Outside, a slight breeze replaced the daytime heat. The moon hadn't yet made an appearance. Other than the frogs and crickets and the faint hum of traffic on the highway, the subdivision Mac lived in was at peace.

Mr. Jenkins, across the court, was at bingo, his Wednesday night ritual. From the way he told it, he was a lucky man. The ladies at the senior center flocked around him because there were three women to every man. And he had at least one bingo every week. Mac had never seen him bring home a lady friend, but he wouldn't rule it out. Mr. Jenkins was old, but he still had a lot of pep.

There were five houses on Mac's court. On one corner was a young couple with a baby. On the other corner was a middle-aged couple with two four-legged kids, large Mastiff dogs, who were sniffing friends of Roxy's. The fifth homeowner sandwiched between Mr. Jenkins, and Mac was a widow in her early seventies. She was a church-going woman, who baked cookies for Mac on a regular basis. One time, before Mac started at Blackstone Academy when he was arriving home from a hike, he saw the widow exiting Mr. Jenkins home. She waved as if nothing inappropriate was going on, so Mac made the assumption it was Mr. Jenkins' cookie day.

Mac watched Roxy attack her dog bone and considered his conversation with Coach while golfing. He'd shared as much as he felt necessary about the conflict between him and Mr. Jackson. Coach told Mac about the time he'd had a run-in with Mr. Jackson. He said Mr. Jackson played dirty and called influential friends to rally behind him and complain to the boss. The pissing match slowly disappeared after Kevin dropped out of sports.

When Mac asked about Stu, Coach had glowing remarks for both the boy and his family. Stu had never been in any trouble that Coach knew of and Stu's father was a well-liked attorney in town, not the stereotypical sleaze-ball on late night commercials.

Roxy had heard the car approach before Mac saw it. Her ears were at attention, and she stopped gnawing on the bone. The all-too-familiar red sports car turned onto Hilltop Court and was inching toward Mac's home. *It's difficult to stay twenty-five feet away when the prick comes to my home*, Mac thought.

The only light in the cul-de-sac was from the dim streetlight at the corner that shone down on the community mailbox, and Mr. Jenkins's porch and garage lights. Roxy was up on all fours her hackles were up, and she was making a deep growling noise. They watched the car pass by their yard and continued around the curve of the cul-de-sac. The red sports car Mac was accustomed to seeing in front of the school stopped across the street in front of Mr. Jenkins' house. The driver parked with the engine idling. Mr. Jenkins' garage lights spotlighted the sports car, but the dark tinted windows made it impossible to see who the driver was. Mac had little doubt.

Mr. Jackson had somehow figured out where he lived and wanted Mac to know he knew.

"It's okay, girl." He spoke with a calm voice. "Roxy. Come." Always obedient, she trotted to him. Mac gave her a calming scratch behind her big hairy ears. He wasn't worried about Jackson, so there was no reason for her to be.

Mac wasn't sure if Mr. Jackson could even see them in the darkness. If he could see them, it was a stalemate, neither side moved. The driver revved the engine a few times like he was a drag racer waiting for the green light on the Christmas tree.

Even with the windows up on the sports car, Mac could hear music playing loud from inside.

Mac was contemplating how to handle the intrusion when Mr. Jackson drove off fast, screeching his tires as he turned the corner to leave Mac's little court.

"Real mature, huh, Roxy?" He kept scratching her and she loved it. Her hind leg kicked, kick, kick, kick on the porch. "Okay, girl, get your bone."

Mac's cell phone rang. He shook his fist into the air. "Dammit. Can't a man enjoy an evening cigar in peace?" he asked nobody.

CHAPTER 16

The number was unfamiliar to him. "This is Mac," he said with irritation. And then waited for a response. He could hear someone on the line, but they remained silent.

"Hello?" He tried again, with a little softer tone.

"Mr. Mac?"

"Yes," he said.

"Hello, this is Susan Jackson, Kevin's mom," she said, in a hushed voice.

A vision of Mr. Jackson manhandling his petite wife at the June school board meeting popped into Mac's head. He wasn't concerned for her safety while on the phone, he was pretty sure Mr. Jackson wasn't home yet.

"Why have you called me, Mrs. Jackson?"

"Kevin gave me your cell phone number to call if I ever needed help."

"Do you need help?" he said.

"Would you meet me for a coffee one day? Kevin told me I could trust you," Mrs. Jackson said.

"Did you want me to help you with something?" he asked, again.

"Yes." She paused. Her words came quicker. "I have to go. Will you meet me?"

"Yes," he said regretting his answer as it passed through his lips.

"Thank you. I'll call back." She hung up.

The asshole must have returned home.

He stomped his foot and scared Roxy. "Damn it." He lowered his voice to a mumble. "What the hell? He files a restraining order to keep me away and then drives by my home. Shit, shit, shit. Then his wife calls...Why? Why did I get involved?" He shook his fist at the sky again and said, "I hate family drama."

He snuffed out his cigar and pushed the swing a few more times.

Roxy gnawed on her treat with a purpose. She kept one eye on him and one eye on the bone. Her guilty pleasure was still providing her some satisfaction.

He pondered, *What do I do with this turn of events? Call Dr. Sawyer? Call Jason? If I call Dr. Sawyer, she'll get even more pissed off at me than she already is, and she'll need to share the developments with the school board members. And my guess is she'll push for my dismissal. If I call Jason, he can't do anything because the asshole didn't do anything illegal.*

Maggie answered on the second ring. "Hey, Mags," he said.

"Hi. To what to do I owe the honor?" Maggie said.

"Funny, I need some advice. Do you have time?"

"I always have time for you."

"I'm so far out of my comfort zone on this."

"What happened?"

"First, I've had a couple of shitty days. Monday, I was served a restraining order in front of parents and students. I have to stay twenty-five feet away from the father I confronted."

"Because of the assault?"

"I assume so. And then tonight, I was sitting on the front porch, enjoying a cigar, when all of a sudden the same father drove by my house."

"Since when do you smoke cigars?" Maggie said.

"The point was not the cigar."

"Sorry… Continue…"

He could hear her smiling on her end.

"So, I'm on the porch, and Roxy's on the lawn, and the dickwad drives by my house real slow. And it's not like it might have been a wrong turn," he said.

"Why would he drive by your house?" she asked with concern in her voice. "And are you certain it was him?"

"Positive. He drives an expensive red sports car. It's kind of hard to miss. The engine has a distinct sound. I hear it twice a day. He did a lame juvenile stunt and stopped across the street while he revved the engine a few times and then peeled out."

"Oh… My… God… That's so high school," Maggie said.

"Right. My moment to enjoy a cigar and Roxy's moment to enjoy a bone, both ruined. But wait, there's more," he said, and she laughed. They've always said that to each other. "As he peels out my phone rings, and it's his wife."

"The kid's mom? Are you shitting me?" she asked. "Wow, this is like a soap opera. What'd she want?"

"She asked if I'd meet her for a coffee sometime. She had to cut it short. I guess because the dickwad arrived home."

"What have you gotten yourself mixed up in?"

"Hell, if I know. The mom sounded scared."

"That's crazy. I think you have to share all this with Jason," Maggie said.

"Why? The dude hasn't done anything illegal. Maybe this job was the wrong thing for me to do. Maybe I don't know how to work in the civilian world," he said.

"Nonsense. Don't even go there. Meet Mrs. Jackson for coffee. Hear her out, and then decide," she said.

CHAPTER 17

It had been two days since Mrs. Jackson called. And it was finally Friday. Tomorrow, his sister, Maggie turns forty-three. Mac promised his nieces he would spend the weekend with them at their house.

Maggie's life was stable and for the most part traditional except that her husband Bobby, was killed in the line of duty three years earlier. Bobby had been a deputy with the County Sheriff Department. Bobby and Mac were the same age, they grew up together, went to the same schools, and had been best friends since kindergarten. Bobby went straight from high school to the sheriff's academy to become a deputy like his father was. Mac went straight from high school to the air force to get away from his father.

The girls were the glue that kept Maggie together after Bobby died. Lindy was seven and Bella was five when they lost their dad.

Mac parked on the familiar driveway of his parents' home. Memories of a volatile family life came to his mind. Every aspect of the street, the yard, the driveway, and the house brought back memories. He remembered riding bicycles on the street after dark when the streetlights lit their course. Life was good in the evenings after his drunken father passed out.

The house looked the same, for the most part. The big fruitless pear tree that was in the center of the front yard was gone. It blew over in a storm. There was a new roll-up style garage door in place of the heavy wood one you had to lift.

Over the years, Mac had parked an assortment of vehicles in the exact spot on the driveway where his truck now sat. His mom always at the kitchen window watching for him. Now it was Maggie who looked out, along with Lindy, and Bella's little head bouncing up and down trying to see.

If he were a better brother and uncle, he'd see Maggie and the girls more often. After all, they only live on the other side of Brookfield. He'd lived alone for most of his adult life. If you called life in the dorms before he made E4 or bunking with the guys when deployed, living alone. He was the loner type. His sister understood how he was and didn't push for more than he could give.

The front screen door flew open and slammed against the blue siding on the old country style house making a loud crash.

"Uncle Mac. Roxy." Two voices screamed in unison as the girls ran to him. Their faces looked like neon signs of happiness, and their hugs were better than any he'd ever had.

Lindy was at the awkward tween phase and was losing her little-girl look. When Mac told her he liked her short hair, she rolled her eyes. Bella was still at the age when it's okay to tickle her and toss her around, the only thing she'd lost since he saw her last was a front tooth.

Roxy ran in circles on the front lawn, burning off some pent-up energy.

"Wow, she runs fast," the younger niece, Bella, said.

"She does. How are my favorite girls?" He scooped them both up in his arms.

"Come inside. Hurry. We've been waiting for you to get here. Mom has an ice cream social set up for us," Lindy said followed by licking her lips and wiggled her eyebrows.

Bella added, "We had to wait for you and Roxy. I didn't think you'd ever get here. Can Roxy eat ice cream?"

"No, Roxy can't eat ice cream. But we can let's go. Come on. I'll race you," he said.

The girls jumped from his arms and ran for the door.

They beat him as usual.

"My sister," he said when he hugged Maggie.

"My brother," she replied.

He didn't want to let her go from the hug. Hugging her felt like he was home. He felt his mother's and his sister's love all rolled into one. "When are you going to replace the pear tree?"

She laughed and pushed away.

Maggie looked more and more like their mother every time he saw her. From her brown hair, warm speckled brown eyes to her beaming smile that was contagious. She was also nurturing and caring like their mother was. It was no wonder she became a nurse.

He could feel Bella and Roxy watching them and waiting. Lindy had already gone inside and was making clanging noises and slammed the freezer. Roxy sat next to him waiting for a command. Bella ran into the house but came right back.

"Come on." Bella yanked on his shirt. "Lindy scooped the ice cream already, and it's going to melt."

He countered his eight-year-old niece with equal enthusiasm and whininess. "Okay then, let's eat ice cream."

She laughed at him.

He took a deep cleansing breath as he walked into his childhood home.

They sat at the dining room table and gobbled ice cream. Bella's was more chocolate syrup and whipped cream than ice cream. She had a chocolate ring around her lips.

With her fingers, Bella wiped the last trace of ice cream from the inside of her bowl and then licked them one at a time. Between licks, she said, "Uncle Mac, can we go to the library and watch a movie? They play movies on a big screen outside. And they make popcorn. And we take pillows and a blanket to lay on and watch."

"Is that something the birthday girl wants to do?" he asked his sister.

Before Maggie answered, Bella said, "Her birthday's tomorrow."

Mac looked at Maggie. "I'd love to go watch a movie at the library."

Mac said, "What movie?"

Lindy turned from the sink where she was rinsing her bowl, she rolled her eyes and said, "Toy Story 3."

"Haven't you two seen that before?"

"Yes, but we want to see it again," said Bella.

Lindy shrugged.

"Let's get some pillows and a blanket before they start the movie without us," Maggie said.

By the time they arrived, the library parking lot was almost full.

Mac's phone rang when they were gathering their belongings from the back of Maggie's mini-van. "You go on. I'll be right there." He sat back in the driver's seat and pressed the answer button.

He heard a hushed voice say "Mr. Mac, this is Susan Jackson, Kevin's mom. I don't know who else to call. Randy's been drunk since last night. He didn't sleep. He's been angry since the assault happened. Today he's bad, the worst I've ever seen him. Would you please…"

The call ended.

He pressed the call back button. It rang and rang and never went to the voicemail option. Mrs. Jackson didn't answer on the second try either.

Mac drummed his fingers on the steering wheel as he watched his sister lay out their blanket on the grass and fluff pillows. Lindy and Bella made a path straight to the popcorn machine and stood in line which allowed him an extra minute or two to call Jason.

"Hey, it's Mac," he said.

"How're you doing, man? Are you up for some more basketball?" Jason asked.

"Not tonight, I'm at my sister's."

"Tell her hello for me," Jason said.

"I'll do that," he said and then he told him about the call from Mrs. Jackson and that he wasn't able to reach her when he called right back.

"Man. That's a tough one. If the husband is abusive and he doesn't know she called, maybe she wants to keep it that way. But then there's always the possibility he's hurt her, and that's why she isn't answering her phone," Jason's voice trailed off as he contemplated the scenarios in his mind.

Mac had nothing to contribute. Jason was the husband, the dad, and the detective.

"Let's try this. I'll speak with the supervisor on shift at the guard house out there and ask him to do a welfare check, but say he's checking the neighborhood because of the assault," Jason said.

"That's perfect. Make sure the security guard sees Mrs. Jackson. Tell him not to trust the husband's word that she's fine," Mac said.

"Okay. But dude, what the hell are you doing? You need to stay on track, find out who the drug source is. If you get mixed up in other issues you might miss something crucial," Jason said.

"I know. I know," Mac said, "She just sounded so helpless."

"I get that. Domestic disputes are ugly," Jason said.

"I'm glad I'm only a wannabe cop. Doing this kind of shit every day would be depressing," Mac said.

"Yea, I know. What was I thinking, right?" Jason said, "It's too late now. It's in my blood."

"Thanks a lot, brother. I'm sorry to involve you," Mac said.

"No worries. You saved my ass more than a few times. I'll let you know what security said as soon as I know something," he said, "Now focus on the assignment. The Chief and Michael Stromberg are counting on you. Plus, my ass is on the line, I gave you a glowing recommendation."

A pint-sized Bella marched toward the mini-van. She stopped alongside the driver's door with her hands on her hips and shoulders squared.

She said nothing. She didn't need to.

Bella had inherited the same look her mother had when she expected you to do something.

Her stance and facial expression reminded him of Training Instructor Gomez in basic training twenty years ago at Lackland Air Force Base in San Antonio, Texas. Gomez couldn't have been more than five feet tall with dark pockmarked skin, a bald head, and bulging black eyes, but when he spoke, the recruits listened. He was a hothead with a booming voice. He reminded them daily that he was fifty percent Puerto Rican and fifty percent deranged pit bull and if they wanted a taste of what he could dish out, he'd be happy to serve it up.

Mac exited the mini-van, "Okay. Okay," he said, "Let's go watch the movie."

Bella ran ahead of him to the blanket.

After they had settled into their comfortable places on the large quilt, Maggie gave his arm a gentle yank. "Who called? The president? You looked like it was something important," she said with concern.

"It was Kevin's mother again, the kid at the school I told you about."

"Why did she call?"

"She was worried about her husband's drunkenness. And then the call ended in mid-sentence. I called back twice, and the phone rang and rang. No option to leave a message." He stood. "I'm going to get some popcorn. Would you like me to bring you some?"

Maggie looked at him. She yanked his arm so he wouldn't stand up.

"Oh, my gosh, Mac. You have to do something." Maggie said.

"What the hell can I do? I didn't want to get in the middle of their fucking drama in the first place."

"Shhh." Maggie held her finger to her mouth and pointed with her eyes to the girls.

"Sorry," he whispered. "I should have listened to my better judgment. I hate family shit."

Maggie grimaced. "She sounded afraid, right? You have to do something."

"To be honest, I don't know the woman, so I can't say if she sounded afraid or not."

"What if that was me reaching out to someone for help?" Maggie asked.

"That's different. I know you." He winked. "And besides, you wouldn't marry an ass who abused you and the girls," he countered.

Maggie's facial expression told him she wanted him to find out what was going on at the Jacksons' home. She kept looking at him, waiting for him to give in.

"I called Jason and asked him to snoop around," Mac said.

"Why didn't you say that, jerk. I thought you were too cavalier about it. Thank you. She reached out to you. If Mr. Jackson's abusive to Mrs. Jackson, her reaching out to you was huge," Maggie said, "I see so many abused women at the hospital who deny it happened out of fear the abuse will get worse. I wish mom would have reached out to someone like you for help."

CHAPTER 18

So far, Saturday had been quiet regarding the Jackson family. Mac enjoyed playing with his nieces and Roxy earlier in the front yard while Maggie indulged herself with a bubble bath.

It was after Maggie's birthday dinner and cake when Mac received a call from Jason.

"Mac. The guard called me back late last night, sorry I didn't call you sooner. Today has been one of those days."

"No problem. What did the security guard say?"

"He told me Mr. Jackson answered the door around ten. The guard asked to speak with him and Mrs. Jackson. Mrs. Jackson peeked out the door wearing a bathrobe and slippers as if she'd already gone to bed. She looked fine to the guard. They both confirmed they'd been home all evening and there were no disturbances."

"That's odd. Did Mr. Jackson appear inebriated? She sounded distressed when she called," he said.

"I don't know what to tell you, man. The guy said everything looked fine to him. He didn't say anything about Mr. Jackson appearing drunk."

"Hmmm. Thanks for getting back to me."

"Say hi to Maggie."

By the time Mac hung up from speaking with Jason, the girls were in the living room tucked into their sleeping bags and munching popcorn. They were watching an animated kid's flick.

Because Mac was sleeping in Bella's room, Mac's old bedroom, the girls camped out in the living room. They said they wanted to be in the living room instead of Lindy's room, so they didn't miss anything.

Maggie was at the opposite end of the familiar worn leather sofa that had once belonged to their parents. She was sipping a glass of wine while Mac drank a beer.

She pointed to Bella. Bella's eyes were getting heavy, and her blinking was in slow motion.

Lindy looked at her mom. "Can I change the movie to something else? I only said I wanted to watch this movie for Bella. I'm not into those movies anymore. They're for little kids."

She sounded older than ten.

"Slow down, Lindy, you're growing up too fast," Mac said before Maggie could respond.

"That's what I was thinking too," Maggie added. "Watch whatever you like as long as it's age appropriate. Uncle Mac and I are going to sit in the dining room and talk."

"Okay, but Mom, Uncle Mac, can I ask you a question?"

"Sure, what?" Maggie said.

"Why don't you guys ever talk about Grandma and Grandpa MacKenna?" Lindy asked.

Maggie looked at Mac. "There's nothing to talk about," she said, "I don't talk about your dad much either. They're all in heaven, and it hurts to talk about them because I miss them so much."

Lindy turned her attention to Mac, "Uncle Mac, is that why you don't talk about them?"

"No...well, yes and no," he said, "I miss Grandma, and I miss your dad. I don't miss Grandpa so much because he was a mean dad."

In his peripheral vision, he saw Maggie's eyes bulge. She must not have liked what he said, but he thought why sugarcoat it?

"Uncle Mac, which is worse, having a mean dad or having no dad?" Lindy asked.

"That's a tough question. Can I think about it and give you an answer tomorrow?"

"Sure." Her curiosity satisfied, at least for the moment, Lindy grabbed the remote control and started surfing for a show that suited her.

Maggie and Mac fled to the safety of the dining room before Lindy asked about 'the birds and the bees.'

They sat at the big oval oak dining room table where they'd had many great dinners with their mom. And more than enough not-so-great dinners with a drunken father sitting at the head of the table.

Maggie still used mom's brown corduroy seat cushions, the kind that tied to the chair back to hold them in place.

She'd hung a large framed wedding photo of her and Bobby in the dining room. They made a handsome couple.

It had been a happy day until their father drank too much and mouthed off to some of the guests.

Bobby left his wedding reception and drove his father-in-law home. Their father had been madder than a wet cat, but he'd gone with Bobby. Bobby never said how the ride went.

Mac's beer, his second, was icy cold and hit the spot after another warm day. "Is it weird living here?" he asked his sister.

"It was at first. It felt like it was Mom and Dad's place still. Now it feels like ours. I like that it's filled with their stuff, though, it keeps me close to Mom. I try not to think about Dad. He was a mean dad. You were right. He was also a mean husband. Poor Mom, she was so nice, and kind, and deserved to be with a man who treated her right," Maggie said with tears welling up in her eyes.

"I know." He patted her hand. "Your older daughter has your inquisitive nature, and Bella received a double dose of stubbornness from you and Bobby," he said.

She smiled. "I know. So, tell me more about Mr. Jackson. What a shit. Serving you with a restraining order." Her voice bumped up in volume.

The wine was loosening up Maggie's mouth.

She lowered her voice and leaned forward. "Mr. Jackson will go apeshit if he finds out his wife called you last night," she added.

"Not much I can do about how crazy he reacts to everything. They're a weird family."

Maggie held her glass by the stem and watched the Merlot as she swirled it around and around.

"Oh, I know. We get plenty of weirdos at the hospital. It's like they wait until after doctor's hours and go to the emergency room."

Maggie drank the entire bottle of wine. She told Mac about a doctor she worked with at the hospital. He'd asked her out a few times. She always said she wasn't ready. She wanted to go out with him, but was unsure how to tell the girls.

Mac was feeling no pain himself after more than a few beers. He told her about Rita.

It was close to eleven-thirty when Mac's cell phone rang, he grabbed it fast so as not to wake the girls. The number was Mrs. Jackson's. "Hello?" he waited. "Hello?" Silence on the other end. "Mrs. Jackson, are you there?" He could hear someone breathing on the other end of the call. "Kevin, is that you?"

Maggie's eyes were large and she sat as still as a statue.

"I told you to stay the fuck away from my family," Mr. Jackson slurred. "You didn't listen."

"Mr. Jackson, have you done something to your wife?" He tried to keep his voice quiet.

Maggie's hand covered her gaping mouth.

"How's your sister, Military Man?" he asked. "She's a pretty lady. The girls are too. Did you have fun playing with the girls today? Oh, and tell your sister I left her a little something in her mailbox."

Without hesitation, Mac ran to the front door, yanked it open and ran out onto the front lawn.

Tail-lights disappeared down the long street. A dark SUV. "Are you still there, motherfucker?" he said into his phone. Click. The caller hung up.

Mac called Mrs. Jackson's phone back, but there was no answer. It just rang, and rang, and rang. There was no option to leave a message either.

"What's going on?" Maggie stood behind him on the front porch.

"He was in front of your house."

"Who was in front of my house?"

"Mr. Jackson."

Her eyes bulged, and her hand covered her heart. "Oh my God."

Roxy must have sensed trouble. She pushed her nose against the screen door hard enough to open it so she could squeeze through. She was by Mac's side, prepared to protect him if necessary. Roxy and Mac walked around the front of the house and along the street.

Maggie stood on the porch and watched.

He was unsure what Mr. Jackson had left for Maggie. He shone a flashlight into the mailbox and peeked inside. There was a photo in the mailbox, taken today when he and the girls were playing with Roxy in the front yard.

There was evidence that someone sat across the street long enough for the air conditioner to dribble. The driver smoked several cigarettes and flicked the ashes on the street. There were no butts, though.

To my knowledge, Mr. Jackson doesn't smoke cigarettes. Mac thought to himself.

CHAPTER 19

Mac heard the alarm on his cell phone. *Is it Monday already?* He thought with a groggy brain. Time to wake up? The alarm sounded different. He forced his brain to engage. It wasn't his alarm. It was a call from someone on his favorites list ringing through the nighttime do not disturb setting.

"Hello." His voice crackled. He cleared his throat and looked at the clock. *Three in the morning.*

"Hey Mac, sorry to wake you, it's Jason."

"What happened?" Mac said knowing full well it was something bad for Jason to call in the middle of the night.

"The mayor's son, Seth, overdosed again. He was at a party Saturday night, a party-goer called 911 and reported that he was unconscious. An ambulance took him to the hospital, and it looked like he was going to pull through yesterday. He died about an hour ago. The Chief was on my ass because we haven't figured out where the drugs are coming from."

Mac listened while he scratched Roxy's head.

"That's horrible. Has anyone considered Seth was getting his drugs from someone not associated with the school?" Mac asked. "What'd he OD on?"

"We won't know until we get back the toxicology results. They think it's heroin again. The Chief wants an update. Call me later."

"Okay, I will," Mac said.

The house was quiet. He heard the faint hum of the light traffic on the highway through the open bedroom window. The crickets along the bank of the creek behind his home sang loudly.

"What happened?" Rita asked.

"Seth Eastland overdosed again. He didn't make it."

"Oh my God. His poor family."

Mac sat on the side of his bed contemplating the news he'd just received and whether he would be able to fall back asleep or not. Roxy waited to see what they were doing. "I'm going to work out for a bit. You stay in bed," he said.

"Okay," Rita said as she sniffled and blew her nose.

Mac, with Roxy on his heels, went to the bedroom he'd set up as his home gym and worked out for an hour. He thought about why teenagers turn to drugs in the first place. When he was Seth's age, his life was less than stellar. His alcoholic father was a monster to live with, and yet he never considered taking drugs. He and Bobby sneaked a beer from his parent's refrigerator now and then. That was to see what they felt like after drinking it, not as a coping mechanism.

Mac concluded it was all about the friends you chose. The guys who were doing drugs or the guys who weren't. There were many times when his father was yelling obscenities at his mother, and she was crying, that he may have taken something to dull his senses had he known about drugs. Instead, he and Maggie retreated to their bedrooms. They'd sit in their closets with the doors closed and talk through a small hole they each bore from their sides until they had a hole straight through their shared wall.

Mac wondered, *Why was Seth so unhappy he resorted to drugs? Was life so bad at the mayor's home? And who were Seth's friends?*

CHAPTER 20

It was six-thirty when Clarence, Coach's uncle, let himself into the home Coach and his mother shared. He poured a cup of coffee and joined his nephew at the table.

Coach scattered the newspaper and began reading the sports section.

"What has you up and out so early?" Coach asked.

"You haven't heard?" his uncle asked.

"I guess not. Heard what?"

"Seth Eastland overdosed again, this time, he didn't make it," his uncle said.

Coach put the newspaper down. "Shit. How're the Mayor and Leona doing?"

"Not good. Leona's inconsolable. Ozzy's angry beyond words. He wants the person who sold Seth the drugs."

"I suppose if it were my son, I'd want the same thing," Coach said.

"You should call the Ozzy to see if he needs anything. We've known the Eastland's many years. They would welcome a call from you," his uncle said.

"I'll do that. Mother will want to go to the funeral," Coach said. He felt exhausted to think of the ordeal of helping his mother attend a funeral.

"Is she up yet?" Clarence asked.

"She's moving around up there. I've heard the floor creak a few times," Coach said.

"I'll tell her."

As Coach's Uncle Clarence went up the back stairway from the kitchen to the second floor to visit with his sister, Coach's phone vibrated. He hadn't turned on the ringer yet.

It was Stu calling. "Hello," Coach said with a quiet voice.

"It's Stu. Did you hear about Seth?"

"I did. It's a damn shame and sad beyond words," said Coach.

"I was at the same party with Seth on Saturday. I called 911 for the ambulance, and then I hung up so they wouldn't trace my phone."

"You've watched too much TV. I don't think it works like that. Did you tell your father this?" Coach said.

"Fuck no. Dad would ground me for life. Are the cops going to know I called 911? I didn't think Seth would die."

"Were you doing drugs at the party?"

"No, I was just drinking. Dad won't believe me if he finds out I was there."

"Would you like me to talk to him for you?" Coach said.

"Just feel him out, don't tell him I was there," Stu said, "I gotta go."

Coach heard the elevator begin its descent. The door was in plain view from where Coach sat. He felt his stomach twist into a knot.

His uncle stamped down the stairs and appeared in the kitchen before his sister made it to the ground floor.

"She's upset and crying, be gentle with her. I've got to get the pharmacy opened. Call me if you have a problem with her," his uncle said.

"Thanks," Coach said with frustration.

Coach was waiting when the door opened, and his mother pushed her walker into the kitchen. "Chucky. Poor Leona and Ozzy." She went to the table and sat with a thud.

"I remember how sad I felt when…when your brother…" She reached for a tissue to blow her nose. "Order some flowers for the family, a big expensive bouquet. I'm ready for breakfast."

Coach prepped to make his mother an omelet. He felt overwhelming gratitude when the front doorbell rang. He knew it was Lucy, his mother's personal attendant who stayed with her while he was at work.

He updated Lucy on what had happened as they walked to the kitchen.

"Chucky, you can't leave me here with Lucy. I'm too sad. Lucy doesn't know the Eastland's."

"Mom, Lucy understands. I told her what happened," Coach said.

Without saying anything, Lucy took over at the stove.

Coach paid Lucy much more than the standard for her position. He needed her more than she needed the money.

He could hear his mother's tantrum brewing.

"NO. I can't stay here with Lucy. Call the school and explain

I need you."

This exit scene was a recurring frustration for Coach. Seth's death gave his mother what she considered to be a valid reason for insisting he stay with her.

Coach thanked Lucy while his mother screamed at him not to leave. When he shut the kitchen door and was in the garage, he could still hear her screaming his name.

CHAPTER 21

Mac and Rita sat in the kitchen with fresh coffee. The TV was set to Sacramento Channel 7 news. They'd expected to see something about the mayor's son's death.

For two hours, they drank coffee, watched the repeating loop of news, and listened to it rain. They talked about the drug use amongst the students at Blackstone Academy and how tragic it was when a young person died before they experienced all that life had to offer. The death was big news, and the station was sending a crew to Brookfield for more details.

Sometime around six o'clock, Rita went to her place to get ready for work, Mac showered and left for work shortly after. He expected he might need to deal with crowd control issues.

As he expected, news crews were setting up along the sidewalk in front of the school. They had pop-up canopies protecting them from the rain. Parked news vehicles were in the way of where parents would drop off their kids. Mac analyzed the situation as he walked closer.

"You need to move your vehicle," Mac said to the first reporter.

"Who are you," he stuck a microphone close to Mac's mouth.

Mac moved the microphone away and turned his back to the cameraman.

"You need to move your vehicle. Now," Mac said again over his shoulder.

"Why?" the reporter yelled to him.

Mac walked back under the canopy. "Parents need to drop off their kids and your vehicle is in the way. Move the van to the parking lot across the street and set up your crew over there," he said as he pointed.

The reporter looked at him with disbelief. "This is a public sidewalk and a public street."

"Is that how you want to play this? Go ahead, be difficult, you won't get many interviews like that. Wait here while I call Police Chief Contee to request police support to manage the media," he said as he walked toward the school entrance. He added under his breath, "I'm sure the mayor will be…"

"Fine. We'll move. But you better make everyone else move also," the reporter hollered at Mac.

Mac repeated the same conversation to the next reporter and the next and the one after that. After he had the sidewalk cleared, he waited at his post for the parents and students to arrive.

Parents formed in clusters under large umbrellas all along the sidewalk in front of the school and across the street near their vehicles. They talked with their heads close. He imagined they were talking about poor Mayor and Mrs. Eastland. A short young woman who arrived later than the other reporters and who Mac had not needed to speak with was talking with some parents in the parking lot. She balanced her umbrella with her chin and shoulder while she wrote in a notebook.

"Excuse me, sir," the woman said, as she walked toward Mac. "I'm Selena Ramirez with the Mountain Tribune. I'm writing an article for the Wednesday paper about the tragic loss for the mayor. May I ask you a few questions?" She spoke fast, not allowing him an opportunity to shut her down.

"No, you may not ask me any questions, and I suggest you show some respect and take your set-up across the street. I better not see you pestering parents or kids either."

"Sir, what's your name?" she asked.

He pointed his index finger toward the cluster of canopies. "Move it, lady."

Dr. Sawyer tapped his shoulder, two women he didn't recognize stood behind her. All three held personal-sized umbrellas over their heads.

"Marshal MacKenna," she said, "Who was that woman?"

"A news reporter trying to get an angle on the mayor's son's story for the Wednesday paper. I think she's got it straight not to bug the parents."

Dr. Sawyer touched the older of the two women on her back. "This is Mary and Alice, school psychologists from Brookfield High School. Because of what happened to Seth, this morning they'll be here to help us to talk with Seth's friends or staff members, if needed."

"I'd like them to stand here with you and Roni this morning. If you overhear anyone speaking about this tragedy, parents, students or staff for that matter, please let Mary or Alice know and they'll start a conversation. And stay visible today. Keep an ear out for any conversations about Seth or his family, and let Mary or Alice know who says what."

"Sure thing, boss," he said.

Mary appeared to be at the end of her career, whereas Alice seemed to be at the start of hers. Both women were solemn.

Dr. Sawyer touched his arm, held her hand there a long minute. "It's a difficult day, Mac. Please stop by my office after the tardy bell rings." Dr. Sawyer said in a sweet tone unfamiliar to him.

"Will do." He was suspicious about why she was acting so friendly to him.

"I've cleared my calendar for the rest of the week, I'll be on campus and available anytime," she said.

He tipped his head. There was nothing more to say.

Roni wasn't her normal self, not as chipper nor as friendly to the parents and students. She held a large umbrella over her and Mac. Mary and Alice stood near them all morning without speaking. Mac was grateful for that.

"Mr. Mac. Ladies," Teddy said, as he approached. His jacket hood was pulled down so far it covered his forehead. His sister, Savannah, had a new purple cast on her arm. Savannah went inside the school.

"What happened to Savannah's arm?" Mac asked, Teddy.

"She fell off the swing set at home and broke it. She's playing it up to get whatever she wants. Girls," he said shaking his head.

"Where did the school kittens go on their field trip?" Teddy asked the four of them with a serious look. He even furrowed his brow in concentration.

"I'm not sure Teddy. Where'd they go?" Mac said.

Roni watched and waited for the punch line.

"They went to the mew-seum. Get it? The mew-seum. Ha ha ha!" Teddy laughed out loud, slapped his thigh, and doubled over.

The four smiled and chuckled a little. Mac doubted Teddy was aware of what had happened to Seth. He was too young to understand.

Mac gave him a high five.

"Good one, Teddy," Roni said, as she dropped to her knees and hugged him. "You stay as sweet and innocent as you are today," she said with a cracking voice filled with emotion.

It was going to take more than a joke from Teddy Ross to lighten the mood.

Roni started to cry after Teddy left. She went inside to pull herself together.

"Mac," Coach had come from behind him, "terrible day, terrible. What a tragedy." Coach shook his head.

"Bad scene, for sure," Mac said.

"I spoke with Mayor Eastland and Leona this morning. They're in shock. Parker won't be in school for the rest of the week. He's taking this pretty hard. After Seth's near overdose in April, Parker thought Seth had straightened himself out. Terrible day," he repeated.

"Hang in there, Coach," Mac said. He patted him on his slumped shoulder.

The flow of people slowed, kids went inside the school, moms and dads off to do what they did while their kids were away.

Mrs. Ross stayed in the parking lot long after Teddy and Savannah had gone inside. She seemed to revel in the limelight.

CHAPTER 22

When Mac turned the corner, Marlene reached for a tissue and blew her nose. She had a blotchy face. Large teardrops pooled in her eyes. She went to Mac and hugged him.

"I can't believe it, Mac. Seth was such a nice boy. How'd he get mixed up with drugs?" she said while she continued to hold him in a squeezing hug.

Mac patted her back to comfort her. "I don't know Marlene."

She released him and stepped back to look up at him. "You're wet. Didn't you use an umbrella?"

"I stood under Roni's with her," he said.

She went back to her desk and sat down. She grabbed two more tissues.

"The boss asked me to stop in to see her," he said.

"Oh. Okay. Let me buzz Dr. Sawyer first," Marlene said.

Given the green light to enter the boss' office, Mac went inside and closed the door behind him. He sat in the usual spot and waited for a butt-chewing.

"Did you have any interaction with Seth Eastland?" she asked. Her tone had returned to a more familiar agitation.

"No, I didn't know him," Mac said.

"What the hell do you do? You should be getting to know all the kids," she said, "Seth was a darling boy." She choked up and had to pause for a moment.

"I've not been here long enough to know every child," he replied.

She cleared her throat. "That's ridiculous." She waved her hand to dismiss the subject. "Do you know if we have drugs circulating?"

"I haven't seen anything suspicious," he replied.

"Because one of our students has died from an overdose, the school looks like we have a drug problem. The mayor wants answers. He suspects Seth purchased the drugs from another student here at the school. Do you have any idea how that makes me look? I'm the leader of a prestigious school with a drug problem. You need to get off your ass and find out what's going on."

"How do you propose I do that? Kids won't tell me they're doing drugs."

"Offer an incentive," she threw out.

"What incentive?" he asked. "Money?"

"Sure, why not?"

"Can a school do that? Offer a reward for information?" he asked.

"Have the Police Chief make the offer, the school's foundation can donate to their efforts," she suggested. "You do know the Police Chief, don't you?"

"I've never met him," Mac said.

"My God. Do I have to do your job for you? The Police Chief was the one who convinced the board we needed an armed marshal. I thought by now you would have taken the time to meet him. He was your biggest supporter."

He didn't like it, but he was becoming accustomed to her ranting.

"He wasn't supporting me. He supported the position and the job description," he replied.

She stared at him for a few seconds. He wasn't sure if she was about to implode. Her face reddened and a vein on her forehead bulged.

She said, again, "The mayor wants answers, and you better find some. Now, get out." She swiveled her chair around to face the French door and look toward her private patio. The rain pounded down on the cement hard and loud.

Marlene stared at Mac as he closed the office door.

"What happened?" she asked. Her face had recovered from crying. She looked normal again.

Mac sat on the chair at the end of her tidy desk.

"She asked, or I should say she ordered me, to find out if Seth bought the drugs from someone here at school," he replied.

Marlene gasped. "Do you think he did?"

"Do you? Does anyone stand out as a suspect to you?" he asked.

"Hmmm," she said, as she tapped her index finger to her lips. "Stu and Kevin are wild boys."

"That doesn't make them drug dealers," he replied. "Do any of the staff seem suspicious?"

"Oh my…no," she shook her head.

CHAPTER 23

Coach was deep into grading papers at his desk when there was a knock on the frame of the opened door. He looked up and saw Stu Collins.

"Come in, come in. Make it quick. I need to take my mother to an appointment." Coach said as he waved his hand to Stu. "Have a seat. How're you doing Stu? It's a tough day."

Stu closed the door, dropped his backpack and then placed the binders on the floor so he could sit down.

"Did you talk to my dad?" Stu asked.

"I've been a little busy. I haven't had a chance. I'll stop by his office on my way home."

"If he finds out I was at that party he's going to kill me." Stu said. Sweat beads covered his brow. His cheeks were redder than normal, and he seemed to be hyperventilating.

"Stu, take a deep breath and calm down. Your dad won't kill you," Coach said, "Were other kids from the school at the party?"

"A bunch of kids were there, like a hundred. There was even a band," Stu said.

"Where was the party? Take a deep breath," Coach said.

"It was at the old abandoned barn out by Durdenberger's," Stu said.

"Were you still there when the ambulance arrived?" Coach asked.

"I split after I called it in. My dad thought I was staying over at Kevin's," Stu said.

"Did you give the drugs to Seth?" Coach asked.

Stu's head dropped. He started to sniffle and wiped tears. He sat still for a minute or so. Coach felt him not answering was an answer.

"That Marshal dude's always looking at me and Kevin weird like he thinks we're big-time criminals or something," Stu said, "If he ever talks to my dad, I'm so screwed."

"Why would Mac talk to your father about you? They don't even know each other, do they?" Coach said, "As far as Kevin's concerned, the way he irritates his father in front of everyone makes me wonder if he's up to something. Not because I relate his behavior to drugs, but that kid's like a ticking time bomb."

"I don't know. I don't think my dad knows the marshal. But if he thinks I'm a drug dealer he might tell my dad that," Stu said. He wiped his shirt sleeve across his brow. He was breathing heavy again.

"Stu, calm down. You're freaking out about stuff that hasn't happened. You're paranoid. If you act like this when the subject comes up about who gave Seth the drugs, you won't have to answer the question. Your face will show your guilt."

Stu shook his head. "I'm so screwed," he said.

CHAPTER 24

Someone knocked on Mac's office door. Coach opened the door and poked his head inside and said, "Do you have a minute?"

"Sure. Come on into my cave," Mac said. There was a lone lamp sitting on the corner of his desk in the windowless office. The main light source was the wall of monitors.

"You're able to watch the entire school from here. I had no idea there were so many cameras or that you had so many monitors," Coach said.

Coach stood staring at the wall of screens with slide shows of various views coming and going.

"There are a few spots where there aren't cameras. Sit down, and I'll give you a tour of the campus."

Coach sat on the one option in the room, a hard plastic chair. Mac's desk was tidy, the opposite of Coach's.

Mac clicked his mouse on each of the locations where there was a camera. He zoomed in on a few areas to show the clarity of the close-up views.

"Let's see who's in the locker room," Coach said.

"There aren't cameras in the locker rooms. How about the gym instead?" Mac said.

"Sure," said Coach.

They watched the girls jogging around the perimeter of the gym. The forecast of thunderstorms kept the physical education classes indoors.

"Impressive," Coach said.

"You didn't come here to watch what's happening on campus. What can I do for you?" Mac said.

"It's so sad about Seth. The students are all freaked out and on edge," Coach said.

"It's a sad thing whenever a young person gets hooked on drugs. They don't realize there's so much more to life. What do you want me to do about the students' fears?" Mac asked.

"There isn't anything you can do. Kids at this age are so paranoid and secretive. Stu Collins is afraid you think he has something to do with the drug scene amongst the students," Coach said.

"Do you think he's involved?" Mac asked.

Coach shrugged. "My guess would be Stu seems too cocky. He thinks he's untouchable because his father's an attorney. He'd be flaunting his power position if he had one," Coach said.

"What about his pal, Kevin?" Mac said.

"Is Kevin involved with drugs? Hmmm, he doesn't strike me as the type either. There's not much he can get away with because his father has him on a short leash," Coach said.

"Then we're back to, what can I do for you?" Mac said.

"There have been a few times when Roni had wandered into the gym area when she didn't need to be there, Stu has it in his head, Roni's snooping for you," Coach said.

"Roni isn't snooping for anyone. Her job is to monitor what's going on all over the campus," Mac said, "Why's Stu so paranoid?"

"Stu thinks you're a narcotics officer working undercover for the police department and he thinks you're going to pin the drugs that killed Seth on him," Coach said.

"Wow. That sounds like a good fiction novel. Why would I retire from the military after twenty years of hostility and war to come home and become a cop?" Mac said, "Besides, I'm too old to be accepted into the academy. Stu sounds too paranoid," Mac said.

"You'd have to know Stu. He's paranoid about everything. He doesn't have a trusting personality. Having a criminal attorney for a father doesn't help," Coach said.

"This has been interesting to learn more about Stu, but I'm not hearing why you're telling me or what you want me to do," Mac said.

"You can't do anything. I agree with you. Stu's too paranoid. I needed to hear from you if I should be more suspicious of Stu or continue to treat him as the lamebrain, I know him to be," Coach said.

"If Stu does something out of the ordinary that causes you to wonder what he's up to, let me know, and I'll look into it. Otherwise, I think Stu seems like a typical teenager to me, and Roni's just doing her job," Mac said.

"Good to know. I'm watching the students more than before Seth died. You may not know this, but I've been friends with Mayor Eastland and his wife for many years. Seth's death has rocked their world. Leona won't eat. She doesn't leave her bedroom. Ozzy's on a mission to find out who sold Seth the drugs. He asked me to poke around at school to see if it was another student here."

The bell sounded to change classes. Coach had to hustle to the gym. His prep period was over. "Gotta run. Let me know if you hear of anything or if there's anything I can do to help get to the bottom of this," Coach said as he opened the door to leave Mac's office.

"You do the same, Coach. Thank you," Mac said.

Mac put in a call to Jason.

"Hey bro, what's happening?" Jason answered knowing who was on the other end of the phone call.

"I just had an interesting conversation with Coach Andrews. He wanted to know if I was an undercover narcotics officer and if I thought Stu Collins was the source for the drugs that Seth overdosed on," Mac said.

"That's interesting. Were you able to squash the narc rumor?" Jason said.

"I think so since the truth is I'm not an officer," Mac said, "Before he left, he asked me to keep him in the loop. He said he was close to the mayor and his wife and he wanted to do his part to end the drugs on campus," Mac said.

"We don't know for sure whether Seth got the drugs from a kid at the school or somewhere else. I find that odd he assumes the drugs came from a classmate," Jason said.

"His concern seems genuine," Mac said.

"That may be the case; you still keep your assignment secret. I don't trust anyone," Jason said.

CHAPTER 25

Coach sauntered into his mother's suite to show her how dapper he looked in his tuxedo. He'd hoped she'd pay him a compliment.

"You look like a penguin," his mother said.

"Gee thanks, mom."

"I don't want to stay here with Lucy. I spend all week with Lucy. Why can't I come to the Gala as your escort? Mark and Stella Blackstone are accompanying Lyla to the Gala," his mother said.

"That's different. Lyla's late husband founded the school. She has to attend every year," Coach said as he plopped onto his mother's chaise with an exasperated huff.

"I don't think it's different at all. Lyla's an old lady just like me, and Mark's a loving son, unlike you," she said.

"Because I'm not taking you to the Gala, I'm an unloving son?"

"If you loved me, you'd take me." She folded her arms across her generous bosom.

"Mother, I do love you. I'm the one who pays for this lavish home, so you're comfortable. I'm the one who takes care of your needs. I'm the one who drives you to your appointments. Do I need to go on?" he said. His shoulders slumped. Coach no longer felt like the rock-star he had when he walked into her room.

"If you loved me, you'd do all that plus take me to the Gala. You're acting just like your brother used to. A spoiled, selfish brat." She looked at him with the stubborn look of a kid refusing to eat their vegetables.

Before Coach could rebut her comment Lucy walked into the room. She picked up on the tension in the room, "Hello."

"Lucy, go home. Chucky's taking me to the Gala. We won't need your services this evening."

Lucy turned around to leave.

"No. Lucy, please stay. Chucky's not taking mother to the Gala tonight," he said.

Lucy turned back around to face them and then froze at the

entrance of the bedroom.

Coach stood. "Mother, this discussion's over. You're staying here with Lucy. I need to leave. Have a good evening." Out of respect, he waited for one final jab from his mother. She said nothing. Her arms still folded across her chest; her gaze filled with fire.

Coach left the room and went down the stairs to the main floor. He hated how demanding she could be, but also hated to disappoint her. He called Clarence.

"What's up?" his mother's brother said, a little out of breath.

"Tonight's the school's Gala at the fairgrounds. Your sister's in a mood this evening. Lucy's staying with her while I'm gone, but she's going to be difficult. I don't want Lucy to quit. Will you come over and hang out with her for an hour or so to calm her down?"

"Um…Sure… I appreciate that you do so much for her. I'll head over in a few minutes. Enjoy yourself."

They ended their phone call. As Chuck was placing his wallet in his pants pocket and grabbing his car keys, he heard his mother on the intercom system. "Chucky, I know you're still here. I didn't hear the garage door open. I'm sorry, come back to my room."

He reached for the door between the garage and the kitchen.

"Chucky, please. Please, come back. Chucky, if you leave, you'll regret it," she threatened.

Coach stared at the door to his freedom and though, *What will she do?* When he stepped into the garage, he felt a heavy weight lift from his shoulders. When he pushed the button to open the roll-up garage door, his cell phone rang in his pocket. It was his mother. He turned the ringer off and drove away.

CHAPTER 26

The Blackstone Gala was a black-and-white fund-raising event attended by most o7f the parents and many distinguished community members. The event was at The Pavilion, a ballroom located at the county fairgrounds.

Mrs. Blackstone, the founder's widow, her son, Mark, and his wife, Stella, always attended. Mayor Eastland did too. Mrs. Eastland was not attending this year. She was still coping with the death of their son. Police Chief Contee and other dignitaries attended along with all five board members and their significant others as well.

Earlier in the week, Marlene gave Mac a crash course in Gala 101. The gala was the primary fundraiser for the school, the annual parent donations were, of course, the first.

The state and federal money had too many strings attached. Whereas the donations allowed the school to provide programs most public schools had cut.

She told him Mark had overseen the family business since Henry died. Mark went to college to be a stock market guy, but ended up following in his daddy's footsteps and was a land developer. Mark wanted to attend college in San Francisco and marry his high school sweetheart. Henry wouldn't have it. He sent Mark to Boston to attend Harvard. That's where he met his wife. Stella's family was more aligned with Henry's vision for his son's future. "You'll see," she said, "She's what you might call a trophy wife."

Mac asked her what happened to the high school sweetheart.

"She married a local boy."

Marlene's spiel ended with a warning for Mac to stay clear of Mr. Jackson, he had a track record for getting smashed at the event, and he was a mean drunk.

Michael Stromberg called Mac last week to hear how things were going with his investigation. He also gave him some pointers about the gala. Other than the conversation with Michael Stromberg, Mac had relied on Marlene for the gala gossip because

Dr. Sawyer didn't speak with him about it at all. She wasn't happy when she learned he would be working the gala.

Mac backed into a stall at the far end of the parking area. He'd arrived an hour before the shindig was to begin. He sat for a moment and enjoyed the quiet.

He noticed Dr. Sawyer walk out of the ballroom at a fast clip. She crossed her arms over her chest holding her coat closed. She went around to the side of the building where someone waited in a car. Exhaust billowed indicating the car was running and most likely the interior was warm. She climbed into the passenger seat.

And then Mac received a text from Maggie.

Maggie: Woowoo. Lady killer. I like the tux. Thanks for sending the pic.

Mac: I'd rather stay home and watch Fight Night.

Maggie: Have you left or are you home still?

Mac: I'm parked at the ballroom watching my boss do something mysterious.

Maggie: Mysterious?

Mac: She scurried to a waiting car and had been sitting in it for a few minutes.

Mac didn't recognize the vehicle. He checked his watch. He had a few more minutes to watch the intriguing scene play out. Two minutes passed. Then four.

Maggie: A lover? Is she married?

Mac: As far as I know, she's single.

Maggie: How intriguing.

At five minutes, Mac gave up.

Mac: Not really. Time for me to do this.

Maggie: Have fun. It's good for you to get out, even if it's work.

Mac: Not my kind of fun. Have a good night.

Maggie: You too.

Mac was about half-way between his truck and the side of the building where the idling car was parked when the passenger door opened and Dr. Sawyer emerged. She smoothed her hair and shifted her coat into place. She leaned over and said something to the person before she stood up and made eye contact with Mac. She averted her eyes and hurried around the corner and inside the ballroom.

The car made a U-turn and passed by Mac. It was Mayor Eastland. They made eye-contact.

As instructed by Marlene, when he walked inside Mac went straight to her. Dr. Sawyer had managed to disappear with the few seconds lead she had on him. Marlene and two female student volunteers from the senior class sat at a long table inside near the door, waiting to take tickets.

Marlene whistled. "Mr. Mac, you clean up real nice." Marlene stood and examined him from head to toe, front and back. "I approve," she said.

"Good evening to you too, Marlene." Mac bowed. "It's all thanks to you. You look beautiful."

Marlene wore a ball gown tasteful for her age except for the brightness of the color under the harsh overhead lighting, almost required sunglasses.

"Oh yeah right. At my age, you don't look beautiful," she said.

"Will you honor me with a dance later?" Mac asked.

She blushed. "I'd love to. Thank you. The last time I danced was with my husband," she said with a hand over her heart. "Come here." She pulled him away from the two girls at the table.

"Remember what I told you, stay away from Mr. and Mrs. Jackson. They always attend. He always ends up drunk, and he always picks a fight with someone. Since he already has a problem with you, he won't like seeing you here."

"I'm not worried about Mr. Jackson."

"Mac, stay away from him. Please," she pleaded.

"Thanks for worrying about me. I'd better check in with Dr. Sawyer. Where might she be?"

She pointed over her left shoulder to the room where bright fluorescent lights glared. "She came in the door right before you and hurried over to the kitchen."

"Thanks. I'll see you later for that dance."

"It's a date."

As he walked toward the kitchen, he overheard one of the girls with Marlene ask if he was her boyfriend. Marlene giggled.

Mac stepped through the doorway of the kitchen and saw Dr. Sawyer. She had a guilty look on her face. She saw him and walked his way. Mac stepped back into the main banquet room so they could hear each other speak.

"Where would you like me to be?" Mac asked. He decided to keep what he had just seen to himself. He didn't know what went down inside the mayor's car.

"I'd like you to be home, but since my opinion doesn't matter,

I suppose you can hang out near the front door. And please stay away from Mr. and Mrs. Jackson, you've caused them enough drama," she said.

"Okay... The door it is," he said ignoring her accusation.

"Look. We haven't had security at this event. This is the first time. If you see something that catches your attention, speak with me about it first, so I'll know who it is before you intervene."

"I can do that."

They both turned toward the entrance when they heard Marlene squeal. Michael Stromberg and his much younger wife had arrived. Marlene jumped up and ran around the table to hug them.

"Do you remember Michael Stromberg, president of the school board, from your interview last summer?" Dr. Sawyer inquired.

"I do," he said.

"Make a point to say hello..." She left before she finished her sentence.

CHAPTER 27

The kitchen staff moved about the kitchen in warp speed. Mac sidestepped through the assembly line of chefs as best he could without getting in anyone's way. The cooks were arranging shrimp on goblets, and huge cuts of beef sizzled on spits over a low flame.

Mac stopped at a young man preparing salad plates. "Excuse me, would you point me toward the head chef?"

"He's the one over there with the blue scarf around his neck." He pointed to a man at the grill.

"Thank you," he said.

Mac continued to squeeze his way through the food prep area. "Excuse me, sir." He tapped his shoulder. The man turned to look at him with an impatient stare. "I wanted to introduce myself. I'm Mac, security for the evening. If you need me for anything, I'll be in the main banquet room."

"Got it. Now get out of my kitchen." He turned away with a dismissive huff and resumed his instruction to the cook at the grill.

Mac returned to the banquet room and noticed quite a few people had arrived in the short time he'd been in the kitchen. He made a fast path to his post at the door and gave Marlene a wink. She smiled.

He felt like the gatekeeper for Noah's Ark. Two by two, couples of all sizes and colors entered the gala. Tall men with short women, short men with tall women, old men with young women and young men with old women, women with women and men with men.

The atmosphere in the room was festive, the bar was in full swing, and the silent auction items had received bids that far exceeded the value of the item.

Mac extended his arm for Mrs. Blackstone and escorted her to the head table. Her son Mark, and his trophy wife, Stella, followed. And then he ushered the school board members and their guests.

Marlene was right about Stella. She was gorgeous, blond, and thin. She carried herself with an arrogance that seems prevalent among the wealthy.

At seven o'clock sharp, although there was an underlying sadness amongst the gala attendees, the room burst into applause when a poised and elegant Dr. Sawyer took the stage. Her white gown shimmered in the spotlights. A small band was set up behind her.

Dr. Sawyer's voice came across the sound system. "Good evening, ladies and gentlemen and welcome to the tenth annual Blackstone Academy Black and White Gala. For those who may not know who I am, I'm Dr. Sawyer, the Superintendent and Principal of Blackstone Academy."

Another round of applause swept through the large room.

Mac stood near the entrance door and surveyed the crowd. He estimated there were at least fifty large round tables that seated eight. Some people stood at the bar. Some people perused the area that held the silent auction items, and others stood in clusters talking.

Dr. Sawyer continued with her greeting. More politics. She introduced the school board members, who stood and waved at their constituents.

For the first time that night, Mac saw Mr. Jackson. He was standing at the bar with a drink in his hand speaking with Mayor Eastland.

Mrs. Jackson sat at a table with other couples. The woman seated next to her seemed to be talking non-stop. She nodded in agreement to what the woman said. She didn't appear to be saying much if anything.

She was a strange woman. He wondered if she was an introvert, an odd duck, or the abused wife he thought she might be. He wasn't sure what she wanted him to help her with, and he wasn't certain he wanted to help at all.

Mr. Jackson either hadn't noticed Mac or was ignoring him. Mac's bet was he hadn't expected him to be at the gala, so he wasn't looking for him. With a drink in both hands and a bottle of wine under his arm, he made his way to the table where his wife was. He sat in the only vacant seat, which faced the stage and away from Mac. *Perfect*. He thought.

Dr. Sawyer asked everyone to take their seats. She then introduced Mayor Eastland to the audience. With an envelope in hand, he made his way to the stage. He spoke into the microphone with a booming voice. "Coach Chuck Andrews get up here." His tired face showed how difficult it was to be a public figure during a personal loss.

Coach joined the mayor on the stage.

Mayor Eastland gushed about Coach's winning record, about his supportive relationship with his athletes and their families, and about what a wonderful person he was outside of work for taking care of his sick mother. The mayor announced Coach was Blackstone Academy's Employee of the Year. He ended his ten minutes of accolades with a vigorous handshake and then handed coach a framed award from the envelope he'd held.

Coach spoke into the microphone. He thanked the mayor, the school board, Dr. Sawyer, and the parents for the tremendous job they were doing raising their future leaders. Coach received a standing ovation.

The kitchen doors burst open, and the serving staff filed out one after another, balancing large round trays on their shoulders. Mac didn't remember seeing that many people in the kitchen when he was in there. The serving staff must have arrived after he checked in with the surly head chef. Dr. Sawyer was back at the microphone and reminded everyone there would be time after dinner to increase their bids on the silent auction items and that the live auction would take place after dessert.

The roar of conversation quieted down, and the band started playing soft dinner music.

Mac walked around the room for several minutes, staying clear of the Jacksons, and then stepped outside for some cool, fresh air. Three men were smoking cigars downwind of the door and talking loudly, one out talking the next. Michael Stromberg was among them.

Mac joined them. "Good evening gentlemen."

They stopped talking to look at him. Michael responded on behalf of the trio. "Hey pal, join us for some fresh air?" He pumped Mac's hand with extra gusto. "Have you met Mayor Oswald Eastland and Police Chief Malcolm Contee?"

"No, I haven't." They all shook hands. Mac expressed his condolences to the mayor. He glanced at Chief Contee as often as he could to see if there was any sign of acknowledgment the two were working together on his drug ring assignment. He also watched to see if there was any exchange of looks between the police chief and Michael. They were in full stealth mode.

"We'll be right in," Michael said.

In other words, he had dismissed Mac.

Mac tipped his head, did an about-face and thought, *Old habits are hard to break.*

The trio went back to their discussion.

Back inside, Mac watched from the door for a while. Most everyone was eating. Others lingered talking to people as they tried to eat.

They'd passed the halfway mark; staff were serving dessert and nothing exciting to speak of had occurred. Michael Stromberg readied himself to auction the big-ticket items.

Mr. Jackson rose for another trip to the bar. He'd had more than enough booze, and he staggered, pinging off people seated at their tables. He bumped straight into a woman in a fancy red dress and spilled his drink down her front. She jumped up, and her escort stood to help her. Mr. Jackson tried to wipe off her bosom with her dinner napkin. The woman's companion pushed him away. Oblivious to his inappropriate behavior, Mr. Jackson stumbled his way to the bar.

Mac searched the crowd and found Dr. Sawyer on the far side of the room. When he reached her, he touched her bare arm. She jumped. "Dr. Sawyer, may I have a private word with you?"

"Yes."

They walked to a vacant spot in a back corner of the room.

"The only person I've seen worth noting is Mr. Jackson. So far, I've managed to avoid him. He's at the bar now. Watch him walk back to his table, he's tanked. On his way to the bar, he stumbled into a woman and spilled the last of his drink on her dress. Would you like me to do anything about him?"

"Given your recent interaction with him, you should look the other way," Dr. Sawyer said.

"What if he decides to drive?" he asked.

"That's not your problem. I'll ask Michael to intervene and suggest he take a taxi or allow his wife to drive," Dr. Sawyer said.

When Mac looked away from her, he saw Mr. Jackson glaring at him and Dr. Sawyer.

"Don't look now, but he's looking straight at us," he said.

"Shit. You go your way, and I'll go mine, and we both stay as far from him as possible. Given that he's drunk, there's no telling what he might do."

"Ten-four, boss lady," Mac said.

Marlene sat at a table with Mary Sue and her husband, Ralph, and a few other staff members from school. Mac strolled by their table. Marlene gave him a 'how ya doing' smile. "Hi. Are you staying out of trouble?"

"I'm on the verge," he said.

"You know my table mates, right?" Marlene swiped her hand through the air. She assumed he hadn't and pointed to each person as she introduced them. "Mary Sue and Ralph Johannson, Elaina and Ben Porter and I think you know Rita Cortez."

"It's nice to meet you all." He nodded. His eyes lingered an extra moment on Rita. She looked stunning in an emerald green dress that fit every curve.

"Remember you owe me a dance later," he said to Marlene and walked away.

Now that Mr. Jackson knew Mac was there, his safe haven was the kitchen. Like a puppy waiting for a treat, he hung out there for a few minutes. A soft-spoken young lady wearing a white chef's hat and apron asked him if he wanted a piece of cheesecake and a cup of coffee. Cheesecake was one of his favorite desserts, and he never turned down a cup of coffee. Plus, he didn't want to hurt her feelings, so of course, he accepted.

Feeling satisfied and charged from the caffeine, Mac reentered the banquet room in hopes Mr. Jackson in his drunkenness would've forgotten about seeing him. He found the dance floor open for business. Someone tapped his shoulder. He expected it to be Marlene ready for her dance. He turned and found Mr. Jackson, wobbling and glaring up at him. Mac said nothing.

"What the fuck are you doing here?" he slurred one eyelid drooping.

He said nothing.

Mr. Jackson poked at his chest. "I asked you a question, bub," he said

"I'm working," Mac replied.

"Working, my ass," he muttered. "You look like you think you're in the Secret Service or something." A spray of spit flew from his mouth. "We don't need you here. Go back to where you crawled out of, Military Man. I don't care what war you fought in. Your services aren't needed." He stumbled backward and crashed into the wall.

CHAPTER 28

"Hello, Randall. We haven't talked all night." Michael Stromberg turned Mr. Jackson around to face him and away from Mac. "Would you care to join me for a cigar outside?" That was Michael's cue he'd deal with the drama. He had a firm grip around Mr. Jackson's shoulders, guiding him out the door.

Mac made a beeline for the crowded bar, as far away from Mr. Jackson as possible.

The band was decent; they were playing a country love song. There was a crowd on the dance floor. Rita was dancing with Coach Andrews. He was blabbering in her ear. She nodded yes, then no, then yes, then no. He was in her ear for the entire dance. She looked uncomfortable again. Rita made eye contact with Mac and then looked away with a hint of guilt on her face. When the song ended, she hurried back to her seat at the table.

"Hey," Marlene said, as she tapped Mac's shoulder. "What was that about with Randall?"

"Same old bullshit. The night's winding down—how about that dance?" Mac said.

"I thought you'd never ask." She giggled like a school girl.

They danced to a soft rock classic.

"Jackson's drunk as usual," Marlene said, "Don't take him seriously."

"Mmhmm." Mac wasn't interested in continuing to talk about Mr. Jackson.

They moved around the dance floor in silence.

As the song ended and the band transitioned to a slow love song, Mac walked Marlene to her table.

"Thank you, Mac. You're an excellent dance partner. If we can make it another thirty minutes, the place will be empty, and we can put this one in the Blackstone Academy history book."

"That works for me," he said.

Rita watched Mac.

Marlene was perceptive. She said, "Mac, dance with Rita. She hasn't danced much tonight."

"Ms. Cortez, may I have this dance?" He held his hand out to her.

Rita took his hand, and they strolled to the dance floor. Another slow love song played.

"Are you enjoying yourself?" he whispered in her ear.

"I am now. I think Marlene may be on to us," she whispered back.

"You think so, huh? Is there anything Marlene doesn't know?"

"Not much."

"What was Coach Andrews telling you that made you look so uncomfortable when you were dancing?" he asked.

"He asked me if I saw how drunk Mr. Jackson was?"

"That's it?"

"Yes," she said.

"It looked like there was more to it."

"No, that was it."

They fell into a comfortable closeness and enjoyed the song.

"What're you doing after this is over?" Rita whispered in his ear.

"I'm tired. Politics are exhausting. I'm going home and hit the rack."

"The rack?" she asked.

"Bed. I need some sleep."

"What about tomorrow? How about I bring all the fixings and make you dinner at your house? I might even stay over if you play your cards right."

"Dinner sounds delicious, as do you, but I teach the jiu jitsu class at the Training Center Sunday evenings."

"You're worth the wait. And you have to eat at some point. I don't mind hanging out with Roxy while you're gone."

"Is the offer open for Monday since we have the day off?"

"Sure."

Mac walked her back to her table, exchanging nods with Coach, and then stood sentry at the door as guests filed out.

It was ten thirty, and the evening was coming to a much-appreciated end. Those guests who'd won raffle prizes or auction items were picking up their treasures.

Mrs. Jackson approached alone, her eyes on the floor. As she neared the exit, she looked up at Mac and gave him a polite half smile. Her husband walked in at that exact moment and saw her. He grabbed her by the arm and jerked her around, so her back was to Mac.

"Who the fuck are you smiling at?" Jackson spat his words at her and shook his head. He got in her face. "Oh no, you don't, you little whore. If I see you look at him again, you know what'll happen." His beady black eyes bounced from her to Mac. He held her face an inch from his nose the same way he'd done to Kevin.

Everyone looked but chose not to see. Nobody said anything. People squeezed past them and escaped out the door.

It was all Mac could do not to punch the man.

Mr. Jackson shoved his wife out the door. "Wait in the car," he commanded. She scurried off.

Mac backed away. "You're violating your restraining order."

Mr. Jackson stepped closer to Mac. His face reddened and his eyes bulged. Mac smelled perspiration mixed with scotch, Mr. Jackson reeked. "Were you making eyes at my wife?" He poked Mac in the chest, and then wiped sweat beads from his brow with a linen handkerchief. He tried to smooth his hair back into place.

You had to give the guy credit. He wasn't intimidated by the fact that Mac was retired Special Ops or that he had a brown belt in jiu jitsu. And he didn't appear to give any thought to the gun resting under Mac's jacket.

Mac said nothing. His pulse pounded in his ears.

Mr. Jackson poked him in the chest with each word he said, "I...Asked...You...A...Question. Buddy."

Mac's focus had narrowed to only Mr. Jackson. The remaining guests had become a blur of movement. He reminded himself, *He was there to find a drug dealer*. This yahoo wasn't worth blowing the assignment.

Mac gritted his teeth and spoke so only Mr. Jackson heard him, "I told you once already, I'm not your buddy."

Again Mr. Jackson poked his chest with each word. "You...keep...your...fucking...eyes...off...my...wife."

Mac's hand was faster than Mr. Jackson's brain could comprehend. He had his finger in his grip, deciding whether to break it when Michael Stromberg stepped between the two men and forced them apart.

"Randall, Mac, you both need to walk away and cool down."

Mr. Jackson swung at Mac with a right hook. Mac dodged, and Mr. Jackson went down with a thud.

Michael Stromberg helped him up. Mac ducked into the men's room to take a piss. When he emerged, Mr. Jackson was no longer in the room.

The kitchen staff was busy clearing the tables. Dr. Sawyer, Marlene, and Michael Stromberg were talking near the main door. The room was a mess. It looked like a kid's birthday party had just ended.

"Mac, I'm sorry about the drunken fool's behavior. Atrocious." Michael Stromberg slapped his back like they were old friends. "The man can't handle his scotch."

"Was he allowed to drive?" Mac asked.

"No…No…Mrs. Jackson tucked him into the passenger seat, and she drove. Every year he gets drunk as a skunk and goes after somebody about something. Last year, he went after Clarence Fotana, the pharmacist at Oakstone Drugs. They argued about whether Governor Brown was doing a good job or not. Randall was so passionate about it."

"Did Mr. Jackson get physical with Mr. Fotana?

"No, he didn't. It was an interesting debate, to say the least. Do you remember, ladies?" he asked Dr. Sawyer and Marlene.

"Oh my, yes," Dr. Sawyer said. Her tone laced with sweetness.

"I've never seen Clarence as angry as he was last year," said Marlene.

"Between you and me, Mac, Randall seems quite threatened by you. Mix that with his inability to pace himself when it comes to liquor, and he's a hot mess," Michael Stromberg said.

Mac had nothing more to add on the subject. They both waited for the other to speak.

"If that's all, Michael, I believe I'm no longer needed here." Mac began to turn around when Michael extended his hand to him.

"Thank you, Mac, for keeping our little event safe and for watching over the students and staff at Blackstone. On behalf of the school board, I want you to know we appreciate you." He continued to pump his arm. "Don't you worry about Randall, he's full of hot air. We don't put much credence in what he says. Hell, he's filed a harassment charge almost every year since his boy was in kindergarten. His hostility toward you will all blow over. It always does."

Mac nodded and thought, *Dr. Sawyer told Stromberg about the harassment charge.* From his perspective, whatever 'this' was, it didn't feel like it was going to blow over.

CHAPTER 29

"Good morning, Mother." He used his most cheerful voice as he entered his mother's bedroom with a tray of her favorite breakfast foods.

She lay in bed and didn't respond. Her eyes were open and focused on him. The look on her face made him shiver.

"I brought your favorites for breakfast." He remained cheerful despite her surly demeanor.

"What did you bring me?" she asked, her tone curt.

"Pumpkin pancakes, crispy bacon, fried brown sugar and cinnamon bananas, and a vanilla latte." He busied himself setting up her breakfast at the table near the French doors which provided a lovely view.

"Help me up," she said. Her tone hadn't softened.

He moved her walker out of his way so he could get close to her bedside. When he tossed the bedding off of her, he was overcome by the smell of urine. She was lying in a large puddle.

"Mother. You've wet the bed. Are you okay?" The concern in his voice was genuine.

"I did? Oh, my goodness. I didn't even know I'd done that," she said with surprise.

Coach helped his mother out of bed and into the bathroom where he sat her on the shower seat. He helped her undress and tossed her putrid clothes into the hamper. She was smiling as he fussed over her.

Using the hand-held shower wand, he wet her down with warm water and then handed her the bar of soap.

"I don't know what's wrong with me, I don't have the energy to lift the soap. Will you please suds me up?" she said.

Coach soaped his mother's withering body, concentrating on her genital area to clean all traces of urine from her thin skin.

He'd never showered his mother before and he hoped he wouldn't have to again anytime soon.

He managed to dry her, dress her and help her to the table where her breakfast sat. The sun was shining in and the vista from her room was spectacular.

He left the room to retrieve fresh linens for her bed. As he walked into her bedroom, she spat her food back onto the plate.

"My breakfast's cold. Reheat it, Chucky," she said, as she pushed the tray of food aside.

He dropped the sheets on a chair. He walked with heavy steps carrying her food tray down the stairs to the kitchen. The two minutes it took the microwave to reheat her breakfast was the best part of his morning so far.

He returned to her bedroom with a hot breakfast and a forced smile.

She sat in the sun waiting.

They went about their business in silence. Her gobbling food as if she hadn't eaten in days. Him changing the sheets on her bed.

"I'm done. Please bring me another vanilla latte, and then help me back to bed," she said in a sweet tone unfamiliar to him. He wanted to talk about the Gala and the award he received, but she hadn't yet asked how the Gala was, so he assumed she was still angry about him making her stay home.

He did as she commanded. When he returned with her second latte she was already in bed. He set the coffee on her bedside table.

"Are you sure you're, okay?" he said.

"I think I need to use the bathroom, help me up," she replied.

He tossed the fresh linens off her to find she had soiled the sheets again.

"Mother. You've soiled the sheets again. Are you okay? What's wrong?" He feared her kidneys were failing.

She said with a calm voice, "You listen to me you ungrateful little prick, I gave you your life. I could have aborted you and your brother, but I didn't. If you ever leave me with a babysitter at night again, it'll be the last time you do. Now change my sheets."

CHAPTER 30

Always cheerful Roni bounded out the main entrance of the school. Her blond pony tailed swung back and forth. "Good morning." she said to Mac, as she approached him. Her hands were deep inside her sweater pockets.

"Hey there, why didn't you go to the gala?" Mac said.

"It was my mom's birthday, and we had a family thing," she replied. "I heard you and Mr. Jackson got into a fist-fight. What happened? Do-tell. The one year I'm not at the gala and I miss a fight."

"There was no fight. He was drunk and took a swing at me. He missed and fell to the floor. End of story."

"Why'd he take a swing at you?"

"Because that's the kind of stuff drunks do. I don't know."

"Hmmm," Roni said with a little skepticism in her voice.

Teddy and Savannah's crazy mom didn't get out of her car. She dropped the kids off at the curb and allowed them to walk into the school all by themselves.

"Good morning, Savannah," Mac said, "Teddy."

Teddy stopped in front of Roni and Mac. "Hello, Mr. Mac. Miss Jacks. Speaking of good mornings, what happens when you eat yeast and shoe polish?" he asked.

"You go to the hospital?" Roni said.

"What happens?" Mac asked.

"You rise and shine." His eyes twinkled with amusement, as he laughed all the way into the school.

"That Teddy's a funny little guy," Roni said.

"He sure is," Mac replied.

Approaching the school from all directions, mothers and fathers walked holding hands with their kids.

"Back to the Gala," Roni said, "Tell me more about the fight. Mr. Jackson had to have a reason he took a swing at you besides being drunk."

Mac told her about the scene with his wife making eye contact with him as her husband walked inside. He downplayed it as much as he could in hopes of squelching the rumor of a fight.

"Hey, let me ask you something. Can you keep this conversation between us?" he said.

"Of course, I can. Remember, I'm going to school to be a cop, secrecy's part of the job," she said.

"Okay. What do you think of Stu Collins?"

"What do you mean?"

"Coach told me there are some students who think I'm a planted undercover narcotics officer. He asked if I thought Stu sold Seth the drugs he overdosed on."

"I've heard the kids think you're a narc, is it true?"

"No. I'm not a cop, I'm just a marshal. Stu. What do you think of him? Why would he be so paranoid? Do you think he's involved in the drugs that Seth used?" he said.

"A good question. I think Stu's too immature to be a key player in any type of business. I see drug sales as a business," she said.

"Good point. Keep your eyes open and let me know if you see him doing anything suspicious. Even if you're not sure something's weird, let me know."

She jabbed him in the ribs. "Because you're an undercover cop, right?"

"No. Because Coach piqued my interest," he said, "What's your take on Kevin Jackson?"

"I told you before, he creeps me out. I get a weird vibe from him," she said.

"You need to toughen that up if you're going to be a cop. You'll be spending most of your on-duty time with creepy people," he said.

She jabbed him in the ribs again. "Do you know this because you're an undercover cop?" she said.

The foot traffic had slowed to a trickle signaling the morning bell was about to ring.

He shook his head and smiled at her. "Let's go," he said. They walked into the school together.

CHAPTER 31

Mac sat alone in his office eating lunch at his desk. He watched the various surveillance views fade in and out. Both lunch periods had ended and everyone was back in their classes. Except for the occasional student walking to and from the restroom, the halls were quiet.

There were two physical education classes sharing the gym. A class of freshmen and sophomores played half-court basketball at one end. At the other end were several classes of elementary students playing Simon Says. Marlene typed fast on the keyboard at her desk.

Sudden movement near the high school restrooms caught his attention. Kevin walked into the restroom. He locked the camera to stay with the feed. Less than a minute later Stu shuffled down the hall looking in all directions before entering the same restroom. Mac checked the time. It was twelve minutes after one. Mac waited and watched. Growing impatient, Mac locked his desk, secured his handgun in its holster, put two long zip-ties into his pocket, and grabbed his two-way radio. He locked his office door as he exited.

Roni turned the corner coming from the opposite direction.

"Where's the fire?" she joked. Her face lit up with a big smile.

"I'm headed to see why Stu and Kevin are out of their classes. They've been in the boys' restroom for longer than seems necessary," he said.

"Can I come?" She put her hands together as if she were begging.

"Sure, but not into the restroom."

"Yuck, I have zero interest in going into the boy's restroom," she said.

They walked fast to reach the far end of the maze of hallways leading to the high school section of the building.

"If you hear anything going down in the restroom, use my radio and ask Marlene to call 911." He shoved the radio into Roni's hand. She had a serious look on her face, all traces of silliness had vanished.

Mac pushed the enter side of the double doors and walked in. He'd caught Stu and Kevin in the midst of what looked like a serious conversation. Their eyes were large and round when they saw it was Mac at the entrance.

"What're you two up to in here?" Mac got straight to business.

Kevin said, "Taking a leak."

Stu said, "Taking a shit."

"It doesn't look like either of you are using the restroom for what it's intended," Mac said, "You've been out of class for at least five minutes."

"It's none of your fucking business how long it takes to shit," Stu said, "Are you the shit patrol now?" Stu laughed out loud.

Kevin didn't respond to Stu's sarcasm.

"Do you speak like that to your attorney father, Stu? How do you suppose he'd respond if I call and tell him what you just said?" Mac asked.

"I don't care. Call him," Stu challenged. "He thinks you're an idiot."

Kevin's face remained deadpan.

"Empty your pants pockets, turn them inside out," Mac said.

Kevin complied. All he had was a lint ball.

"Go fuck yourself," Stu said. He steadied his stance in preparation for a fight.

Roni knocked on the restroom door. "Is everything okay in there?" she said.

"We'll be right out, Roni," Mac said over his shoulder.

"Stu, either turn your pockets inside out or I will," Mac said.

Stu guffawed.

Mac grabbed Stu and flipped him over his leg, threw him to the floor with a thud, face up. It was a basic jiu jitsu take-down. Kevin left the restroom. Stu wiggled around while Mac flipped him over, held him down with his knee and slipped one of the zip ties around his wrists. He hopped off and stood Stu up as fast as he'd taken him down.

"Let's go see Dr. Sawyer and see what she wants to do with you," Mac said.

Mac and Stu exited the restroom and found Roni pacing. When she saw Stu with his arms secured behind his back she covered her mouth.

"Should I have called Marlene? I didn't hear a commotion," she said.

"There was no commotion. Just Stu here being defiant," Mac said.

"My dad will sue your ass for this," Stu said, "This is police brutality."

"I'm not a police officer, Stu. If you're going to make threats, get the terminology straight, I'm a marshal."

Mac, Roni, and Stu rounded the corner into Marlene's office in a whoosh of momentum that startled her. She jumped and almost fell off of her chair.

"What's going on here?" Marlene asked.

"Caught Kevin Jackson and Stu in the bathroom when they should have been in class. They were up to something. Stu became defiant causing me to take control of him and bring him to speak with Dr. Sawyer," Mac said.

"I see," she said. Marlene looked at Roni. She shrugged.

Marlene knocked on her boss' door and then entered closing the door behind her.

"You're so fired, asshole. My dad's going to sue you for everything you've got. Kiss your job goodbye," Stu said.

Dr. Sawyer yanked open her office door. She had a look of pure hate on her face. "Cut those zip ties off of Stu's wrists," she said.

Marlene handed Mac a pair of scissors. Stu gave Mac a smug look.

Dr. Sawyer said to Stu, "Turn your pants pockets inside out."

Stu looked at her, and then at Marlene. He complied. There wasn't anything in his pockets.

"Into my office. Now." She pointed to her office.

Stu walked into Dr. Sawyer's office in front of her. Dr. Sawyer turned and looked at Mac with fury in her eyes. Through gritted teeth, she said to Marlene, "Schedule a meeting with Marshal MacKenna for this afternoon."

CHAPTER 32

Mac felt frustrated, playing out in his mind the meeting with the boss yesterday afternoon. As usual she was irritated that he'd gotten involved in whatever Kevin and Stu were doing in the restroom.

He wondered if her inability to ruffle feathers brought about some of the troubles the school was experiencing.

He was half-way through the stack of security reports highlighting anything that looked suspicious when Susan Jackson's number scrolled across the caller ID on his cell phone. In the background, the voice on the PA blared, "Happy Bulldog Tuesday everyone…"

"Mac," he said brusquely.

The familiar hushed voice of Kevin's mother said, "This is Susan Jackson, Mr. Mac. Would you be available to meet me for coffee in thirty minutes?"

"Will you be alone?" he asked.

"Yes."

Mac didn't want to know what she needed him to help her with, but Maggie's wishing their mother had reached out to someone like him ran through his mind. "Sure. Where?"

"Handley's Coffee Shop. Do you know where that is?"

"East of town on Highway 12?"

"Yes. Thirty minutes?"

"I'll be there," he said.

He watched the monitors. Some young kids with papers were walking toward the front office. They went to Marlene.

"Thank you. And please don't tell anyone you're going to meet me, especially Kevin," she said.

"Okay… I won't."

He checked his watch; it was eight thirty. Before he left, he tucked the security reports into his desk's top drawer and locked it.

"Marlene," he said, as he rounded the corner to her office. She was seated behind her desk with her nose in a thick reference book. She looked up and jumped at the same time.

"God. Mac. You scared me." She scolded him right before her whole face turned into a smile.

"Sorry about that. How's your day going so far?" he asked.

"Fine. How about yours?"

"I haven't been served with any official papers yet, nor have I been arrested. All in all, doing good so far," he said.

"What's up?" she asked.

"I'm going to be off campus for about an hour on personal business," he said.

"Well, that's a first. Thank you for letting me know. Is it a top-secret spy mission?" she probed.

"Yeah, something like that," he said.

Mac sprinted to his truck, taking the crosswalk in three leaps. He had twenty-two minutes to get to the coffee shop. Before leaving the staff parking lot, he looked around for the red sports car, black sedan or dark SUV. Nothing.

Sixteen minutes later he parked his truck in front of Handley's Coffee Shop.

When he pushed on the metal bar that spanned the width of the heavy plate glass door, a small bell at the top of it jingled. He stepped inside and scanned the room for Susan Jackson.

The patrons looked to see who had entered the coffee shop. A small woman wearing large sunglasses, seated at a corner table in the back, waved at him. Susan. He surveyed the other patrons, who had resumed eating breakfast or drinking coffee or reading yesterday's Mountain Tribune. She looked even smaller than she had at the Gala.

The only person still eying him was the aging waitress, who always had a scowl on her face and coffee pot in her hand. Her face broke into a big smile. "Y'all here for some cinnamon rolls for those nieces of yours?" Her Alabama roots came across loud and clear.

"Not today. Meeting a friend for coffee." Mac nodded toward Susan. The waitress followed him with her coffee pot and a mug which she plunked down on the Formica table and filled to the brim.

"Hello, Mr. Mac." Susan's voice was hushed, as he'd come to expect. He decided that she wasn't speaking in a hushed voice, she just had one of those voices that always sounded like a whisper.

"Hello, Mrs. Jackson," he said as he sat on the hard chair next to her with his back to the opposite wall. His chair legs scraped the floor when he scooted in.

"Please call me Susan," she whispered, before she removed her sunglasses. She wasn't wearing any make-up. She extended her hand, and he accepted it in his. It felt frail, like the hand of a much older woman would feel.

"Okay, Susan, why am I here?"

She looked nervously around the small coffee shop. "Is that woman at the counter staring at me?" she asked.

"The older woman reading the newspaper?"

"Yes."

"No, she's reading the newspaper."

"What about the one next to her?"

He looked again at the patrons seated at the counter. Two gray-haired women were together in the middle section, and a uniformed package delivery man sat at the far end. All were engrossed in their world paying no attention to them whatsoever.

"No, she's eating breakfast."

"She was staring at me, but looked away when you looked," she said.

Paranoia oozed from her pores.

She kept her gaze moving about the room rather than looking at him when she spoke. "Kevin told me to trust you. Can I trust you?"

"Kevin told you to trust me? That's interesting seeing as Kevin seldom speaks to me. And when he does, he's rude. I can't imagine how I made him feel I was trustworthy."

"Yes, Kevin said you were someone I could trust," she said with exasperation. "I only have fifteen minutes. Randall works from home a lot so I don't get out much. Today, he has a meeting in his office. He thinks I'm shopping for a new dress. I have one hour until he's home and I still need to stop and buy a dress to show him," she said.

"What happens if you're gone longer than one hour?"

"That woman at the counter's looking at me again. Do you think she knows Randall?" she said, "Randall can't know I'm here. He's jealous of you. And the restraining order. He can't know we met."

The woman was still minding her own business. The two women had switched their attentions. The one who'd been reading the newspaper was now eating her breakfast and the one who'd been eating her breakfast was now reading the newspaper. They were also chatting.

"She's not looking at you, Susan. What happens if you're gone longer than one hour?" he repeated.

"Do you think she knows Randall?" she asked, again.

Her hands were shaking and she was rubbing them together.

"Susan, what happens if you're gone longer than an hour?" he asked, for the third time.

"Randall will know I've been gone longer than I said I would be because he checks the home security system for the arm and disarm times. He thinks I don't know," she said.

"And then what?" he asked.

"I think the waitress knows Randall. She looks like she's texting him," she said. Tears welled in her eyes.

The waitress was looking at her cell phone.

"She's looking at her phone, Susan, not texting Randall," he said.

"How can you be sure?" she said.

He grasped her trembling hands with a gentle grip. "Susan, what happens if you're gone longer than one hour beside Randall knowing?" he asked.

"I'd be in trouble."

"'Trouble?' You're not a kid. What would he do?"

She hesitated. She seemed conflicted about what she should say. She pulled her hands from his grasp, pushed up the right sleeve of her sweater, and removed an expensive wide gold bracelet from her wrist. There was a smooth pink scar about a quarter of an inch wide that went all the way around her wrist.

With a gentle finger, Mac touched the healed skin, the scar felt tight and bumpy. From his pararescue days, he knew it wasn't a fresh wound. And it wasn't a single wound either. The injury occurred numerous times in the same spot. She averted her eyes and quickly replaced the bracelet.

When she looked into his eyes again, he saw emptiness. She said nothing. Then she pushed up her left sleeve and removed an identical bracelet to show him the same type of scar. Both of her wrists had been cuffed or restrained in some manner. And not once, but numerous times to make scars of that size. Again, she quickly replaced the bracelet and looked away.

Mac's blood was heating up. "What happened?" he asked with genuine concern.

"There's too much for me to tell you in fifteen minutes. I need help to get away from the hell I live in. I'm so afraid Kevin will be damaged from the things he's seen. This isn't how he should treat his wife," she said.

He didn't come out and say it, but if life at the Jackson home was as bad as he imagined, it was too late. At Kevin's age, the damage was done. Only years of therapy would help.

"Do you mean you need help to get you and Kevin away from your husband?" he said.

"No, no, no." She shook her head. "Kevin has to stay there. Randall said he'd kill Kevin if I ever tried to take him away."

"Those are just 'heat of the moment' things people say when they're fighting. He doesn't mean it," he said, "Try telling your husband you want a divorce," he said.

"Oh no, I can't do that either. He'll kill me first," she said.

"He wouldn't do that. It's a bluff," he said.

"I believe he will. He's told me if I try to leave him, or if I tell anyone about our private business, he'll kill me and nobody will find my body," she said.

"He's trying to scare you is all," he said.

"No, he means it," she assured him. "He killed his mother."

"What're you talking about?"

"When he was a boy, his mother tumbled down the stairs in their home and died. His dad was found guilty of manslaughter and went to prison based on Randall's testimony. I think it was Randall who killed her," she said.

His gut wrenched. His thoughts spun from the accusation.

"Why haven't you told the authorities?"

"Who would believe me over Randall?"

"How can I help you?" he asked.

She looked at the pendant watch on a chain she wore. Panic spread across her face.

"That woman's looking at me again. I…I…I have to go. I think she knows Randall and will tell him I'm here. Thank you for meeting me," she said.

"Wait. You haven't told me what I can do. Are you sure you're safe?"

"If we abide by his rules, we're safe," she said, "I'll call you again when I can."

"'His rules'?"

She touched the back of his hand. Her hand felt cold, and soft, and light as a feather.

"Thank you, Mr. Mac. I'll call you soon," she said and then stood.

She clutched her purse to her chest and scurried out the door with her head down. The bell over the door chimed as Susan ran outside.

The salty waitress slapped the bill for Susan's and his coffee on the table. "She was in a hurry."

He downed the last of his coffee and then texted Maggie.

Mac: I met the mother for coffee. She wants me to help her leave her husband.

Maggie: Oh my. How are you supposed to do that?

Mac: She didn't have time to elaborate. She had a curfew.

Maggie: A curfew?

Mac: It's twisted. I'll call you in a day or two and tell you all about it.

Maggie: Okay. Thank you for meeting her.

He noticed Susan had left a small, cream-colored envelope next to her coffee mug. He thought there was money inside but instead, he found a small key. For a moment he pondered what Susan told him. *His rules? What are his rules? And what the fuck am I supposed to do with this key? How do I walk away from this helpless woman?*

CHAPTER 33

Mac spent the afternoon considering how he should proceed with Susan Jackson and stay focused on his assignment. He decided he would not contact Mrs. Jackson; he'd leave the ball in her court and stay focused on connecting Coach to the drugs or removing him from the potential drug dealer list.

Mac waited in his truck for Coach to leave the school. Coach blasted out the main door, like he was jet-propelled. He was at his car in record time and left the parking lot with reckless regard for the students and parents lingering about.

Mac followed at a safe distance. Coach swerved in and out of traffic lanes. Mac had entered Coach's home address into his GPS in case he lost him in traffic.

It was no surprise to Mac that Coach lived in Blackstone Estates. What did surprise him was the size and grandeur of his home. He remembered the mayor's speech at the Gala, commending Coach for taking care of his sickly mother. Mac wondered if his mother was a wealthy woman.

He parked across the street and down a house so he could watch Coach's home. After several minutes, he wondered what he thought he might see happening at Coach's house. Perhaps a semi-truck park and offload crates of drugs? His phone vibrated with a text from Maggie.

Maggie: Hey bro. Have things calmed down at the school?

Mac: It seems that Seth's death is yesterday's news.

Maggie: I saw Jason when he came in to question the emergency room staff. He looked tired.

Mac saw in his side mirror a red sedan speeding toward him. He blew past him and screeched a turn onto Coach's circular driveway. A man was driving. He jumped out of the car and ran into the house without stopping to knock.

Mac: That's how life is when you have twin babies.

Maggie: True. Are you still at the school?

Mac: I am. Did you need something?

Maggie: Have dinner with us. The girls would love to see you.

Mac: Sounds great. See you later.

Maggie: Woohoo. (Emoji - horn blowing confetti)

Mac heard the ambulance siren blaring before he saw the red lights flashing as it approached from the same direction the red sedan had come from. The ambulance also turned onto Coach's circular driveway. The driver and passenger ran to the rear of the ambulance and flung the doors open. They grabbed the gurney and rolled it fast toward the front door. The wide door opened before the paramedics were on the stoop and then shut as soon as the paramedics were inside.

About ten minutes later, the paramedics exited Coach's home with a patient on the gurney. Coach and another man walked alongside the gurney and the group approached the rear of the ambulance. The paramedics slid the gurney into the rear area and one of the paramedics along with Coach hopped into the rear with the patient.

The ambulance driver hit the siren as it pulled away from Coach's home. The red sedan followed the ambulance. Mac jotted down the license number of the red sedan and then sent Jason a text asking him to look into who the man was.

CHAPTER 34

Coach sat next to his mother's hospital bed. He felt drained and tipped his head back to rest. The noises in the hospital became a soothing hum. He dozed off to thoughts of time long ago.

His head throbbed and his eyes burned. When he was eight-years-old with an ear infection he felt like he was dying. He was happy to stay home alone while his twin brother and mother went to the Saturday morning church service. He liked staying home alone the day before also, while his brother went to school and his mother to work.

He laid on the sofa watching cartoons. He could hear them moving around in their bedrooms. It was a small two-bedroom apartment. He propped his bed pillow behind his back and sat up. The only good thing about an ear infection was he could drink lemon-lime soda pop anytime of the day. He slurped the last of his bubbly beverage through the straw in his plastic Scooby-Doo cup.

"Chucky, stop slurping." their mother yelled from her bedroom.

Chuck cringed when he heard his mother's voice.

"Kent, are you ready?" she bellowed.

"I have to go to the bathroom first," his brother said before he slammed and then locked the bathroom door.

Their mother entered the living room dressed in her church clothes. She sat on the easy chair and placed her purse and gloves on her lap. She drummed her finger on the arm of the chair.

"Chucky, turn off the TV, you've watched enough," she said.

"But mom, I…"

"I said turn it off." She glared at her son.

He walked over and turned it off.

"Kent, it's time to go." She stood and smoothed her dress. Kent remained in the bathroom. She went around the corner to the bathroom and pounded on the door. "Kent, it's time to go."

"I can't go poo, mom. I have to, but I can't. My stomach hurts, too," Kent said through the door.

He heard his mother reach for the weird little key she kept

above the bathroom door. She unlocked the door, went inside and slammed the door behind her. Chuck stiffened. Chuck buried his head in his bed pillow and pulled the sides tight around his ears. He stayed there until he felt a light tap on his back.

Chuck's twin brother Kent was looking down at him. He had a red face and tears pouring out of his eyes. Chuck was a minute older than his brother, but he always felt older than that. Kent was a bit of an underdog. "We're leaving now," he said, "I'll see you later." He had the saddest look on his face Chuck had seen in his eight long years of life.

"Where's mom?" he asked.

"In the car. I have to go," he said.

"Do what she says," Chuck warned his younger brother.

"I will," he said.

As Chuck hugged his brother, they heard the car horn sound. Kent ran out the front door.

Chuck fell asleep after his mother and brother left for church. He awoke when his mother opened and slammed the front door. Without saying a word, she went to her bedroom.

Chuck sat up on the sofa and waited for his brother to open the door. He felt he waited a long time. He looked out the window. She'd parked the car on the street in front of their apartment. There was a small patch of dying grass between him and the car. He'd see Kent if he was still in the car. He wasn't. He jerked around to face forward when he heard his mother's bedroom door open. She entered the living room with a big smile on her face.

"Where's Kent?" Chuck said.

"He asked if he could walk home from church. He'll be home soon. How're you feeling?" She asked. Kneeling in front of him she pressed the back of her hand to his forehead. "You're still running a fever. Are you hungry?"

"No, I'm not hungry," he said.

His mother went into the kitchen and fixed herself a fried bologna sandwich. She sat alone at their small kitchen table and ate her lunch. She yelled from the kitchen, "Chucky, would you like some more pop?"

"No, thank you," he said. He turned around without making a sound and looked out the window.

The sun had set and parents were calling out to the neighborhood kids to go inside. Chuck watched the street in front of their apartment in silence. His mother watched the news on TV.

He had a terrible feeling in the pit of his stomach.

"Mom, where's Kent?" he asked with trepidation.

"I don't know where that boy is. He should have been home hours ago. I'm getting worried," she said, "He was mad at me for spanking him before we left for church. Maybe he ran away from home," she said with a sparkle in her eyes. "You know how he is, always joking around. He'll be home soon."

Chuck and his mother watched TV in silence until it was time for Chuck to go to bed.

His mother leaned down and kissed his forehead. "Mommy loves you. Have sweet dreams," she said.

"I'm worried about Kent," he said.

"I think he's hiding in a neighbor's car trying to make us worry. I'm sure he's fine. He'll be home in the morning," she said.

Chuck woke when he heard a man's voice inside the apartment. Kent's bed was still made and he wasn't in their room. He put on his robe and slippers before leaving his and Kent's bedroom. He peeked around the wall and looked in the living room and saw a police officer seated on their sofa. He recognized him from the time his mother took him and Kent to the emergency call center where she worked. He was writing in a notebook. Chuck stayed where he was and listened.

His mother dabbed her eyes with a handkerchief. "He wanted to walk home from church. I thought he'd be fine. We don't live far from the church," she said sniffling and wiping her tears. "Where could he be?" She blew her nose.

"We'll use this photograph of him and post copies around town. Someone knows where he is. We'll find him, Donna. We'll find him," the officer said. He patted her hand.

Chuck went back to his room and started to cry. He knew the officer wasn't going to find his brother. He knew it last night. He was connected to Kent like that. He knew something bad had happened to his brother and that he may never see him again.

Images of his brother flashed in his mind like a slide show. Teaching Kent how to ride a bicycle without training wheels. The birthday cake they shared each year. Playing catch on the street in front of their apartment. Riding the school bus together.

Chuck jumped when his cell phone rang. He grabbed it fast so it wouldn't wake his mother. "Hello," he whispered.

"Coach, it's Stu. Something terrible happened."

CHAPTER 35

His cell phone woke him at three twenty-two. The blinding light from the screen of his phone made his eyes hurt. He heard Roxy stretch, groan, and shake her entire body starting from her big head down to her tail. Her dog tags jangled.

The caller ID said it was Jason.

"Hey, Jason," he croaked, his vocal cords dry from sleep. He could hear a lot of commotion in the background.

"Mac, I'm at the Jacksons'. I wanted you to hear it from me before you got to school tomorrow, well, technically today," he said in a loud, muffled voice.

"What happened?" His mind raced. *Did Jackson hurt Kevin? Did he hurt Susan? Did Susan hurt Jackson?*

"I also need to get a phone number for the superintendent. What's her name again?" he asked.

"Jason, what happened? What did you want me to hear from you first?" he turned on his bedside lamp. Roxy lumbered toward him. She looked like she wanted to know what had happened as well. Her big head turned one way and the other as she watched him.

"It's Mrs. Jackson." He paused to give directions to someone near him. "She fell down the stairs in her home tonight. She's dead, Mac," he said.

"What. Are you fucking kidding me?" he gasped. "There's no way in hell she fell. He fucking pushed her. Jason, you have her checked for any signs of a struggle," he said.

"It looks pretty clear-cut brother," he said, "I'm sorry."

"Where's Kevin? The son?" he asked.

"He's with his dad right now. They're still here at the house," he said.

"He's not safe with his father, Jason. Put him in protective custody," he said.

"Mac, you're talking crazy. He seems quite concerned for his son's well-being. He hasn't left his side since I arrived," he said.

"Of course, he hasn't left his side. He doesn't want you asking him questions when he's not present to hear his answers. Please keep an eye on him, and I'm telling you—have the coroner check her for signs of a struggle."

Mac felt pissed and sad at the same time. "We need to talk. I have information about the Jacksons I need to tell you. Can you come to the school today?"

"What kind of information?"

"Information that may be relevant to your investigation," he said.

"I'm not sure there will be much of an investigation," he said.

"I think it's more than a weird coincidence that Jackson's mother died the same way when he was a kid," he said.

"What the fuck are you talking about?" Jason said. There was so much background noise and activity that Jason yelled into the phone.

"Randall Jackson's mother died from a tumble down the stairs when he was a kid. So don't conclude it was an accident until after the autopsy, all right?" he pleaded.

"We'll talk. Hey, man, I gotta go," he said, "I'll see you at the school later. Can you text me the number for the school superintendent?" he asked. "What's her name?"

"Yeah, yeah, I will. Her name's Dr. Sawyer. And Jason, thank you for calling me," he said.

"What happened, Mac?" Rita asked, from behind him.

Roxy stared at him. His world was calm and quiet while Susan Jackson lay dead at her house.

"That fucking rat bastard, Mr. Jackson, Kevin's father, did it, Rita," he said, "He pushed his wife down the stairs and killed her. Accident, my ass. No fucking way. He probably didn't mean for her to die. Or maybe he did. My God, I had no idea he would fucking kill her. That little prick better not get away with this. I'm sure he pushed her. As sure as I'm sitting here, he fucking pushed her."

"I'm sorry, Mac, I didn't know you were so fond of Kevin or his mother," Rita said.

Adrenaline pumped through his veins like he'd witnessed a gruesome car accident.

Rita and he gathered in the kitchen once again. They drank fresh coffee and watching the Sacramento Channel 7 News.

Mac gave Rita the abridged version of his involvement with Kevin and his parents.

It was around six when Rita left to get ready for work.

He was glued to the TV. There was no mention of a death at the Jacksons' home on the five o'clock news, or the five-thirty, the six, or the six-thirty news. A scumbag shooting a scumbag was newsworthy, but a nice woman tumbling down a staircase to her death wasn't.

At six forty-five Mac gave up on the news and called Maggie.

"Mac?" She answered on the first ring, her voice hushed. "What happened? You never call me this early. Are you all right?" Rapid-fire questions flew across the airwaves.

"I'm fine," he said, "I needed to tell somebody what happened."

"What happened?"

"Remember the family drama I involved myself in? The mother who called me when I was at your place? The father who hired someone to park in front of your place when I stayed over?" he asked.

"Yes, the woman with the abusive husband? Yes, I remember," she said, "I asked you to help her."

"That's the one. The mother died early this morning. According to Jason, she fell down the staircase in their home," he said.

"Oh my God. That's awful. You don't believe she fell?"

"Not for a single second," he said, "Her husband pushed her. I can feel it in my bones. She called me to meet her for coffee where she asked me to help her get away from her husband. And then she's dead less than 48 hours later?"

"Oh my God, Mac. Do you think he killed her because he found out you two met?" Maggie sounded choked up.

"I'm going to push Jason to consider it. I told you she was paranoid, and she led me to believe her husband was capable of killing her."

Maggie gasped. In the background the girls were chirping like baby birds waiting for breakfast. They chirped for outfits to wear, one chirped for a ponytail, and the other for braids. There was too much distracting chatter going on at her house. They agreed to talk later.

Mac fed Roxy, and let her run in the backyard while he showered and got ready for work.

He wasn't sure what to expect when he arrived at work.

He locked the house up and hurried toward his truck. Roxy

followed him to the backyard through her over-sized dog door. He secured the gate to corral her in for the day. She was free to go outside or stay inside.

Mac watched Roxy watch him as he drove away. His mind focused on Susan Jackson. *Would parents at the school know of the tragedy? Would the staff know by the time he arrived? Did Susan Jackson matter to anyone else? Would the media be there like they had when the mayor's son died?*

When he arrived at the academy, there were clusters of parents along the sidewalk in front of the school talking with their heads close. He imagined they were talking about poor Susan. The same young reporter from the Mountain Tribune approached him.

She said, "Hello. I'm…"

He finished her well-rehearsed introduction, "Selena Ramirez, with the Mountain Tribune. I remember you."

"I'm writing a piece on the mother of your student who died in her home this morning. Did you know Susan Jackson?" she asked.

Because this reporter cared enough about Susan to look into the story, he decided to give her a moment of his time.

"No, I didn't know her," he said.

She wasn't much taller than a fourth grader and she spoke fast. "Do you know her son?"

"Not really," he said, "Sorry, you may speak with some parents if they agree to speak with you, but I want you out of here in fifteen minutes."

"Thank you. What's your name?" she asked.

"Mac."

Dr. Sawyer tapped his shoulder. "After the bell rings, I'd like a word with you in my office."

CHAPTER 36

Mac walked into Marlene's office. He could tell she had been crying. She blew her nose and said, "She's expecting you."

He walked into Dr. Sawyer's office and stood near the door. She was typing on her computer keyboard. Without looking at him she said, "Close the door and take a seat." Her tone was terse.

He sat in one of her wingback chairs and waited while she continued to type. He remembered Jason's words of caution, "trust no one." He watched her typing fast. He thought she was an attractive woman when she wasn't acting like a bitch. He wasn't sure why she'd disliked him from the moment they met.

She pushed her keyboard into the computer cabinet and then turned to look at Mac. The visible part of her chest and neck was mottled with redness.

"I'm going to get straight to it. Were you and Mrs. Jackson having an affair?" She didn't seem sad; she was furious about something.

"No. God, no. Why would you ask that?"

"That's the rumor. You and she were having an affair. Her husband found out and they fought about it last night. Something upset her and she stumbled on the stairs... you know the rest."

"I didn't even know her," he said, "I resent the accusation." The volume of his voice clicked up a notch.

"Something was going on between you and the Jacksons'. I told you to leave them alone. And now look what's happened." Her hands were trembling.

"Are you insinuating I had anything to do with her death?" He took a slow deep breath through his nostrils and kicked into Pararescue mode. Service before self. He had the assignment to complete. He knew the truth, and nothing she said changed what his involvement was with the Jackson family.

"If you had an inappropriate relationship with Mrs. Jackson, it will come out," she said. Her nostrils flared and her pupils dilated with fury.

"Let's calm down and focus on the issue at hand. Kevin's

mother died in a terrible accident and we need to help Kevin during his time of grief," he said with a calm that even surprised him.

She glared at him. They locked their sights on each other.

"I'll need to speak with the school board about all this," she said. Her hostility still present.

"All what? You'll need to speak to the school board about all what?" he said.

"What happened with Mrs. Jackson. The rumors about you," she said.

"If I, were you, I'd take a step back on spreading that rumor about me. Just because it's a rumor doesn't make it true. You're acting like a school yard bully. I get that you've never had to deal with something like this before. Stay focused on what your student needs, and let the police decide if there was more to her death," he said with the calmness of a yoga instructor.

She looked at him like he had three eyes. "Get out." She pointed to the door.

He closed the door behind him when he left her office. Marlene was still blowing her nose. He sat in the chair next to her messy desk. She looked at him as a new tear spilled over and streamed down her cheek.

"I can't stop crying," she said.

"Did you know Mrs. Jackson?" he asked.

"No. I'm super sad for Kevin," she said, "If I was going to predict something like this happening to one of our families, the Jacksons would have been on the list."

"Why?"

"As you saw at the Gala, they're the definition of dysfunctional." She blew her nose.

"Why do you think the boss is angry about Mrs. Jackson's death? She all but accused me of playing a role in it," he said.

She stopped wiping her nose and looked at him. "She did? Maybe because she doesn't like it when the school looks bad."

"Why would the tragic death of one of our parents make the school look bad?" he said.

"That's a good question," Marlene said.

He could see the wheels in her brain twirling.

Dr. Sawyer's office door opened. "I hear you talking about me." She scolded. "Stop it and get back to work." She slammed her door as fast as she had opened it.

CHAPTER 37

B rookfield P.D. cruisers made the Jacksons' driveway look like a parking lot. A crime scene van was parked adjacent to the walkway that led to the front door. There was no crime scene tape stretched from tree to tree like you'd see on TV, since it wasn't considered a crime scene. Not yet.

Mac parked his truck on the street behind the Mountain Tribune van. Curious neighbors congregated on both sides of the wide street. They sipped from travel mugs and endured the cold to appear concerned, when it was the gory details, they hoped to learn. Mac recognized a few women from Blackstone Academy.

With no regard for the onlookers, both sides of the Jacksons' glossy black front doors were wide open, exposing the large foyer for the world to see.

Officers and crime scene specialists moved in and out of the marble foyer, busy doing their jobs. Jason stood on the front stoop, talking with two uniformed officers. They met in the middle of the walkway where a three-tiered fountain trickled water.

"Hey, Mac, thanks for coming," Jason said. He reached out to shake his hand.

"Sure, anything for you. I'm not sure how I can help, although I'm intrigued," he said.

"You're the only person I've found aside from Mrs. Jackson's sister, Jane, Mr. Jackson, and Kevin Jackson who spoke with Mrs. Jackson in the last week," Jason said, with his open notebook in one hand and a pen in the other.

"Seriously? She had no friends?"

"Not that I've located thus far," Jason said.

"It's not like we spoke much. We weren't friends, so I still don't think I'll be of much help. I'm a little pissed off at Dr. Sawyer, she all but accused me of having an affair with Mrs. Jackson and contributing to her stress, which according to her, may have led to her misstep and then tumbling down the stairs."

"She said that?" Jason asked.

"She did. She's had it out for me since I started working there,"

Mac said.

"Is she on your list of potentials?"

"She sure as shit is," Mac said.

"Forget about her. You've always had a keen eye for detail. You might not realize what you know," he said.

An older, heavyset man with a full beard and wearing a baseball cap hopped out of the Mountain Tribune van and began to photograph the two men.

"Okay, can we go inside to finish this?" Mac asked.

"Damn reporters," Jason said, "We'll go into the living room. Tell me everything you remember, all of the details, as if we'd never spoken about the Jacksons," he said.

They sat on an overstuffed sofa, which looked like it had never been used, facing a pristine fireplace. It was one of those gas fireplaces, with fake wood strategically placed to resemble a pile of real logs.

"I was at Maggie's the first time Mrs. Jackson called me. That was a Friday night. We took the girls to the library for outdoor movie night and we had just arrived when she called," Mac said, "she said Kevin gave her my number and told her to call me if she needed help. She said her husband had been drunk since he was assaulted and he hadn't slept and he was angry, yadda, yadda, yadda. Before she could say why she was calling me, the call was disconnected. I tried her back, but there was no answer or message option."

"How did Kevin have your cell phone number?" he asked. He took notes in between giving orders to the officers who were processing the house.

"After his dad grabbed him at school, I gave him my business card and wrote my cell phone number on the back. I told him to call if he ever needed anything," Mac shrugged and said, "I thought he threw it away."

"Keep going," Jason said, "Didn't you say you talked to Mrs. Jackson again after that?"

"She called me Tuesday morning, when I was at school and asked me to meet her for coffee at Handley's."

"On the school phone or your cell phone?"

"On my cell phone. I drove out there and met her. She was at a corner table, looking all nervous and jittery, and she kept thinking people were looking at her and those people were going to tell her husband she was there."

An officer caught Jason's attention. "Sorry, I'll be right back," Jason said. He disappeared into another room.

Mac went to the foyer.

There was blood on the carpeted stairs, and a pool of Susan's blood had congealed on the polished marble floor, at the bottom where the staircase curved. There was also splattered blood on the wall toward the bottom of the stairs. The business of cleaning up death moved much slower in real life, than it did on TV. There were several bloody smudges along the staircase wall and some small jagged holes in the sheet-rock at the curve.

"So, you can see where Mrs. Jackson ended up. And you can see where she bashed her head into the wall on the way down," Jason said from behind him.

"Doesn't seem like enough to kill her."

"She was banged up from the fall, and her neck was broken," Jason said.

They went back into the living room and sat on the sofa.

"So, where were we?" he asked.

"We were at Handley's," Mac said, "She asked if I would help her to get away from the hell, they lived in. Her words, not mine. I asked her why she didn't get a divorce. She said Jackson would kill her if she tried to leave him. She believed he would, because she believed he killed his mother and blamed his father, who subsequently went to prison. And for the record, his mother died the same way Susan did."

"That's interesting," he said, "Did you agree to help her?"

"I didn't have a chance. After she showed me the scars on her wrists, she freaked out about being gone from home too long, said he'd check the security reports and she had rules to follow. She ran out and said we'd be in touch."

"Anything else you can think of?"

"She stiffed me for the coffee and left a small key in an envelope on the table."

Jason said, "A key? To what?"

"I have no idea. It's in my desk at school," Mac said.

"Hang on to that," he said.

"Do you have time to walk through the house with me? I'd like to show you something."

"Sure. Okay," Mac said.

"Let's go up to the second floor, there's another stairway in the kitchen," Jason said.

Mac nodded. The stairway was more like a freeway, officers ran up and down two stairs at a time, passing by them.

On the second floor, they walked past four or five closed doors. Beyond the landing at the top of the formal staircase were wide open double doors. The master bedroom. It was tidy, except half of the bed was slept-in.

"So, Mrs. Jackson was in bed, that's obvious." Jason pointed to the king-size bed. "Mr. Jackson has not been very cooperative so far. He was drunk when the paramedics arrived, blew a point one three on the Breathalyzer test at the station. He had to have been more than that, at the time Mrs. Jackson fell down the stairs."

"It doesn't surprise me that he's being uncooperative. He's a jackass through and through. It also doesn't surprise me that he was drunk," Mac said.

Jason nodded.

"The son isn't saying much. He's with his Aunt Jane now, Mrs. Jackson's sister. Jane said he's not saying much to her either. She also said her sister told her Mr. Jackson was physically abusive to her and had recently started in on Kevin. She said she didn't have many opportunities to speak with her sister when Mr. Jackson wasn't around," Jason said.

"You still haven't said how I can help." Mac said.

"I wanted you to see the environment they lived in and get your take on all of this," Jason said.

"Okay. Let me ask you this then, what about the scars on Mrs. Jackson's wrists? Any ideas on how those happened?" Mac asked.

"Get this," Jason said, "The sister asked to see Mrs. Jackson's body to confirm it was her sister. She was in shock and having a hard time believing her sister was dead. Their parents are deceased. So, the sister took a long look at her sister, at the coroner's office and I'm talking minutes. She touched her wrists like she couldn't figure out what the scars were. She told me her sister told her Mr. Jackson restrained her as punishment when she broke the rules, and then she burst into tears and ran out of the viewing room."

"Did anyone ask Mr. Jackson about the scars or the rules?" Mac asked.

"Yes," Jason said, "Mr. Jackson said his wife liked sex play in the bedroom, and her favorite was to be a captive with real handcuffs on and have Mr. Jackson pretend to rape her."

"That's fucking bullshit." Mac hissed.

"I thought the same thing. But look here," Jason said. He

opened one of the bedside table drawers on the side that was clearly Susan's and showed him a set of standard police handcuffs, sitting right next to a romance novel, a fingernail file, and some face cream.

Mac could feel his pulse throbbing in the back of his head. "There's no fucking way that's true. No fucking way. Why would she have shown me the scars on her wrists if they were from sex play?" Mac asked.

"Maybe she was setting the stage to make claims against her husband, to get a restraining order or alimony?" Jason offered with a shrug.

"No fucking way. There's more to it than that. You didn't see the way she looked. Her spirit was broken. She was not a hellcat in the sack. Jason, please, tell me you aren't buying that bullshit story."

"Nothing surprises me anymore. I follow the evidence, and so far, there isn't much to follow," Jason said.

"Humor me then. Let me take a look through the house," Mac said.

Jason nodded. "We have a couple of hours before Mr. Jackson's released. We don't have a reason to keep him at this point, and as best we can tell there was no crime and no crime scene. Unless we turn up some evidence, this will be classified as a tragic accident," Jason said, "So go for it."

Mac and Jason walked through every room in the house, and looked in closets. On the main floor, they looked around the pristine formal living room again.

Susan's kitchen was as clean and tidy as the rest of the house. Too clean. It had the look of a model home, the ones in a new subdivision tempting buyers with a beautifully decorated home where nobody lived. The kitchen was large and built for a gourmet chef. There was even a pizza oven, which did look used.

Mac knocked on walls, looking for a hidden room similar to his gun room, and found nothing. Two hours went by in a blink, and his time was up. He hoped he was wrong about Mr. Jackson, for Kevin's sake.

CHAPTER 38

S aturday morning was Coach's favorite time of the week. He always woke early. His mother slept in a little giving him time to himself. Over the droning of the vacuum, Coach heard the front door bell chime a melodic tune. He skirted around the cleaning lady in the hallway to reach the door before the person rang the bell a second time and woke his mother.

Coach didn't expect to see Stu and Kevin at his front door. He looked left and right to see how they had gotten to his home. Stepping aside, he motioned for them to enter.

"What's up?" Coach asked.

"Can we talk?" Stu said.

"Sure." Coach turned and then walked back to his den where he'd been enjoying a cup of coffee and reading about Susan Jackson's death in yesterday's newspaper. The boys fell into step behind him. The three of them slid around the cleaning lady who seemed oblivious to their presence.

"How'd you guys get here?" Coach asked, as he closed the door to his den. "It's raining out."

"We got a ride," Stu said.

"Chucky, who's here? I heard the doorbell?" his mother's voice boomed through the intercom.

"Ignore her. So, what's up?" Coach asked, as he guided the boys to chairs facing the sofa. The newspaper was scattered on the coffee table next to his cup half filled with coffee.

"Chucky, who's here?" his mother repeated herself.

Coach went to the intercom panel on the wall near the door. "Just some kids from school," he replied. He was two steps away from the intercom when she chimed in again.

"What kids from the school?" she asked.

He spun around and turned off the intercom. He patted Kevin on his shoulder, as he passed by. "I'm sorry about your mother Kev. What can I do for you two?" he asked.

"Thanks, my dad did it," Kevin blurted out.

"What?" Coach asked.

"My dad pushed my mom down the stairs." he said without emotion.

"You need to tell the cops." Coach scooted forward to perch on the front of the sofa.

"I will."

"Why wait? He might hurt you next," Coach said. His forehead wrinkled with concern.

"My dad said I can't talk to them without Stu's dad present and the time isn't right. If it looks like he'll get away with it, I'll figure out a way to tell what I know. Trust me, my dad will go down for this."

The room was quiet.

"I'm sorry Kev." Coach felt bad for the kid. He also felt frustrated about why they were at his home on a Saturday morning. He turned his attention to Stu. "What can I do for you guys?"

Stu jabbed his thumb toward Kevin. "He won't be in school for a while. He told his dad he's too upset about his mom's death and can't handle school. His dad told him he can stay home as long as he needs to."

"Okay," Coach said.

"He doesn't plan on returning until next year. And he needs you to help him pass his classes, so he won't be held back a grade," Stu said.

"Why are you taking the rest of the school year off? We aren't even finished with the first semester?" He looked at Kevin to answer the question, instead of Stu who had taken on the role as spokesperson.

Kevin sat quietly looking at Coach.

Coach had a chill run down his spine.

Stu responded, "Why not? If I could get out of going to school, I would."

"How am I supposed to help him pass his classes, when he isn't doing the work? Are you talking about homeschooling?" Coach talked to Stu, as if Kevin wasn't present.

"Whatever it takes. You'll need to provide the work for him to turn in for grades." Stu looked at him square in the eyes.

Both boys looked at Coach and waited for his reply.

"You're both nuts. I can't do that. You think I have more clout than I do," Coach said.

"We know too much, Coach, and we know what's been going on with you and Ms. Cortez. It would be a shame for Dr. Sawyer to find out what you've been up to," Kevin spoke up.

The door to the den crashed open. Coach's mother scooted in pushing her walker. Her caftan billowed behind her. Rather than put on a wig, she had wrapped a scarf around her head. Her face said it all, she was pissed off. She stopped at the doorway to turn on the intercom.

"Chucky, I wanted to meet your students," she said so sweet.

"Mother, this is Stu Collins, Fred's and Vanessa's oldest boy, and Kevin Jackson, Randy's and... um... Susan's boy."

She scooted her walker across the room and stopped next to Kevin. "I'm so sorry about your mother."

"Thanks," Kevin said.

"We're gonna take off, think about it and we'll get back to you. We can find our way out," Stu said. The boys left the den.

"Mother. How dare you barge in here like that, it was a private meeting with those boys," Coach said.

"How dare I?" she replied. "How dare you turn off the intercom, you little prick. I thought about cruising in here naked. How would you have liked that? You pull a stunt like that again and I'll do more than embarrass you. It's time for my breakfast."

He stared at his mother in disbelief.

"Chop, chop. I'm hungry," she said.

CHAPTER 39

Coach's day began with a visit from Stu and Kevin, and went downhill from then on. His mother demanded he cater to her every whim as a punishment for him turning off the intercom. The day couldn't end soon enough for him.

He and his mother were eating dinner in the kitchen in silence. He could tell by her body language she was still angry with him.

"I have a treatment tomorrow," his mother reminded him.

"I know. It's on my calendar," Coach replied.

"You better not be late like you were the other day," she scolded.

Coach was about to defend himself when his Uncle Clarence arrived.

"Hey. How're you doing? Sit down and join us for dinner," Coach was ecstatic to have someone besides his mother to talk with.

Clarence gave his nephew a thumbs up. Coach jumped up to get a place setting for him.

"Hello, Donna." Clarence kissed his sister on her cheek. "How're you feeling?"

"I feel like crap," she replied before taking a bite of her steak.

Chuck shrugged.

"Steak, baked potato, and asparagus—what a feast," Clarence said.

Clarence and Coach talked about football. Coach's mother ate without saying much.

Coach was about to take a bite when his mother pushed her plate forward. "I'm done. Chucky, help me to my room," she said a little terse.

Clarence said, "I'll help you. I came to visit with you too."

"You're so sweet," she said with a loving tone. "Get some cookies from the pantry and bring them with you."

Coach finished his dinner in welcomed silence, comforted by the sound of the elevator going up.

About an hour later, his uncle thundered down the stairs from his sister's bedroom. Coach was sitting at the kitchen table reading.

"I wrapped your plate and stuck it in the fridge," Coach said.

"Thanks. I'm starved," Clarence said. He removed the wrap from his plate and placed it in the microwave for two minutes.

Coach set his book on the table. "How was Mother?" Coach asked.

"Surly, as always. She's asleep now," he replied. "So, how're things going at school?"

"Fred Collins' kid, Stu, is freaking out because he thinks the marshal's looking at him as the drug source that supplied the stuff to Seth. And, well... you know about Randy Jackson's wife's death?" Coach said.

"Are you kidding? Susan Jackson's death is the talk of the town. I heard it twice from every customer; once when they dropped off their prescription and again when they pick up their meds. It's quite sad. Why's Stu so paranoid?" Clarence said.

"Stu has it in his head, that Mac, the new marshal, is an undercover narcotics officer looking for the person who supplied Seth with the drugs," Coach said.

"Did Stu sell the drugs to Seth?" Clarence asked as he shoveled food into his mouth.

"He didn't answer when I asked him that same question. So, I assume he did. He was also the one who called 911," Coach said.

"Do you think the marshal's an undercover cop?" Clarence asked.

"We've golfed together and I've talked with him plenty. I don't think he is. I asked Marlene, the secretary, she knows everything and she also doubts he is. I think Stu's the son of a criminal attorney and he's learned to suspect everyone," Coach said.

"Did he start at the school before or after the mayor's boy died?" he asked.

"Before," Coach said, "What're you thinking?"

"Just wondering."

"He grew up here. He was away for a long time because he was in the air force for twenty years. He was still in high school when you left for college," Coach said.

"Was he in the military police in the air force?" Clarence asked.

"No, he was some type of special ops that are also trained as paramedics," Coach said, "He's cool."

"I would think, by now, the cops would have already talked with Stu if they had evidence that he was the supplier," his uncle said, "I have the sports cream for the boys in my car. Walk me out. Why didn't you go to the school board meeting tonight?"

"Nothing too exciting on the agenda." Coach said.

Coach and Clarence walked to his car that was parked on the circle driveway near the front door steps. He unlocked his car and handed Coach the medium size cardboard box from the backseat floor.

"That should last them for a while," Clarence said, "How about I take your mom for her treatment tomorrow and give you a break?"

"Hell, yeah. You don't have to ask me twice. Be sure to get here early. I'll have her cooler packed." Coach felt like it was his birthday.

CHAPTER 40

There were a lot of reports given at the board meeting. After the public meeting, the board went into a closed session for almost two hours. It was close to midnight by the time Mac left the school. He put the window down and let the fresh air blow in as he drove. It was a cool night with a clear sky. He didn't enjoy board meeting nights, especially when they ran this late. Watching the school get smaller in his rearview mirror felt good.

The court was quiet as it should be at that late hour, all porch lights were off, except his. His house was lit up as if there was a party going on. He didn't remember leaving so many lights on, but it was still daylight when he'd left and he didn't pay much attention.

He touched the clicker and the gate at the end of his long driveway slid open. His diesel truck rumbled down the driveway to his detached garage. He expected Roxy to blast out the door with her usual excitement to see him, but she didn't. As soon as he opened the back door, he saw why Roxy hadn't greeted him.

She laid lifeless on the kitchen floor. Her tongue hung out the side of her mouth. There was a bandanna tied around her neck with a piece of paper attached. The words cut from a magazine and glued onto the paper said, "Back off NARC. Next time she's dead."

He felt for a pulse. Roxy had one. It was faint, but she had one. He called Maggie regardless of the late hour.

She whispered. "What happened?"

"Somebody gave something to Roxy. Drugs. Poison. I don't know what. I need to flush her system. Or a 24-hour vet," he said, as he sat on the floor next to his beloved dog.

"The closest 24-hour vet office is in Sacramento. I'll be there as fast as I can. I have to wake Lindy and tell her where I'm going, and then stop by the hospital," she said, as she hung up on him.

Maggie was at his front door in less than fifteen minutes. Her arms filled with medical supplies.

"Where's she?" she asked.

"In the kitchen. I got her to throw up most of what was in her stomach. There was some meat that I sure as hell didn't give her. Somebody laced it with something," he said.

Mac and his sister sat on the cold tile floor next to Roxy.

"Why would someone poison sweet Roxy?" she asked, as she prepared the PICC line for insertion. "Shave her leg over her main cephalic." She tossed him an electric shaver. "And then clean the area."

"There's a rumor going around the school that I'm an undercover narcotics officer. This note was around her neck." He showed her the piece of paper in a clear sealed baggie.

"Grip her leg so I can insert the IV catheter." She handed Mac the bag of saline solution while she taped the needle and wrapped Roxy's leg so when she woke, she wouldn't yank it out.

"Are you working undercover for Jason or something?" she asked.

Unsure how to respond without lying to his sister, he said with sincerity. "I'm not a cop."

"This is serious. Did you call Jason?"

"No, and I'm not going to. They don't get enough sleep as it is with the twins," he said.

"Then call 911. Someone came to your house and poisoned Roxy. They knew where you live and that you'd be gone."

"Let's focus on Roxy. Tomorrow I'll talk to Jason about this." He continued to hold the bag up.

He looked at the clock. It was almost one in the morning.

"Okay. If you think you can handle this, I'm going home," she said.

"I've got this. Thank you for being a nurse and for saving my girl," he said.

"Do you have oatmeal in the pantry?" she asked.

"Why?" he said and gave his sister an odd look. "You decided you're hungry?"

"I'll be right back," she said as she dashed off. Returning with a canister of oatmeal. She set the oatmeal next to Roxy's paw and then stuck her hand out for the IV bag. She set the bag atop the oatmeal allowing an elevated unrestricted flow of fluid. She smiled at her brother.

"There, hands-free. You still need to watch it because she could start moving around."

"You're the best." he said.

"I know." She beamed. "Text me as soon as she wakes up. It

doesn't matter what time. I want to see that she's okay as soon as I wake up. That's of course if I can get back to sleep. This was a bit of an adrenaline rush. And call Jason."

"I will."

She bent over and kissed her brother on his head before she left.

He watched Roxy for a few minutes. She appeared to be in a deep sleep. He hurried to his gun room to retrieve his laptop and security video from the evening. He was up and down the stairs in record time. Roxy hadn't moved in the short time he was gone.

He grabbed a bottle of water from the fridge, plugged in his laptop and sat next to Roxy on the floor once again to check her line. Glancing at the kitchen clock validated his fatigue. It was one-thirty in the morning.

Mac fired up the laptop and then started the video recording from the moment he walked out the back door. As usual, Roxy went inside to gobble her food shortly after Mac had driven away. After she inhaled her dinner, she went back out the dog door.

Mac was unable to see her when she was outside. He made a mental note to *update security coverage on the backyard.* She stayed outside for about thirty minutes.

When she came inside, she went straight to her water bowl where she lapped, and lapped, and lapped more water. Next, she staggered toward her pad in the alcove off of the kitchen near the breakfast table. She fell with a plop right where Mac had found her.

Roxy was out cold when the dog door flapped up and a head poked through. The person wearing a black ski mask climbed into the kitchen through the dog door like a baby being born. A twin-like person followed the first.

From their build, Mac was certain they were men.

They looked at Roxy. One of the goons kicked her in the ribs. She didn't move. Mac's blood began to boil.

They cruised from room to room. They looked in closets, and they took photos. They spent most of their time in Mac's bedroom. They looked in the drawers of his night stand. They didn't look under his nightstand or they would have found his loaded Bersa Thunder Pro .40 caliber.

When they walked into his closet, he held his breath for a moment. They walked back out and Mac exhaled. They didn't notice that he had a secret room beyond the rear closet wall. Not the brightest goons. He thought as he watched.

They returned to the kitchen, gave Roxy another kick. One goon looked in the fridge and grabbed two beers. They took their beers with them and left. All together they'd been inside his home for twelve minutes.

He stroked Roxy's side. Checked her line. She blinked. He scratched her in her favorite spot. She opened a lazy eye and looked at him, her tongue was still flopped out of her mouth. He scratched her some more and held the IV bag in hopes she would move. She pulled her tongue in and closed her mouth. She looked at him with a glazed look. She wagged her tail a few times.

He vowed, *Whoever did this to Roxy was going to be sorry. They messed with the wrong guy's dog.*

"Roxy," Mac soothed her as he stroked her side. She blinked once and then fell back to sleep. It was a good sign that she kept her tongue in her mouth. He texted Maggie a progress report.

CHAPTER 41

There was a knock at the front door. Bella yelled, "I'll get it." A minute later she ran to her mother's bedroom where Maggie was ironing.

"Who was at the door?" Maggie asked.

"A big scary tattooed man. He gave me this," Bella said. She handed the envelope to her mother.

The outside of the envelope was blank. She ripped it open and read the single piece of paper on the inside. She ran to the living room at the front of the house to look out the window. A scary tattooed man sat in an old beat-up looking truck parked across the street from their home. Maggie jumped to the side of the window and closed the curtains.

Maggie called her brother; the call went to his voicemail. "Mac," she whispered into the phone with her hand cupped around the microphone. "Some creep was just here. He parked across the street. He knocked on the door and then gave Bella an envelope for me. It warns me to tell you to back off. Please come here as soon as you hear this message. I'm scared," she said. She next called one of the guys Bobby worked with. When he was killed in the line of duty, all of the deputies at his office promised they'd take care of her.

Bella and Lindy were hugging each other standing next to their mother while she made her phone calls. Bella quivered and tears flowed down her little cheeks.

Maggie peeked out the kitchen window. The truck was gone. She kicked herself for not getting a better description or a license plate or even a description of a tattoo. "Bella, can you describe the scary man's tattoos?"

"I saw a picture of a gun on his neck," she said between gulps of air.

"Any others?" Maggie probed.

Bella started to sob, "I'm sorry mommy, I'll never answer the door again," she said on the verge of hyperventilating.

Maggie hugged her girls. All three jumped when there was a

forceful knock at the front door.

Still attached, the three shuffled to the door. Maggie stretched on her tippy-toes to look out the small leaded glass at the top of the door. She saw Deputy TJ Rizzo and threw open the door.

"Oh my God, come in, come in." She pulled him inside and then craned her neck to look up her street. There was comfort in seeing TJ's patrol car parked in the driveway. "Thank you for getting here so fast."

Lindy and Bella hugged TJ.

"Tell me more about what's going on," he said.

"Girls, go play in your rooms," Maggie said.

Lindy replied, "No, mom. Whatever's going on involves us too."

Bella waited for further instructions.

"Sorry, sweetie. You're right. Take a seat at the dining room table." Maggie checked the time and realized it was past their dinner time and she didn't have a plan.

Maggie started with the innocent knock on the door. She'd learned a lesson about leaving her door unlocked. The guy could've walked in without knocking.

Bella quietly cried. Lindy had tears pooling, waiting for the final drop to tip the bucket. Maggie showed TJ the note which looked like a classic cut-the-letters-out-of-a magazine-type threatening note you'd see in a slasher movie. "Tell your brother to back off or you and your girls will pay the price." And then she told him about what happened last night to Roxy and the threat Mac received.

Lindy said, "Someone poisoned Roxy?" Her tear-filled eyes were opened wide.

Maggie pressed her finger to her lips. "I'll tell you more later."

TJ asked Bella to describe the man. She did her best, but hadn't paid enough attention. Why would she? In her eight-year-old world, there wasn't crime, or line-ups, or arrests. She described the gun tattoo on his neck and said he had tattoos all over both arms. She couldn't describe the truck because she didn't look at it.

Maggie was describing the truck when someone rattled the front doorknob and then knocked. Maggie and the girls froze. TJ went to the door. The gear hanging from his duty belt clanked as he walked.

Maggie followed and pointed her finger at the girls giving the mother command to stay put. She stayed behind TJ when he opened the door.

Her brother and Roxy were on the other side of the door. "Sorry, the door is usually unlocked."

"Not anymore," Maggie said, as she gave her brother a tight squeeze. She whispered in his ear, "Roxy looks good."

Mac nodded in agreement.

Mac and TJ shook hands and did the bro-hug thing. Mac hugged the girls. The girls squealed in happiness to see Roxy.

"Fill me in," he said to TJ.

Mac examined the artistic threat. "This looks just like mine. Gee, I wonder if the same person did yours," he said with attitude.

"Mac, it's not funny," Maggie scolded her brother.

"I agree. This fucking... sorry girls. This pisses me off."

"What's going on at the school, Mac," TJ asked.

"Since the mayor's son died of an overdose, somebody thinks I'm an undercover narcotics officer planted at the school to bust whoever sold the drugs to Seth," Mac said.

"Are you?" TJ asked.

"Am I an undercover cop? No. I'm a marshal hired to be a deterrent to ward off anyone considering crimes against students, parents, and staff," Mac said.

"You're a threat to somebody's drug business," TJ said.

Maggie, Lindy, and Bella sat quietly watching and listening to the conversation. Roxy sat between the girls. One scratched her head while the other scratched her neck.

Maggie didn't often use her alarm system. She agreed to have it on every time they left the house and put it in stay mode when they were home.

TJ said he will have the guys cruise the neighborhood and they'll be on the lookout for the truck the tattooed man drove. He filed a report on Maggie's threat and Mac's from the previous night. He had to respond to a call and left.

Maggie asked her brother if he'd stay and have pizza with them.

Bella ran to her uncle and put her hands together as if praying. "Please stay, Uncle Mac, please," she begged.

"It's Friday, no school tomorrow. I'm staying all night," he said.

The girl's sad faces turned to blotchy red happy faces.

Maggie ordered the pizza and then asked the girls to do their homework. She asked her brother to talk with her in her bedroom while she finished ironing her uniforms.

As soon as they were alone, Maggie said, "Spit it out."

"Spit what out?" he replied.

"You're keeping something from me. The two threats are serious stuff. Whatever you've got going on, now involves us too. The least you can do is clue me in." She stood firmly in front of him and gave him 'the look'.

"Fine. Iron." He dove onto her king size bed. He told her about the secret assignment he was on and that she had to keep it super quiet. He wasn't supposed to tell her. He told her the only people who knew.

"The school superintendent doesn't know?" she asked.

"No, and it better stay that way. She's on my list of potential drug dealers."

CHAPTER 42

Coach tucked his mother into her bed and then pulled a chair from the table to her bedside. She liked to talk before she watched TV in the evenings. Since she didn't socialize much, she seldom had anything new to offer.

"It was so nice of Clarence to take me to my treatment yesterday. He arrived here thirty minutes earlier than I expected him," she said.

He thought she wanted to drive home her disappointment that her son couldn't or wouldn't leave his work in enough time to do the same.

"Maybe he can take you from now on. Then you'll never have to worry about my tardiness," he said.

"He can't do that. He owns his business and has to be there. People depend on him to fill their prescriptions," she said with some hatred in her voice.

"Since I wasn't there, did anything out of the ordinary happen at your treatment?" he asked.

"They were training a new girl. She had a little diamond pierced on her nose. I'm going to tell them I don't want her as my patient care tech," she said.

"Because she has a nose piercing?" he asked.

"Yes, she's reckless," she replied.

Coach wanted to say more on the subject, but thought it better to keep his mouth shut. She was going to do what she wanted to do regardless of his opinion.

"Madeline's coming over for brunch tomorrow. I need you to be a dear and run up to the Apple Farm for some fresh hot cinnamon apple donuts. Be back here by ten, she'll be here at eleven and you'll need to bake a quiche and cut up some fruit."

"I thought you didn't like Madeline." he said.

"Madeline's one of my dearest friends," she rebuked his criticism.

"We don't have a frozen quiche." He decided to let go of the debate about whether she did or didn't like Madeline.

"Then you'll need to stop at the store on your way to get the donuts. Allow enough time so brunch will be ready when she arrives. And…try to be punctual. I'm ready to watch TV now. You can leave," she said, as she reached for the remote control.

Before Coach stood up, his Uncle Clarence walked into the bedroom. "So, this is where the party is."

"Oh, what a nice surprise," his mother said. Her faced beamed with happiness. "Chucky, get up and let Clarence sit. He was just leaving," she said, shooing him away.

Coach retreated to his den with a fresh cup of coffee and a novel. He'd enjoyed the peacefulness for at least an hour when he heard his uncle walking toward the den.

"Is she asleep?" He took a sip of his cold coffee.

"God, no. She's wide awake and engrossed in some cop type TV show."

Coach shook his head. He kept his feelings to himself and decided not to invite his uncle to his pity party.

"She invited me to a brunch you're making tomorrow for her and her friend," he said.

"And?" he asked. "Will you be joining them?"

"No, I've got things to do tomorrow. I heard the marshal guy had a break-in at his home. That's scary," he said, "Where does he live?"

"I didn't know he had a break-in and I don't know where he lives," Coach was short with his uncle.

"What's your problem tonight?" he asked. "I thought since I took your mom for her treatment yesterday, you'd be flying high today."

"You have no idea how difficult she is to live with," Coach said.

"Are you kidding me? I grew up with the bitch," his uncle said.

"She treats me like I'm the hired help. Like she pays the bills. You're lucky I didn't run off like my brother did or she'd be living with you," Coach said.

"Oh, hell no," he said, "She'd be living in a home somewhere. She might not appreciate that you provide a lavish lifestyle for her, but I do."

"Thanks, she's not supposed to eat the donuts she wants me to buy for her tomorrow. Every time I remind her that she shouldn't eat something she does it anyway out of spite," Coach said.

"So, let her eat what she wants, maybe she'll die sooner rather than later," his uncle said.

"I'm embarrassed to admit this, I'm not sure I know how to live without her. Yes, we have a dysfunctional relationship, but it's all I've ever known," Coach said.

"Look at the bright side. When she's gone, you'll be able to have a real relationship with a woman," he said.

"The only woman I'm attracted to is dating someone else," he replied.

"Man, you need to perk up. Are you talking about Rita? You and she have a special friendship. When you can pursue her, you may learn she was into you all along."

"Doubtful. She's dating Mac," Coach said.

"The marshal dude?"

"Yup. Mr. Good-looks with rippling muscles," Coach said.

"Back to his break-in. I heard it was gang members from the east side of town. That should make the boys at school less paranoid about him looking at them for the drug thing, right?" his uncle said.

"I guess. Who do you hear all this gossip from?" Coach said.

"The customers. They like to tell me juicy gossip I may not know, so I play like I don't know anything. It's amazing what you hear. Did you know the mayor is having an affair?"

"What!?"

"You'll never guess who with," he said, as proud as a news reporter with a scoop.

"Who?"

"Your boss," his grin spanned from ear to ear.

"Are you shitting me?" Coach said.

"That's the gossip. But there's also gossip your marshal dude's an undercover narcotics officer. And that Mr. Jackson murdered his wife," he said.

"I'm not sure I believe any of it," Coach said, "Based on when Mac retired from the air force, he wouldn't have had time to attend the police academy to be a cop. There's one rumor discredited. Ozzy wouldn't cheat on Leona. They just celebrated their twentieth anniversary and still act like they're newlyweds. Two down. Plus, their son just died. I've got nothing on Randy and his wife. I'm sure we'll know if that's true soon enough."

"Maybe, Mac isn't a cop, but some bad dudes think he is. I'd keep your distance from him," his uncle counseled.

"Chucky. Bring me some cherry pie," his mother bellowed on

the intercom, "A la mode."

CHAPTER 43

Mac couldn't stop thinking about poor Susan. Sacramento was a two-hour drive. At three o'clock in the afternoon commuter traffic was going in the opposite direction. Mac thought he'd be home by eight.

Mr. Jackson, Sr.'s address was easy enough to find on the Internet. The neighborhood he lived in was rough, especially compared to his son's neighborhood. Most of the houses had barred windows to safeguard against break-ins.

A local gang had tagged a few garage doors and wooden fences. One house, in particular, Mac and Roxy drove past appeared to be the gang's headquarters. A chain-link fence surrounded the small home, tough looking guys were standing around drinking beer and smoking something. Mac didn't make eye contact. The last thing he wanted was an altercation with gang members. He hadn't considered what type of neighborhood Mr. Jackson, Sr. lived in when he left Brookfield.

Senior's street was several turns away from the gang activity. He lived in a small white stucco bungalow style house with a small patch of dead grass in front and two strips of cement that led from the street to where the garage must have been at one time. Mr. Jackson senior had the blinds on the windows closed. There was a small multi-colored pick-up truck parked on cement strips. The rear bumper was missing and there were quite a few dents, some small, some not so small. He thought, *Maybe he's in construction. Maybe that's his work truck. Maybe he's a terrible driver.*

He left the windows half down so Roxy would appear even more frightening to anyone who came near his truck.

The metal security screen door rattled in response to his knocking. A TV blared inside.

Someone yanked open the door, but Mac couldn't see the person through the screen.

"I ain't buying nothing," a man said.

"I'm not selling anything," Mac said, "I'm here to talk about your son, Randall, your daughter-in-law, and grandson."

The man was silent. Behind him, someone had just won a new refrigerator on the game show he'd been watching.

A short man with a ring of shaggy gray hair on his otherwise bald head opened the screen door wide enough for Mac to see him. He wore dirty jeans and a tight dingy, cream-colored thermal which revealed a round ball of fat sitting at his waistline. He looked pregnant. He wore no shoes, only socks. Dirty socks. The man looked like he hadn't shaved for several days.

"Who are you? And how do you know my son and his family?"

"May I come in? I'll tell you what you want to know," he said.

The man opened the door wider and motioned Mac inside. He made no excuses for the pigsty condition his home was in.

"You want a beer?" he asked.

"No, thank you," Mac said.

He shrugged and took a long drink of his beer before he plopped onto his well-used recliner. He pulled a lever and catapulted himself to a reclined position, his feet flung up in the air. Five empty beer cans sat amongst the debris on the side table next to him. The TV remained on, although he did turn the volume down.

"Sit down," he said pointing with his beer.

Mac slid the disheveled mass of newspapers on the sofa over to reveal a stained plaid cushion. Yesterday's open pizza box with its hardened pizza slices stared at him from the coffee table.

"Well? Spit it out," he said, "What'd you come here to say? How do you know them? Are they dead?"

"No, Mr. Jackson, your son and grandson aren't dead. Your daughter-in-law, she died four days ago," Mac said.

"How'd she die?" Mr. Jackson, Sr., said.

"She fell down the stairs in their home."

He slapped his thigh. "That son of a bitch. Damned if he did it again," he said.

"What're you talking about?" Mac said.

"Who'd you say you are? You a cop?"

"No, I'm not a cop. I didn't say who I was. I work at your grandson's school. My name's Mac," he said, thinking, *This may be crossing the line, may be grounds for dismissal. What the fuck am I doing?*

"What do you want?" he said.

"I think your son pushed his wife. I don't believe it was an accident. I wanted to know what you thought since your wife died the same way. Did your wife fall? Or did you push her like the jury verdict said you did?" Mac said.

He stared at Mac, returned his chair to the upright position, and stood up slow. Mac readied himself to grab the gun he'd tucked in an ankle holster under his pant leg.

Mr. Jackson senior walked into the kitchen. A slow, arthritic walk that gave Mac time to look around the place. Dishes and frozen food cartons littered the section of kitchen countertop he could see. It was afternoon, but his blinds were all closed. Streaks of filtered light shone through onto the walls.

He popped open another beer as he swayed from side-to-side walking back into the living room. Some of the foam from his beer spilled onto the carpet and blended in with the many other stains.

"Hell no, I didn't push my wife. My wife was a nut job, but I loved her. I was never sure if she loved me or hated me, though. She'd have made one hell of a poker player. She never showed emotion on her face." He shook his head. "Man, she had one mean temper." He took a long guzzle of beer and then belched. "That son of a bitch kid, though. He pushed his mother and blamed me. I'd bet he pushed his wife too. What was her name?"

"Her name was Susan," Mac said.

"Poor Susan, she didn't know married a monster. He was mean like his momma. I locked our bedroom door at night to keep him out. I was afraid he was going to kill us in our sleep," he said, "He killed my dog; I'm sure of it. When he was about seven years old, for his birthday, my wife's father gave him a bow and arrow set. Randy claimed it was an accident when he shot an arrow through my dog's head. It was no accident. I watched him practice shooting birds with arrows."

"How was it the jury found you guilty of manslaughter if you didn't do it?"

"That damn Randy. He lied about what happened. He said Claire and I were fighting in our bedroom. Said he heard our voices get louder. Then he heard Claire scream, and ran out to see what happened. He said he saw me standing at the top of the stairs looking down on her bloody, twisted body. He turned on the water works and was real convincing."

"What's your version?"

"I was asleep when I heard Claire scream. She must've gone to get a sleeping pill or something. I ran into the hallway and saw Randy staring down at his mother. I called 911, but by the time paramedics arrived, it was too late.

Randy stayed in his room until the cops came asking questions. You can fill in the rest."

"He pushed his mom for the fun of it?"

"Hell, if I know. Ask him."

"Why would he do the same thing to his wife?"

"Maybe he hates women cuz his mom was so mean. I don't know. Do I look like a shrink? Where's the kid now?"

"He's with his aunt, his mother's sister. Who did Randall live with when you were in prison?"

"He was in foster care. Became emancipated at sixteen. Are we done here?" he asked, before he drained his beer.

CHAPTER 44

The Brookfield Police Department was downtown in the same block of government buildings as the superior court and building department. It was Mac's first official visit to the Brookfield PD. After his conversation with Mr. Jackson, Sr. last night, Mac had a hunch and it paid off big time. He had an appointment with Jason and his partner, Detective Ruiz to discuss what he'd discovered. When he placed the truck in park, he received a text from his sister.

Maggie: Hi. What's going on?

Mac: I'm at the PD to meet with Jason and his partner.

Maggie: Why?

Mac: So much to tell you. I'll call you later. Mr. Jackson may have a hidden room in their home where he made his wife stay as punishment and his mother died the same way his wife died. His father went to prison, but he said his son did it.

Maggie: WTF. Did you talk to Mr. Jackson's dad?

Mac: I did. He's in Sacramento. Does TJ still have cruisers watching your place?

Maggie: Yes. And I'm using the alarm like a good girl.

Mac: Good. I'll call you and tell you everything.

Maggie: Be careful.

The husky female officer at the front counter directed him to a meeting room. He had the Jacksons' house plans in a cardboard tube he kept close to his side like it was his third leg. The meeting room, if filled, sat about thirty people, some around the table and others seated along two walls. Jason came in with a notepad and Detective Ruiz with a large accordion-style file.

"Hey, how're doing?" Jason shook Mac's hand. "This is my partner, Detective Dan Ruiz," Jason said and waved his hand in his partner's direction.

Detective Ruiz and Mac shook hands. He had a firm grip, a cop's grip. He was a tall man, about six foot and muscular. He gave off a shy vibe. Maybe he was more of a thinker than a talker.

"Before we look at the drawings, I have a confession to make,"

Mac said.

Both men watched him in silence and waited.

"I looked up Mr. Jackson's father and paid him a visit yesterday."

"Oh, you did," Jason said, "And?"

"Mr. Jackson Senior, of course, said he was innocent of killing his wife all those years ago. He said his son pushed the wife down the stairs. He said he was asleep and heard her scream. When he went to see what happened, Junior was standing at the top of the stairs looking down at his dead mother. Does the scene sound familiar? He also said Junior killed their dog with a bow and arrow."

"That's interesting," Jason said, "You should have let us speak with him."

"Would you have? Was he on a list of people to talk with? I doubt it. I seem to be the only person who wants justice for Susan Jackson's murder," he said.

"Now, wait a minute. We have to keep an open mind and follow the evidence," Detective Ruiz said.

"That's why I spoke with Senior. I knew you weren't going to, there was no reason you would. You have no evidence that pointed you in his direction."

Detective Ruiz wrote notes.

They spread out the architect's floor plans for the Jackson home onto the conference table between them. Mac flipped to page nine where he pointed out the wine cellar beneath the fireplace in the living room. Detective Ruiz continued to take notes and seldom looked up from his notepad.

Jason nodded his head. "I thought that fireplace looked too clean. Never would have guessed it was the access to a hidden room. Smart thinking to check out the house plans. Remember, though, because it's on the plans doesn't mean it's there or that it has anything to do with Mrs. Jackson's death. Let's see what the coroner thinks the scars on Mrs. Jackson's wrists were from, and if he thinks your theory of bondage is plausible, I'll take it to the sergeant and see if we have enough for a search warrant."

"And remember Mrs. Jackson's sister said Mr. Jackson restrained her as punishment when she broke the rules," Mac reminded his long-time friend.

Detective Ruiz continued to scribble on his note pad.

"Any way you could ask Kevin about the wine cellar and the

scars on his mother's wrists?" Mac asked.

"Negative. Mr. Jackson told us we'd need to go through his attorney if we have more questions for either of them," Jason said

"Of course, he did," Mac said, "Who's his attorney?"

"Fred Collins."

"Of course."

"Mac. Leave the Jackson case to us. You focus all your attention on your assignment. If Mrs. Jackson's death wasn't an accident, we'll figure that out. The Chief wants us to wrap up the drug case," Jason said, "How's Roxy? Any more trouble?"

"She's good. No more trouble," Mac said, as he began to roll up the drawings and left them with Jason. He'd had enough bureaucracy for one day.

He felt frustrated when he left the police department. His guard was down when he stepped one foot into the crosswalk and heard tires screech. The front grill of a red sports car was inches away from plowing over him. Mr. Jackson's red sports car. He looked like a maniac gripping the steering wheel his beady eyes bulged, his perfect hair tousled, and Mac saw the sheen of sweat glistening on his face.

He leaned out his window, "You're wrong about me. I didn't hurt my wife."

CHAPTER 45

Mac said nothing to Mr. Jackson. How'd he know where to find me? He wondered as he stared at him through his windshield.

Of course, he wasn't going to run him down in front of the police department. Mac crossed in front of the fancy sports car like he owned the road.

"Can we talk for a minute? Please?" Mr. Jackson hung his head out the window.

"Sorry, that'd be a violation of the restraining order," Mac replied.

"I withdrew it this afternoon. Please?" Mr. Jackson asked, again.

Mac jabbed his thumb toward the parking garage.

Mac hopped onto the driver's seat of his truck. He pulled his handgun out from the glove box and placed it under his seat. He called Jason.

Mr. Jackson walked to the passenger side of Mac's truck. Mac put the window down a couple of inches. "Hang tight," he said to Mr. Jackson.

Jason answered, "Miss me already?"

"Something like that. Can you check on the restraining order Mr. Jackson has against me and see if he withdrew it?"

"Sure. Hang on."

A few seconds passed and then Jason was back on the call. "Surprise, surprise, he did. What's going on?"

"I'll tell you later, gotta go. Thanks," Mac said.

Mac unlocked the door and Mr. Jackson climbed onto the passenger seat in Mac's truck.

"We got off to a bad start. Am I a bad father? Yes. Was I a good husband? No. But I didn't push my wife down the stairs. Kevin did. He's a bad seed, you have to believe me." His breath smelled of alcohol.

Mac listened.

"He's a lot like my dad. My father killed my mom. Look it up, you'll see. He went to prison for it," he continued. "Kevin killed his mother, the same as my dad did my mother. And then Kevin blamed me." He rambled

"Why would Kevin do that?" Mac asked.

"He doesn't want to follow rules. He wants to be independent. But he needed money to live so he killed his mother and wants to put me away. He'll get her inheritance. You have to believe me," he pleaded.

"What rules are you talking about?" Mac asked.

"Huh?" he said.

"You're the one who said Kevin doesn't want to follow rules. What rules?" Mac clarified.

He waved his hands in the air. "Any rules. Emancipation. He wants to be on his own," he replied. "I was working in my office downstairs when I heard Susan scream and then thud sounds. I ran to see what happened. Susan was at the base of the stairs and Kevin stood at the top smiling at me. He was smiling at me."

He began to cry.

"Why are you telling me this? You need to tell your attorney," Mac said.

He stopped crying and looked at Mac. "I did tell my attorney. He said I'm screwed because Kevin's a good actor and he's a child," he said.

"I can't help you, man," Mac said.

Mr. Jackson slid out of the tall truck.

Mac watched the hunched man walk away hunched over to his sports car.

He left the area first, and Mac followed, watching his mirrors more than usual on the drive home.

When Mac turned off the main road into his neighborhood, Mr. Jenkins, Mac's elderly neighbor, stood near the community mailbox. They usually exchanged niceties when their paths crossed, him walking his white miniature poodle, Mimi, Mac walking Roxy. Even though they didn't socialize, Mac kept an eye on all his neighbors. For their benefit and his.

"Mr. Jenkins. How're you doing?" he said in a loud voice.

"I'm still kicking, even though my kids can't wait to get their hands on my money," he said, "Somebody was snooping around your place about an hour ago. Mimi barked her head off. Do you know someone who drives a red sports car?"

"What do you mean snooping?" he asked.

Mr. Jenkins said, "He parked in front of my place and then walked into your yard through the gate at the walkway. He peeked in the windows then went around to the side of the porch. I couldn't see him then. Mimi kept barking and barking. I couldn't get her to shut up." He shook his head as if remembering his agitation.

"Did the man stay out of sight for long?" Mac asked.

"No. I pretended to take Mimi for a walk. I stopped at your driveway where I could see him, and yelled at him to get out of there." He beamed with pride. "When I hollered, he looked up, but he didn't acknowledge me."

"Thanks for watching my place, Mr. Jenkins," he said.

"Sure thing. But that guy seemed crazy. When he walked back down the walkway and over to his car, he was mumbling and shaking his head the entire time. He never even looked at me. And believe me, he had to have known we were there because Mimi was still barking."

Did he know I wasn't home or did he want to confront me? Mac thought.

"I'll figure out who it was. Thanks again. Next time, call 911 and report it," he said, "He could have been dangerous."

CHAPTER 46

Jason and Mac rode together in his unmarked police car, a newer white Ford Explorer. The backseat had accordion-style file folders packed full with papers. There was a police radio and a scanner chattering on low volume. There wasn't a weapon that he could see, although he was sure it was there somewhere.

Jason's partner, Detective Ruiz, followed in his unmarked car, another white Explorer, with a uniformed officer riding shotgun, and a cruiser with two uniformed officers brought up the rear of their caravan. It was hard to tell if anyone was home at the Jacksons'. No vehicles were visible and they had closed the curtains.

"Don't engage Mr. Jackson in conversation. Let us do all the talking," Jason cautioned. "He's a loose cannon."

"No problem. I've got nothing to say to that jackass anyway." Mac hadn't seen Mr. Jackson since they talked in the police department parking lot a few days ago.

Mac stood behind Detective Ruiz, shielded by his height. The uniformed officers were to his left. Jason stood on Detective Ruiz's left and rang the bell.

After what felt like minutes, Mr. Jackson opened the left half of the double door a few inches and peered out. Mac couldn't see him, he only heard his squeaky voice.

"What do you want? My wife just died. Why won't you leave me alone so I can grieve?" he snarled and tried to slam the door.

Jason placed his foot upon the threshold of the door to prevent the door from closing. And then he held out Mr. Jackson's copy of the search warrant. "We have a warrant to search your fireplace in the living room and anything attached to or beneath it."

"You can't barge into my home when my attorney isn't here." His squeak was getting squeakier.

"Yes, Mr. Jackson, we can. The warrant allows us to enter. Feel free to call your attorney while we're looking at your fireplace. These two officers will go with you to another room while we're here." Jason had a strong authoritative voice and demeanor.

Jason stepped aside to allow the uniformed officers to enter first. Jackson fell back several steps while the six of them plowed inside. Mr. Jackson and Mac made eye contact. Mac kept all expression off his face.

"What the fuck's he doing here?" Mr. Jackson screamed at Jason while pointing at Mac.

"That's none of your concern, Mr. Jackson. Mr. MacKenna works for us as a consultant," Jason softened his voice.

"Oh no. No fucking way. He has it out for me." He hadn't taken his eyes off Mac. His face reddened and the veins in his neck bulged.

Mac noticed Kevin upstairs standing outside his bedroom. He looked down at them, his face void of all expression. He looked tired.

Jason stepped between Mr. Jackson and Mac and broke Mr. Jackson's stare. He pointed to one of the uniformed officers. "This officer will escort you to the kitchen and stay with you while we look at the fireplace."

"No. No. No. I will not allow this." Jackson screamed in Jason's face.

"Mr. Jackson." Jason kept his cool. "We're going to conduct our search now. That includes Mr. MacKenna. You can either allow us to do what we're here to do or the officers will place you in the backseat of a patrol car. It's your choice."

"No. No. No. He's not allowed inside my home."

Jason directed the officers to wrangle Mr. Jackson into their patrol car. "Stay with him, and allow him to use his cell phone to call his attorney." The third uniformed officer entered the home with them and went upstairs to locate Kevin.

When the front door closed, they could still hear Mr. Jackson screaming obscenities at the officers.

"What a nut case. Let's get this done and get out of here," Detective Ruiz said.

They stood in front of the fireplace and did a visual inspection. It looked like a normal gas fireplace.

The stone surround looked like the stone on the front of the house. The firebox had an iron grate with realistic looking split oak logs with embers underneath to replicate a real wood fire. There was a glass panel adhered to the face of the firebox, protecting fire gazers from getting burned. It looked authentic.

"According to the house plans, the mechanism that opens the

access is behind one of these stones," Jason said. He pushed on the stones in the region indicated on the architectural drawing until a larger stone popped open like a kitchen cabinet door with hidden spring hinges. Inside was a panel with five rectangular boxes marked for fingerprints.

"Shit," Jason said, "That's fucking great. Dan, get Mr. Jackson in here. Tell the officers what we need him for. He's going to put up a fight, so hog-tie him if necessary."

Several minutes later, two uniformed officers carried Mr. Jackson headfirst into the house. He looked like a human battering ram. He must have spat at an officer because he also had a mesh sack over his head.

"Here he is," Detective Ruiz said.

The two officers wrestled Mr. Jackson to get his right hand free and pressed his fingers on the biometric panel. He screamed profanities as the firebox slide sideways, revealing a trapdoor in the floor. Jason opened it up to expose a set of stairs leading into darkness.

Mr. Jackson screamed more obscenities as the officers hauled him back outside.

Jason, Detective Ruiz and Mac clicked on their flashlights. They had to stoop to fit into the short space where the firebox had been and then descend the stairs. The light from their flashlights bounced off the narrow cinder block stairwell. When they reached the bottom three wide beams of light bounced off the walls in the small room.

It looked to be five feet wide by five feet long by seven feet high, as indicated on the architect drawings. Racks of wine bottles lined both sides. The room shrank in size when the three of them stood side-by-side. There was an overhead light, which Detective Ruiz pulled the chain to turn on. It looked like an innocent wine cellar.

Detective Ruiz went through the unlocked door leading to the next room. Jason and Mac crammed in close behind him and peered into the adjoining room.

They shone their lights all around the room. The three of them breathed an audible gasp.

Jason spoke first, "What the hell?"

"What the hell's right," Detective Ruiz agreed. "That's messed up."

There were heating and air conditioning vents in the ceiling.

The walls were the same cinder block as in the wine room. In one corner, was a large pillow on the floor and handcuffs attached to the wall. In the opposite corner was a heap of something, perhaps blankets. The room was completely dark with no windows or light of any kind, and it felt damp and cold.

Mac was speechless, wondering, *How many hours had Susan spent handcuffed in this room over the years?* Then Kevin came to mind.

"Dan," Jason said, "What's that piled in the other corner?" Jason and Mac shone their flashlights on the pile.

Detective Ruiz flipped it over. It was a straitjacket. Again they let out an audible gasp.

Jason looked at Mac and said, "So now we know why Kevin doesn't have scars."

Jason and his partner took photos of the small space, the walls, the latches on the doors, the handcuffs, and the straitjacket from every angle possible.

"Here's that weird little key Susan left on the table at the coffee shop. She never told me what it went to. I thought maybe a jewelry box," Mac said the first words he'd uttered since entering the Jackson home.

Jason took the key. "That's a handcuff key, they're unique, but distinctive." Jason locked the cuffs and then tried the key, they sprang open. They looked at each other.

"So, Mrs. Jackson gave you the key to the handcuffs Mr. Jackson forced her to wear while she was in his special made - and hidden from view - torture chamber? Is that about right?" Jason asked, not expecting an answer from either his partner or Mac.

As they were exiting the fireplace, the Jackson family attorney, Fred Collins, Stu's father, burst through the front door.

Jason handed Mr. Collins a copy of the search warrant. "Have a look at the wine cellar, Fred, I left it open for you. And then you can speak with your client at the jail, we're taking him there for questioning."

Mr. Jackson was still screaming obscenities from the back of the squad car when they walked past.

"Every time I think I've seen the worst I'll see in my career something comes along and tops it," Jason said when he and Mac settled into his Explorer for the ride back to the police station.

"He's a sick person. Will he spend the weekend in jail?" Mac said.

"No. Even if we charge him, Fred will bail him out. But thanks to your insistence, we now have enough to take a closer look at a murder charge. Will you now leave this alone and focus on the drug case? I'm begging you," Jason said.

"In all fairness, it's not like I have ignored the drug case. I've got a short list of suspects. To answer your question, I'll let it go," he said.

CHAPTER 47

It was around six early Saturday evening when Mac noticed Roxy had heard someone approach the front door. She went to the door and waited. When the doorbell rang, she barked.

Mac saw a yellow Volkswagen Bug parked in front of his home. He opened the door to a smiling Rita.

"Surprise." Bags filled with something hung from her arms.

They kissed. Roxy wagged her long hairy tail with great enthusiasm, she was as happy to see her as Mac was.

"I thought you were going out of town with your girlfriends." He shut the door and followed her into the kitchen.

"I didn't feel well this morning so I told them to go without me," she said.

"And you're feeling better now?" he asked.

"I am. I hope you haven't thought about dinner yet, I brought a homemade lasagna, garlic bread, and wine."

"Even if I did, you win. Sounds delicious. Is there a special occasion I've forgotten about?" Mac said.

"My mom always told me the fastest way to win a man's heart is through his stomach," she smiled.

He gave her a long reassuring kiss. "You're already a winner, Rita." His words muffled as he kissed her neck.

They kissed like teenagers at the end of a date until Rita gave a slight push from Mac's embrace.

"The food's getting cold, maybe we should eat." Her eyes reflected a mix of passion and worry.

Mac forced his mind to change channels.

He opened the wine while she served the food. They sat at the kitchen table in the alcove. Roxy slept on her pad in the corner.

"How's Roxy doing since her poisoning? Have your friends found out who the guys were that broke in?" she asked, before taking a small nibble of her food.

"She's fine. I think it may have been something to knock her out more than to poison her. Since they took nothing, it's not a high priority. It's seen as more of malicious trespass and animal cruelty."

"I'm glad she's okay."

"What's on your mind, Rita? You have something weighing heavy on you," Mac asked.

"Do you remember when you saw Coach and me in a heated conversation in the teacher's lounge? You came in to see what was going on?"

"Yes," he said.

"We weren't talking about the students. I lied to you. I've felt terrible about it since then," she said looking at her lap.

"What were you discussing?"

She didn't answer. She fiddled with her fork, pushing a pasta noodle around on her plate. She hadn't eaten much of her dinner.

Mac waited for her to say what she needed to say.

"There's something I should have told you before we went on our first date."

He waited. He sensed this wasn't going to be a good confession.

"I was married before. We divorced. It was when I lived in Miami. He stayed there and I moved as far away as I could. I saw the opening at Blackstone and applied. I was able to get a temporary teaching certificate in California," she said.

"That's okay, Rita," he said. He rubbed her arm and then refilled their glasses with more wine.

"There's more," she said.

"Okay," he said.

"I became depressed from the divorce and about living so far from my parents…" She took a sip of wine. "Coach was extra nice to me and told me he had something that would help me with my depression," she said.

His ears were at attention.

"He gave me some meth…" a tear escaped from one of her large brown eyes. She took another swig of wine. "It helped. I felt better until it wore off and then I felt as sad as I had before. So, he gave me some more." She paused and took a deep breath. "I'm addicted."

"Are you high now?" he asked.

Her silence answered his question.

"Do you inject it or snort it?" He couldn't believe what he was asking her.

"Snort," she said without looking up at him.

"Since you're being honest, what were you and Coach discussing when I saw you and him in the teacher's lounge?" Mac said.

"I told him I cared about you and I was quitting cold turkey," she said, "He laughed at me and told me I wouldn't be able to. And he was right." She began to cry.

"Does Dr. Sawyer know?" he asked.

"NO. Nobody knows except Coach."

"Where does he get the meth that he sells to you?" he asked.

"I don't know. He just always has some," she said.

"Do you pay for what he gives you?"

"I didn't at first." She dropped her head.

"So let me see if I've got this straight. You're addicted to methamphetamine, your supplier's Coach, and you've been lying to me the entire time we've dated?" he said.

She walked toward the bathroom and returned with a tissue box. She blew her nose several times and threw the tissues in the trash before returning to her seat.

"Yes," she whispered.

"Is he selling drugs to the kids? Is he the one who gave Seth the drugs?"

"I'm not sure."

"That's bullshit, Rita." He pushed his chair back causing the chairs legs to scrape on the floor tile. Roxy jumped up from her pad, ready to follow Mac wherever he went. "You're closer to Coach than you wanted me to know about. Is there more to your relationship?" Mac asked. Disappointment was building inside him. "Have you been playing me all along?"

"No. No." She shook her head. "I'm falling in love with you, Mac. That's why I'm telling you this."

"I think it's best if you don't stay here tonight. Thanks for dinner."

"There's something I overheard Coach talking about that you should know," Rita said.

CHAPTER 48

Rita stayed seated at Mac's kitchen table. Mac leaned back and stretched out his long legs. "What did you overhear Coach say?"

"I saw him give Stu an envelope and heard him warn Stu not to take it home or let his dad see what was in it," she said.

"And how did you happen to be privy to this top-secret conversation?" he replied.

"I was in Coach's office picking up some more... and Stu interrupted," she said. She closed her eyes. The disappointment in herself written on her face.

"Coach keeps meth in his office?" he asked.

"In his briefcase," she said.

"Did Stu see what you two were doing?" he said.

"No, Coach put the stuff away when he heard Stu talking to another kid near his door," she replied.

"So, Stu comes in and Coach gives him an envelope telling him not to let his dad see it?"

She nodded.

"What do you think was in the envelope?"

She shrugged. "If he supplies me with meth, maybe he does for the kids too," she said.

"You just said he hid the drugs when he heard Stu approach," Mac said with agitation building.

"It felt sketchy to me," she said, "I'm going to go."

She packed the remnants of her lasagna dinner back into her carry bag. He helped her. The two said nothing while cleaning up the kitchen.

She looked at him before walking to the front door. He couldn't bring himself to kiss her.

"Rita, on Monday you tell Dr. Sawyer about your drug addiction. If you don't, I will. A drug addict can't work at a school. That's wrong."

He watched her walk to her car a broken woman. There were many things he could overlook or learn to live with in a relationship, drug use was not one of them.

Mac sat on the sofa and turned on the TV. Roxy plopped down in front of the sofa and fell back to sleep before Mac found a show that interested him. He texted Jason.

Mac: Hey. Rita told me she overheard an interesting conversation between Coach and Fred Collins' kid, Stu. Coach gave Stu an envelope and told him not to let his dad see it. Rita thought it was drugs.

Mac waited for a reply. He felt anxious. He poured what remained in the bottle of wine into his glass.

Hearing nothing from Jason he continued with his thought.

Mac: Can we schedule the drug dog to come to the school on Monday and sniff around for drugs? Rita told me a shit-load of stuff. Call me tomorrow. Night.

Mac texted Maggie.

Mac: Hey, you up?

Maggie: I'm sorry to say, yes. Can't sleep. I was reading. What're you doing?

Mac: The woman I've been dating, Rita, showed up with a homemade dinner.

Maggie: So why are you texting me?

Mac: She dropped a bombshell on me after dinner.

Maggie: Do tell.

Mac: She told me she's addicted to meth.

Maggie: WTF. And you didn't know?

Mac: She's not hardcore.

Maggie: Still....... So you broke it off?

Mac: Pretty much.

Maggie: Does she shoot it or snort it?

Mac: Snorts it. Shit. I liked her a lot too. I can't believe I didn't have a clue.

Maggie: Maybe you were falling in love.

Mac: So much for that.

Maggie: Who does she get her drugs from and what other teachers are doing drugs? Geez.

Mac: I'll give more detail in person.

CHAPTER 49

"A re you sure you want to do a surprise drug search?" Jason asked, "You're already on the boss lady's shit list."

"You don't think I should?" Mac asked. "Why?"

"I think you should talk to your boss first. Blindsiding her may have repercussions."

"She's on my list," Mac said.

"I'll call Michael Stromberg and give him a heads-up," Jason said.

"Let me know if we have a green light. I'll be ready," Mac replied. He parked in the staff lot next to a woman dressed as a mummy who was dropping off one of the teachers.

It was Halloween, students weren't allowed to wear anything other than their school uniform. They could 'accessorize' with Halloween earrings, necklaces, etc. Mac and Roni stood at the front of the school admiring the creativity some of the students put into their non-costume adornments.

Mac leaned over and whispered in Roni's ear, "We're doing a surprise drug search this morning. Want to tag along?"

Roni's eyes lit up like it was Christmas morning and she had the biggest gift under the tree.

"Does a bear shit in the woods?" she whispered back to him.

"So, that's a yes?" he confirmed.

"Yes. What time?"

"About half an hour, when the officer and dog arrive."

"Did you have a tip?"

"Yes. I hope it was reliable," he said. The vision of Rita walking away from his home Saturday night popped into his head. He hadn't seen or spoken with her since. She either arrived to work before him or scheduled a substitute to cover all or part of her day to avoid him.

The last of the stragglers were running into the school before the tardy bell rang. Mac and Roni hung out in front waiting for the narcotics officers to arrive. Roni was giddy about observing a drug search.

A black SUV adorned with Brookfield Police Department pulled to a stop in front of them. The rear window was part way down allowing the dog to sniff fresh air. The dog barked at Mac and Roni. The officer said something to the dog in German and it stopped barking.

Mac and Roni led the officer and his dog into the school. First stop was Marlene's and Dr. Sawyer's offices.

"Good morning, Marlene," Mac said, as the group rounded the corner into her office.

"Morn—," Marlene jumped mid-sentence when she looked up and saw Mac wasn't alone. "What do we have here?"

"A random drug search," Mac said.

Marlene looked at the officer and the dog. Then she looked at Roni who smiled at her.

"Was this on the schedule?" Marlene asked.

"No, that's why it's a random search. Will you let Dr. Sawyer know? If she's interested in joining us, we'll start with the lockers, then the gym," Mac said, as he turned to show the officer where to begin.

Walking in stealth mode the foursome arrived at the hallway with two rows of lockers, uppers and lowers on both sides of the hall. The dog handler began commanding the dog in German. The dog got excited and sniffed high and low, they moved fast.

Mac knew what number locker was Stu's and Kevin's, although with Kevin not at school he doubted there would be anything in his locker.

The dog heard the clickity click of high heels approaching from behind before the rest of the group. Dr. Sawyer stopped next to Mac. She was a little closer than he'd like.

She pulled Mac's arm to have his ear closer to her mouth. "What do you think you're doing?" she whispered through clenched teeth.

"Random drug search," he whispered back unmoved by her anger.

"I can see that. Why wasn't I told about this?" she said.

"Random means it's a surprise to everyone," he said.

"Parents are going to be furious when they hear about this," she said.

More German commands distracted both of them.

"They'd rather have drugs in their kids' school?" he said.

Dr. Sawyer moved nearer Roni. "Why are you here?" she

asked, in a not so quiet voice.

"Mac invited me to observe because I'm taking a Criminal Investigation class at the college," Roni said with apprehension.

Mac and Dr. Sawyer looked at each other. He saw she was beyond angry with him. She stood with her arms crossed over her chest. When the group moved forward so did Dr. Sawyer.

They were getting close to Stu's locker. The dog sniffed something and began howling and gyrating and scratching at locker 622. Stu's locker was 626. The custodian who had been following along in silence was asked to cut the lock with his bolt cutter. The officer rummaged around in the locker showing the dog various items. When he showed him an aluminum refillable water bottle the dog began his dance once again. The officer gave a command in German to the dog and the dog sat down and remained still. He opened the bottle and looked inside. When he tipped the bottle upside down three skinny marijuana joints fell out. The officer popped one open and smelled it.

"Smells like pot to me," he said. He tested a little which was positive for marijuana.

Dr. Sawyer said to Marlene over the walkie-talkie, "Marlene, have Zorion Karranza sent to my office."

"10-4"

Mac asked Roni to take the joints to Marlene. He was hopeful the dog wasn't done. If this is all we find my ass is grass and the boss is going to mow me down, he thought to himself.

Once the excitement from having found the pot had subsided, the officer said something to the dog again in German. The dog began sniffing and was uninterested in locker 626.

They moved on to the gym lockers. The students in P.E. were in the gymnasium leaving the locker area free to search. The same was true for the girls' locker area. The dog didn't find anything else. They cruised into Coach's office and let the dog sniff around. Again, nothing grabbed the dog's senses.

The officer shrugged his shoulders. Mac walked the officer out to his vehicle and thanked him for his time. The officer said he had a niece attending the elementary side and he was glad they found nothing. He said he'd come back anytime.

Mac went to Dr. Sawyer's office for the butt chewing he knew he was in for. He cruised past Marlene. Zorion sat leaning back against the wall waiting his turn like a cow at the slaughterhouse. Mac walked into the boss' office, shutting the door behind him. He sat and waited. She was on a phone call, but wasn't saying anything.

She hung up and looked at him. Her face reddened and he could see she was trying to slow her heart-rate through deep breathing.

"That was a parent who already knows we did a random drug search. He threatened to remove his child if he hears there are drugs at our school," she said.

"Sounds like a good parent to me, I'd do the same thing," he replied. "We found some pot, didn't we?"

"My phone will ring off the hook today because you decided to go half-cocked and bring that officer and dog onto the campus without clearing it through me."

"It defeats the purpose of a random search," he said, "For all I know, you have drugs in your office."

She gasped. "Do...Not...Ever...Accuse me of using drugs." She pointed her finger at him and jabbed with every word.

"I wasn't accusing you. I was making a point."

"Your surprise search was reckless. I'm going to speak with the board about your actions."

"Is that a threat? Like you're going to see to it that I'm fired?"

"No, it's not a threat. It's a promise." Her face contorted from the anger running through her veins.

"Then I guess we're done here." Mac stood and exited. Neither said another word.

Marlene turned toward Mac as he left the boss' office. She pulled the headphones from her ears and waved him over to her.

She whispered so that Zorion wouldn't hear, "Well? Did she blow? Should I tread lightly today?"

"If I were you, I'd tread lightly every day and look for a different job," he whispered back.

"Great. I better get busy." She turned her attention back to her computer monitor, adjusted the headphones and began typing.

Mac went to his office to call Jason. He answered on the first ring.

"Hey, did you hear how the drug search turned out?" Mac said to Jason.

"Not yet." Jason said.

"Three joints in a kid's locker who's not on my radar. I didn't know who he was," Mac said.

"Are you shitting me?" Jason said.

"That's it. And I got my ass reamed for pulling a surprise drug search without asking the boss for permission. She's pissed because the parents will call to complain once they get wind of it. She pretty much said she's going to fire me."

"Man, that sucks. I cleared the search with Michael Stromberg. He was cool with it. He'll make sure you aren't fired."

"Great place you set me up with. Not loving my retirement today."

"Hang in there, bro. What's next?" Jason asked.

"I'm going to confront Coach about what Rita said and see how he responds. He's moved to the top of my list."

"You knew going after a drug source wasn't going to be an easy assignment. Just like going into the war zone to pick up a wounded soldier was dangerous. We did it anyway because in the end we saved that soldier's life or gave our best trying to. Think about the kids you're going to save by removing the drugs from their school.

CHAPTER 50

It was almost time for class change. Mac stared at the security feeds and contemplated his next move. The daily announcement yammered on in the background.

"Band clinic starts Thursday for interested seventh or eighth-grade band members. See Mrs. Weeks in the front office for details. Be sure to check the bulletin board across from Mrs. Week's office to see the results of…"

Doors flew open and the halls filled with kids going in every direction. You had no clue it was Halloween by looking at the kids. Mac felt bad for them. He remembered class parties and dressing in costume when he was a kid. The older kids had six minutes to get to their next class. They ran to their lockers to swap out their books. Nothing too out of the ordinary.

As the minutes ticked by fewer and fewer kids were in the halls. Those that lingered began to sprint to class. Mac saw Coach marching toward the front of the school. *Is he going to the boss' office?* He wondered.

Someone knocked hard on Mac's door. Coach opened it. "Got a minute?" he asked.

"Sure," Mac said waving him to come in.

"I heard there was a surprise drug search and you found some pot in Zorion's locker. He's a good kid, I hope nothing too serious will happen to him?" Coach said.

"The school has a 'Zero Tolerance' policy on drugs," Mac said, "It's out of my hands."

"For three joints? He's an advanced placement student, this could affect his college acceptance." Coach pleaded the boy's case.

"Any idea where he got the joints? That may sway the school board," Mac said.

"I don't know," Coach said.

"I had a tip that someone saw you give Stu a suspicious envelope thought to have drugs in it. Any truth to that?" Mac said.

Coach sat up straight and fixed his stare on Mac. "That's preposterous. Who said that?" he demanded.

"Tips are usually anonymous," Mac said.

"Did you find drugs in Stu's locker?" Coach asked.

"The dog didn't smell anything at the lockers other than Zorion's," Mac said.

Coach squinted his eyes appearing to run a few scenes through his mind. His eyes lit up when his memory landed on something. "I remember I did give Stu an envelope. The only person who saw me do that was Rita. Is Rita the one who gave you that tip?"

"I said the tip was anonymous," Mac said.

"That's a strong accusation with nothing to back it up. I may need to speak with my union representative to file a grievance for harassment."

He thought, *What is it with these people and their harassment charges?* Then said, "You do what you need to do. Before you leave, there's something Rita did tell me about you."

"More lies?" Coach asked.

"She told me you supply her with methamphetamine for her addiction," Mac said.

"What? That's ridiculous." Coach yelled and shook his head. "You don't believe that shit, do you?"

"Why would she lie about that? It's not good for her career to admit she's addicted to drugs," Mac said.

"We had a brief fling a year ago, she didn't want to break up. Maybe she's a scorned woman. I don't know," he said, as he paced in the small office.

Mac's irritation with Coach increased. His phone buzzed and Marlene said, "Mac, the boss wants to see you."

"Okay," he said.

Mac and Coach stared at one another.

"Looks like I'm not the only one in the hot seat," he mocked.

Mac didn't take the bait.

"So, that's it? Are you taking that whore's word over mine? I'm not blind or stupid. I know Rita's your fuck-buddy. You might want to check around, you're not her first nor will you be her last." Coach left and slammed the door.

He reopened the door. "For the record, I gave Stu an envelope with tickets to a Sacramento Kings game for him to surprise his dad for his birthday. I didn't know that was a crime." He slammed the door again.

CHAPTER 51

Marlene was eating lunch at her desk. She wiped her mouth with a napkin. The pumpkin earrings dangling from her earlobes bounced around. "Go on in, she's waiting for you." Marlene gritted her teeth giving Mac the cue that the boss was still in a rage.

"Why are you eating lunch at your desk?"

"I'm getting off early, so I'm making up that time."

"It's not lunch time if you eat at your desk?"

"Shush. Go in," she said and fanned him away.

He knocked on the door frame and stood in the doorway. She looked up from the stack of papers she appeared to be examining.

"Come in and have a seat," she said in an eerily quiet voice.

He'd been a marshal for two months, and he'd seen Dr. Sawyer's irritation with him grow stronger each time they spoke.

"Guess how many calls from angry parents I've received since you and I last spoke," she said.

"Four?" he replied.

"Twelve." She gave him a frosty stare.

He waited.

"The parents I spoke with want me to rein you in. They're turning on me because I can't control you. If I were able to supervise you there wouldn't have been a drug search this morning," she took a slow deep breath in and out. She closed her eyes and took another cleansing breath.

He waited.

"I spoke with Michael Stromberg about your little stunt," she said with a smirk of satisfaction. "He didn't think it was a big deal. Tell me about you and Rita." She looked quite pleased to have a credible piece of gossip about him.

"What would you like to know?" he said.

"Are you and she in a relationship?"

"Would that have been a violation of my contract?"

"No," the disgust spewed from her lips.

He waited.

"Tell me about her drug use," she seemed pleased again.

"Why don't you get to what you want from me and quit wasting my time," he said.

"Rita came to me and told me she's been hiding her addiction to methamphetamine from me and everyone at the school. She said she was falling in love with you and confessed to you, her secret. Is that correct?"

"Yes, she told me about her drug use."

"She felt rebuked by you," she said, "She said you told her she had to tell me about her addiction or you were going to. Is that correct?"

"Correct."

"She told me. And then she resigned. I hope you're happy. In two short months you've turned the campus upside down."

"Rita resigned?"

"Yes. She said she was moving back to Miami to live near her parents. She's gone. Thanks to you."

"I didn't get her hooked on drugs, that's on Coach, not me," he said.

She jumped up and slammed her hands on her desk. "That's it. Now you're going after Coach?" she yelled.

"Didn't Rita tell you about Coach?" he asked.

"She didn't say anything about Coach. And I'm not going to stand by and watch you ruin another distinguished teacher's reputation." She glared down at him.

"Wait a minute. I had nothing to do with Rita's addiction. She told me she got the drugs from Coach."

"Well, she didn't tell me that," she said. Both hands were on her hips.

"There will be no more 'surprise' anything without my approval. Consider this a reprimand. I'll fire your ass if you do another random drug search without my knowledge. I'll fire your ass if you spread that vicious rumor about Coach supplying Rita with drugs. And I'll fire you so fast if you go after another parent the way you went after Mr. Jackson. Now, get out." She pointed to the door and stayed in her statuesque position.

Mac stood on the other side of the boss' door reeling from her harsh comments. Blaming him for instigating any part of the recent events. He didn't understand why she felt that way or why she disliked him so.

Marlene looked up from her transcribing. "What? Why do you look like that? What happened?"

"She's something," his tone clarified a possible misunderstanding of the intent of his word choice.

"What did she say?" Marlene's concern seemed genuine.

"Not worth repeating," he said, "See you later."

Mac returned to his office and called Jason.

"Hey, there's a complication," Mac said.

"What's that?" Jason replied.

"The boss reprimanded me for getting involved with the Jacksons, for springing a drug search on her, for getting involved with Rita. She slapped a leash on me and told me I'm not to do anything without her prior consent and if I did, she was and I quote 'firing my ass'.

"Bro, you're right, she doesn't like you at all. Granted the drug search didn't turn out how we'd expected. Your involvement with the Jacksons was a normal reaction to what you thought was child abuse. Mrs. Jackson was ready to reach out to someone for help, it just so happens her son told her you'd be a good guy to turn to. Dr. Sawyer doesn't know the facts. And since when's it any of her business to tell you who you can have a personal relationship with?"

Mac watched the video screen pan through the feeds from all points of the campus. He fiddled with a mechanical pencil while he listened.

"In hindsight, we should have held off on the drug search and not tipped off Coach that we're looking at him," Jason said.

"I agree. I should have investigated Rita's claim. By the way, she quit."

"Rita did?"

"Yes. I don't get why Dr. Sawyer was so pissed off at me because I told Rita either she told the boss about her drug use or I would. Am I wrong to think people who work at a school should be drug-free?" Agitation was creeping back into his voice.

"No, you were spot-on. It's the same for law enforcement, fire personnel, and military. When you serve the public, you're a role model and you should be drug-free," Jason said.

"In regards to the Jacksons, I have to testify at his trial," Mac said.

"I figured as much. It sounds like there's enough evidence against him. I can't imagine the jury will find him not guilty."

"I agree. Poor Mrs. Jackson and Kevin. Talk about role models, that kid is screwed. Let's hope his aunt's a positive influence for him," Mac aimed for Alaska and threw a dart at the map on the wall across from his desk. He aimed the next dart at Florida. A quick check of the time showed the school day was about to end.

CHAPTER 52

There were a few parents hanging out around Mrs. Ross' car in the visitor parking lot. She'd submitted her name for the board position up for re-election on the November ballot. She'd been campaigning for a few weeks. Every day she placed election signs in her windshield like a sun-shield. She arrived early and stayed late to get the most exposure.

Mac didn't hang around after the stragglers left the campus. He locked up his desk and his office before he hurried to his house to pick-up Roxy. She didn't care where they went, she enjoyed riding along. At the highway, Mac went straight across and turned onto Broadway. He pulled into Tres Esposas' parking lot and parked in one of the to-go stalls. He'd forgotten it was Halloween. There was a barricade downtown between Main Street and Rock Street to prevent vehicles from endangering the trick or treaters who stopped at each merchant for a treat of some sort.

He placed an order of tacos, rice, and beans with chips and salsa to take with him to Rita's. The food would be ready in fifteen minutes, so he made a quick trip to the market to buy a large bag of candy just in case Rita also forgot it was Halloween and some beer to go with the tacos.

By the time he returned to the restaurant, his food was ready. They left downtown. Roxy hung her head out the truck window and wagged her tail at all the people walking around.

It was quarter past six when they arrived at Rita's. Her bug was in her assigned parking spot. He knew she was home. Little ghosts and goblins walked down the sidewalk alongside their parents. Roxy was anxious to get out of the truck and sniff the little ones. Mac pulled her in close when he saw one of the mothers do a double take at Roxy and overheard her scold Spiderman for attempting to walk away from her.

Rita opened the door with a bowl of candy in her arms. The smile left her face when she saw it was Mac.

"Trick or treat," Mac said, "May I come in? I brought tacos." He held up the bag of food.

"Sure," Rita said, as she stepped aside.

Her living room looked like she was moving. Empty boxes stacked along one wall. Opened boxes half packed. Contents from cabinets strewn about the floor.

Mac put the food on her kitchen island and the beer in the refrigerator. He went back to the living room and gave Rita a hug. "I'm sorry," he whispered in her ear.

"For what?" she asked.

"You were honest with me about your addiction and instead of supporting you I pushed you away," he said, "I'm not good at situations like that."

The doorbell rang and Roxy barked. Rita grabbed the bowl of candy near the door before she opened it. Roxy was at her side, her tail wagging as she sniffed the group holding out their bags. Rita shut the door and turned to face Mac.

"It's okay, Mac. I'm sorry I didn't tell you I quit and decided to move back to Miami," she said, "It was a spur of the moment decision."

"I've never told you about my father. It's not a subject I like to talk about. He had an addiction to alcohol and he was abusive to my mother. It left me with a strong aversion to an addiction of any kind. I overreacted when you told me about yours," Mac said.

"It's best that I move home and be with my family while I kick this beast," she said giving Mac a half smile. "How about those tacos? I bought candy, but didn't think about dinner."

Rita put paper plates and forks on the island. "Sorry, I packed the plates already."

"Don't apologize."

Mac took his first bite when the doorbell rang again. Rita and Roxy went to the door. Mac heard a chorus of 'trick or treat'.

"That was a large group," he said when she walked into the kitchen.

"I can see I'm not going to get much packing done tonight."

They fell into an uncomfortable quiet. Both focused on their tacos rather than the status of their relationship. After he'd eaten three tacos, Mac popped open a second beer. He watched Rita take a swig of her first.

He'd miss her. He hadn't been in many serious relationships. Rita was the most compatible and easy-going woman he'd ever dated.

"Can I help you pack?"

"No, it's okay. I'm sorting through stuff as I pack."

"I'm going to miss you, Rita. I'm sorry about how I reacted Saturday."

"It's okay, Mac. My dad's health isn't so good. They need me there. Everything works out for a reason. We just don't know what it is until we're looking back."

"When's your last day here?"

"The moving company will pick up my stuff on Friday. I turn in my keys on Saturday and away I go. Road trip to Florida. My mom's happy I'm moving back."

"Can I stop by and see you again before you leave?"

"Sure. Stop by anytime, Mac. And I want us to stay friends. You can't get rid of me that easy," she said with a smile.

"I'd like that," he said, "So, I hear the Jackson trial's winding down. Jason said it should go to the jury on Wednesday."

"That was a fast trial," she said, as her doorbell rang again. She giggled at him, scooped up the bowl of candy and repeated the process again.

Mac followed her to the door to see the kids. He thought it would have been fun for the school to drop the uniforms for one day of fun. But they didn't. It was dark outside and almost eight o'clock. Older kids lined the streets. The boys' costumes oozed fake blood or had knives sticking out of their chest. The older girls wore too little for a cold night and dressed too provocative for their age.

"Ms. Cortez." A playboy bunny sang out. "Where were you today?"

Rita swung her arm around to show the boxes. "I gave my notice and I'm moving to Florida. My parents need me to be closer to them," she fibbed.

The playboy bunny pushed through the gang she was with and hugged Rita. "I'm going to miss you. You're my favorite teacher."

"I'll miss you too, Sarah," she replied, as she tossed several candies into each bag. When she turned around, she had tears in her eyes. "I know I need to move, that doesn't make it easy," she said to Mac.

He nodded. Unsure how to navigate through the whole awkward moving conversation again, he opted to resume where he'd left off. "Jason said the evidence against Mr. Jackson is strong that he pushed his wife down the stairs. Plus, Kevin testified against him."

"And you testified," she said.

"That too," he replied.

"What will happen to Kevin?" she asked.

"Who knows. He's with his aunt for now. She never married and doesn't have kids," he said, "Next week we'll find out if Anna Beth Ross is a new board member." He was running out of things to talk about.

"That's right, I forgot about the election. If she does, oh my goodness... trouble."

They were back in the uncomfortable quiet again only this time without tacos to distract them. Mac looked around at Rita's condominium. He had been here a couple of times. She always seemed to stay at his house. He realized he didn't know much about her other than they got along well. He knew little about her parents or her siblings. He knew her father was from Cuba and had met her mother in Miami. That was about it. She knew less about his family. That was his fault, he didn't share much with her or anyone.

"I should let you get some packing done," he said.

"Okay. Thank you for dinner," she replied. She stood to walk him to the door.

A part of him hoped she'd ask him to stay longer, or to not leave at all. She didn't do either.

CHAPTER 53

It was a cold November morning. A strong breeze caused the last of the dead leaves to drop from the trees and there was the smell of wood burning in the air.

Rita was on her road trip to Florida, she promised to phone Mac when she arrived. He still felt sad about how he reacted to her confession. He sat on his back porch steps with magnifying glasses perched on the tip of his nose and the porch light illuminating the newspaper. He watched Roxy race around the yard while he nursed a cup of lukewarm coffee and read the Mountain Tribune. He thought he'd be elated to see Mr. Jackson get what he deserved, but he couldn't stop thinking about Rita.

On the front page, above the fold, he read the bad news for Kevin. His father was guilty of killing his mother. It was a life changing event for a young boy.

GUILTY! It took the jury two days to reach a guilty verdict in the Jackson murder trial. Local man, Randall Jackson Jr., owner of Jackson Loans, is guilty of Involuntary Manslaughter in the death of his wife, Susan Jackson. Police responded to a 911 call to the Jackson home located in the posh community of Blackstone Estates early the morning of October 13th, where they found Susan Jackson sprawled out in a pool of blood at the bottom of the staircase. Jackson's son testified against his father. A hidden room, a cellar of sorts was the nail in Jackson's coffin. According to testimony, he imprisoned his wife in the hidden room as a punishment, which led the jury to an additional guilty verdict for False Imprisonment. He will be sentenced in two weeks.

There was a photo of Mr. Jackson as he walked into the courthouse included with the article. He looked professional in his business suit. He and his attorney were surrounded by reporters and women's rights activists holding signs that said 'Waterboard Jackson' and 'Jackson Should Get Solitary Confinement' and 'Jackson Should Die—an Eye for an Eye.' The shot was priceless. He had a blank stare even with the signs all around him, and Fred Collins was caught right in the middle of elbowing a man who held a protest sign.

The rising sun painted shades of purple on the clouds that lingered from the weekend rainstorm. Mac gathered his newspaper, coffee cup and Roxy and went inside. He needed to leave early for work, he expected the press might be camped at the school hounding parents for comments.

When Mac turned onto Oakwood Drive, he was a little disappointed to see the same local newspaper reporter and no other news media. He expected more interest in the son of the wife killer. Selena Ramirez was bundled in a winter coat and hat. She approached Mac as soon as he put the truck's transmission into the park position.

She extended her hand to shake long before she reached Mac's truck. "Good morning, Marshal MacKenna. Selena Ramirez with the Mountain Tribune. Do you have time for a few questions about the Jackson murder case?"

"Sure, a few questions," he replied.

"When you were testifying, did you feel like Mr. Jackson's attorney was trying to blame you for upsetting his wife?" Her pad was open and pencil positioned ready to jot down notes. She also had a voice recorder attached to her jacket lapel.

"Isn't that what attorney's do? Try to shift the focus away from their client?"

"But he asked you about a secret meeting with Mrs. Jackson at Handley's Coffee Shop days before she died. He implied you and she were friendly and that your relationship had upset her to the point of her misstep and tumbling down the stairs. Was any of that true?" she probed.

"His attorney was fishing for something that may have swayed the jury toward reasonable doubt. If you were there listening to my testimony then you'd have heard me say under oath Mrs. Jackson and I did not have any sort of relationship. Period," he said.

"What about—."

"That's it. Your time's up, Selena. I have nothing more to say. Remember not to bug the parents and stay away from the entrance of the school, keep your interviews to this side of the street," Mac said before he walked away.

He caught up with Roni who was hurrying into the school. "What's your hurry?" he said.

They stopped in front of Mac's office door.

"I saw you walking away from that reporter so I ran. I didn't want her to try to ask me anything," Roni said, "Can you believe it? Guilty."

"I never doubted his guilt. I'm glad the jury saw through his attorney's shenanigans to try and put reasonable doubt in their minds," he said.

Roni said, "Now that it's over, can we talk about the trial?"

"We can," Mac said.

"I'll meet you out front in five minutes," she said, as she hurried down the hall away from Mac.

Mac saw Marlene sitting at her desk with her nose in the newspaper. He tiptoed into her office and flicked the newspaper.

"Oh my gosh. You scared me," Marlene said.

"That was the point. Are your reading about the verdict?" Mac said.

"Yes. It's scandalous," she said with a sparkle in her eyes. "Are there any news crews out front? I came in early to avoid any of that."

"The newspaper reporter who was here after Seth died is out there. She agreed to stay on the other side of the street and not bug the parents," Mac said.

Marlene said, "Did you know Roni asked a friend of hers to sit in on the trial and record everything?"

"No." Mac shook his head and smiled. "That doesn't surprise me. She's laser focused on being a cop and cops testify in court."

"The day after she'd tell me all the juicy gossip from her recordings," Marlene said. Her face turned serious. "She said you took a beating on the stand. Mr. Collins tried to imply you and Mrs. Jackson were having an affair."

"Well, you can't make something out of nothing," Mac said.

"So, it says here in the article. Mr. Jackson's guilty on both counts: Criminal Homicide and False Imprisonment," Marlene said.

"The coroner received the DNA test results from the handcuffs found in the hidden room at the Jacksons' home. They were a positive match to Susan Jackson. I guess when the coroner testified that Susan's wrist injuries were consistent with continued restraint from the handcuffs Mr. Jackson's goose was cooked," Mac said.

"Are you going to the sentencing?" Marlene asked.

"Hell yes," Mac said.

"Me too. I'm so glad it's during Thanksgiving break," Marlene said.

Dr. Sawyer stormed around the corner and toward her office.

"Mac, get out front. That news reporter's bothering the parents. Make her leave. Marlene, my office," she said without slowing her pace.

CHAPTER 54

With Mr. Jackson behind bars and Kevin homeschooling, Stu had been on his best behavior Mac had seen so far. The weeks leading up to Thanksgiving break were somewhat tame relatively speaking. Roni was standing in front of the deserted school. When she saw Mac she stuck her thumb out like she was hitchhiking. She hopped up on the running board and then into the passenger seat of Mac's truck.

"Burr, it's so cold out," she said.

"You need more meat on your bones, it's not that cold."

She shivered as she settled into her seat.

"I've never been to a sentencing before. Have you?" Roni asked.

"Once. When I was a teenager. A drunk driver killed a friend. I went to see if the guy showed any remorse," Mac said.

"Did he?"

"Remorse about his sentence. No remorse for killing someone," Mac said.

"Do you think Mr. Jackson will say anything?" she said.

"If he's smart, he won't," Mac said.

They turned onto Main Street from the highway and then into the tri-level parking garage down from the courthouse. The first and second level of the parking lot was full, Mac had to park on the top level. He and Roni walked fast down the three flights of stairs. They crossed the street and walked past the delicious smells escaping Trav's Donuts.

Roni grabbed Mac's arm to stop him. "Can we take food into the courthouse?"

"I don't think so," Mac said as he smiled.

They moved along the sidewalk and waited for the green light in front of Collins Law Office at the corner of Main Street and Broadway.

They stood in the slow-moving line along with other court attendees. There was a bottle-neck at the scanning machines looking for weapons and metal objects. All bags, cell phones and pocket contents had to pass through the scanner before you could enter the courtroom. Although there were two machines with an officer overseeing the process, the line still moved at a snail's pace.

The courtroom was almost full to capacity and noisy. Mac and Roni sat in the back row on the state's side. Roni pointed out Marlene, she sat with a teacher friend from Blackstone, Mary Sue, and her husband Ralph. Mac was surprised to see Mr. Jackson Senior sitting across the center aisle from them. He looked like a different man from the one Mac chatted with in his dingy living room. He was clean-shaven and looked sober. He'd been to a barber and had his shaggy ring of hair trimmed and smoothed down with some type of gel. His jeans looked clean, and he wore a dress shirt.

Roni pointed to two Mountain Tribune reporters and a photographer in the front row on the defense side.

Mac thought to himself, *Selena Ramirez must be lower on the food chain than the reporters who were assigned to cover the sentencing.*

"The judge hadn't allowed photographers inside the courtroom during the trial, he must have approved them for sentencing," she said.

There was an electric vibe in the courtroom—a buzz. People chatted with their neighbors. Fred Collins, Mr. Jackson's attorney, sat with his hands in his lap waiting for his client.

The District Attorney and two women sat at the state's table.

Marlene and Mary Sue had their heads together, gossiping and snickering about something. Mac saw Ralph shake his head and scold Mary Sue.

Kevin and the woman presumed to be his Aunt Jane walked into the courtroom. The room fell silent and everyone looked at them. They went straight to the front row where two seats were reserved for them. Aunt Jane resembled Susan. An obvious difference was that Aunt Jane carried herself with confidence with her head held high. She wore a blue dress, and Kevin wore khaki pants and a polo shirt. His look made Mac think he was off to church next or to play a round of golf. If Kevin recognized his grandfather, he didn't show it.

Mrs. Ross, and a man presumed to be her husband, entered the courtroom holding hands. He placed a gentle hand on her back when they turned to squeeze sideways down an aisle on the opposite side from Mac and Roni, where a woman had saved two seats for them. They sat in front of Mr. Jackson Senior.

The bailiff entered the courtroom and stood by the judge's chamber door.

The side door opened, and Mr. Jackson entered the room flanked by two uniformed officers. He shuffled along wearing ankle cuffs and orange plastic slip-on shoes. His hands cuffed in front and connected to ankle cuffs by a chain. His designer suit transformed into an orange jumpsuit with the words BROOKFIELD COUNTY JAIL stenciled in large black lettering on the chest and back.

Mac considered which look he preferred...this or him in a business suit hog-tied with a mesh sack over his head.

Mac felt some satisfaction hearing the jangle of his shackles as he shuffled to the empty chair next to his lawyer. After Mr. Jackson sat, the officers stood at attention at the side door.

Even wearing jail-house attire, Mr. Jackson still wore a pompous look on his face while he talked with his attorney before the court was in session.

Everyone stood for the judge to enter the courtroom. Jangle, jangle. Mr. Jackson stood.

The judge was direct and to the point. She warned the press not to take photographs until after she delivered the sentence.

Then the judge asked if any family members wanted to make an impact statement.

Kevin sat with his back straight, and his gaze appeared to be on the judge. Mr. Jackson turned and stared at his son.

Mr. Jackson Sr. stood from his seat in the back of the courtroom. Mr. Jackson Jr. looked to see who had caused heads to turn. If he felt anything when he saw his father, it didn't show on his face. Mr. Jackson Sr. took his time walking to the front of the courtroom. When he arrived at the podium, he pulled a crumpled paper from his jeans pocket and smoothed it out.

"Good afternoon, judge. I'm Randall Jackson Senior." There was an audible gasp in the courtroom. "That's my boy there in the jail-house jumpsuit, and I couldn't be prouder." He pointed to Mr. Jackson. Kevin looked at his aunt. Aunt Jane shrugged. The court reporter's light press of her stenography keys was the only sound in the room. Mr. Jackson Sr. looked at his son. "Orange is a good color for you, Randy. Long overdue. I hope your cell was as uncomfortable as possible. You and I both know you pushed your mom down the stairs to her death in 1984 and blamed me for it. Just like you blame your boy for what you did to your wife."

Mac saw several women put their hands over their mouths, their faces registering shock.

Mr. Jackson Sr. continued. "You know how hard it was for you to not have your mom or me to raise you, and now you put your boy in the same sad situation. You're an evil man, Randy, and I hope the judge puts you away for life."

Mr. Jackson Sr. shoved his crumpled paper into his pocket and walked back to his seat.

When nobody else stood to speak, the judge asked Mr. Jackson if he had anything he wanted to say to the court. His attorney indicated he did wish to speak. Mr. Jackson stood. Jangle, jangle. He told the judge he did not commit the crime. His son pushed his mother down the stairs and framed him. When he finished with his squeaky dribble, the judge didn't respond to his comments.

What a fucking jerk. Throwing blame on his son, Mac thought.

Kevin squirmed in his seat a little when his father accused him of killing his mother. His Aunt Jane placed a protective arm around his shoulders.

The judge told Mr. Jackson to remain standing for sentencing. She told him how despicable she thought he was. Mac was sure it felt like a knife jab to his gut to be forced to hear a woman berate him for a change. She gave him four years for Involuntary Manslaughter and two years for False Imprisonment. She added that his terms were consecutive.

Mac felt victorious for Susan when he watched the guards escort Mr. Jackson from the courtroom.

The Mountain Tribune photographer started snapping shots of Mr. Jackson Junior jangling out of the courtroom. Everyone filed out to the wide hallway. One reporter ran to Mr. Jackson Senior and the other to Kevin and his aunt. The officers hustled Jackson out the side door. Mac and Roni shuffled along with the crowd to the door and out into the hallway.

Mr. Jackson Senior walked toward the elevator in the same slow manner he walked to and from the front of the courtroom. Mac hoped it was the last time he'd ever see the man.

Mac felt a tap on his shoulder, he turned to see Mr. and Mrs. Ross. She introduced her husband, and then said, "I heard you learned about the deplorable living conditions for Mrs. Jackson and Kevin and tried to help them. Is that true?" Her tone had a gentleness to it he'd not heard before.

"Yes, that's partly true," Mac said, "Mrs. Jackson contacted me and asked me to help her leave her abusive husband. She died before I could do anything."

"Maybe you aren't such a bad guy after all," she said, "I look forward to working with you next month."

She didn't miss an opportunity to remind people she had won the election.

"Thank you, Mrs. Ross," he said.

"You're welcome. I get sworn into office after Thanksgiving break," she said.

She was giddy. Had she been a dog, her tail would have wagged.

"Congratulations," he said.

"Well, that was a surprise," Mac said to Roni. "I do believe Mrs. Ross just sort of thanked me for caring about Kevin and his mother."

"She has her moments," Roni said, "I need to use the restroom. I'll be right back."

Jason saw Mac as he left another courtroom. "Hey there." They shook hands.

"Busy catching more bad guys?" Mac asked.

"Yeah, yeah, something like that. I heard the news. Jackson got six years. You know, we may not have pulled that case together if it hadn't been for you pushing Dan and me," he said, "You'd make a good cop Mac. It's not too late."

"No thanks. That's not for me," he said.

Jason chuckled and patted Mac on his shoulder. "Gotta run. Let's talk soon, I need to give the Chief an update."

"Sure thing," Mac said to his back as he turned toward the stairs.

Mac waited for Roni near a large plate glass window. The sun was setting and pinkish clouds filled the western sky. He looked down on Broadway. It was a normal day for most people outside the courthouse. Cars whizzed along Broadway Avenue going about business as usual. While inside the courthouse lives were ripped apart.

"Mr. Mac," he spun around when he heard Kevin's voice behind him.

"Hi. How're you doing?" he asked. Kevin faced the window; Mac faced the busy corridor. Kevin's face had his usual sullen look.

He stuck out his hand to shake. Mac accepted the gesture. Then his face broke out into a broad smile. A big toothy, scary, eye squinting smile. Like he knew something funny Mac didn't know. "Thanks, man," he said, as he pumped Mac's arm, "Thanks for your help. Without you, my dad would have gotten away with murdering my mom." Then he winked at Mac.

Mac dropped his hand like it had burned him.

"When mom told me she asked you to help her leave my dad and gave you the key I suggested she give you. Oh man, I couldn't believe it. And getting my grandfather involved, that was the icing on the cake. I didn't think mom was going to mention him or that you'd take the bait."

Mac was speechless.

Kevin's face went back to sullen before he turned to walk toward his aunt.

Mac's heart sank, he thought, *Was I wrong about Mr. Jackson? Did Kevin push Susan? Did he set up Mr. Jackson the same way Mr. Jackson set up his own father? Or did the jury have it right when they found Jackson senior guilty? Did he set me up too?*

Mac watched as Kevin walked by his grandfather and the two did a fist bump.

Mac turned away to stare out the window, he felt nauseous and processed what Kevin had just said.

Mac jumped when Roni touched his shoulder. "I'm sorry, I didn't mean to startle you. Are you ready to go?" she asked, "What'd I miss? You look like you've seen a ghost or something."

"I think I've made a huge mistake," he said, "I need to speak with Jason."

CHAPTER 55

It was twilight when Clarence found Chuck on his mother's bed where he'd been for at least three hours, maybe more. His knees were at his chest in a fetal position. The room was church-like quiet.

He touched his nephew's shoulder. "Chuck, I'm so sorry. What can I do to help?"

Chuck opened his eyes and stared at his uncle through a fog of sadness. He remained in his comforting position. He faced the table near the door to her balcony. He noticed there was a faint rosy glow bouncing off the clouds. He thought his mother would expect dinner soon. Then he remembered and began to cry.

Clarence sat on the edge of the bed and touched his nephew's shoulder again. "Chuck, what can I do to help?"

"Leave me alone," Chuck murmured.

"Did you hear Randy Jackson was given six years in prison?" his uncle asked.

"I don't care," Chuck said in a faint voice.

"There are things we need to do," his uncle said in his most sympathetic voice.

Chuck lay still, staring out the glass door, watching the day slip away.

"I'll make you something to eat. Are you hungry?" he prodded.

"No."

His uncle left the room. The peacefulness returned. Chuck rocked on the bed. He was unsure how he would be able to do the tasks his uncle expected him to. He needed time to adjust to his mother's death.

She was a pain in his ass, but he'd never lived apart from her. It had been the two of them since his twin brother, Kent walked off to who knew where. Time stood still for him while he lay rocking, holding his knees tight to his chest. He watched the action on her balcony as birds gathered around the bird feeder his mother insisted, he refill daily.

Chuck released a deep sigh and rose.

He sat at his mother's table when Clarence returned with a

plate of cheesy scrambled eggs and fresh coffee. "Good. You're up." He placed the tray of food in front of him and then sat across the table. He'd brought himself a cup of coffee as well. "I'll get paper and a pen to make a list of what we need to do."

Chuck didn't look up from his food. The eggs were perfect, he hadn't realized how hungry he'd been.

Clarence sat with the pen hovering over a notepad like a secretary about to take the minutes at a meeting. "We should go to the mortuary and retrieve your mother's clothes."

"I don't want her clothes." Chuck blew on his coffee to cool it a few degrees.

"Okay. We still need to go to the mortuary to instruct them what to do with…"

"She wanted cremation. And she was adamant about no autopsy."

"Okay, I don't think that's our call," Chuck said.

"NO AUTOPSY."

"Okay. Okay. Calm down. I'll call the police chief and see what's going on."

"We should draft an obituary for the newspaper," his uncle suggested.

Chucked pushed his plate away from him and then crossed his arms at his chest. He sat unresponsive for several minutes. "You write it," he mumbled.

"Alright, I'll take care of that. We'll need to let the bank know," he added.

"What bank? She didn't have any money." His tone became angry.

Clarence put his hand up. "Okay. I'll clean up the kitchen and work on the obituary there. You come downstairs when you're ready.

CHAPTER 56

As Mac meandered through the aisles at the market, his phone rang. It was Jason.

"Hey, how's it going?" Mac parked his cart next to the frozen vegetables. His contribution to Maggie's Thanksgiving feast was peas and carrots.

"Where are you? Sounds busy," Jason said.

"Along with everyone in town except you, I'm at the market getting stuff for dinner tomorrow," he joked.

"Can you come to the station? You won't believe what happened."

"Don't leave me with that teaser. Tell me, I'll be right there," Mac said, as he tossed the frozen package back into the freezer.

"Did you hear Coach's mother died yesterday?" Jason began his brief explanation.

"No," Mac replied.

"Yes. Coach must have taken it hard. He was in a vehicle accident a short while ago. He ran a red light and T-boned another car. When the responding officer arrived, the front of the Cadillac pinned Coach in his seat, and..."

Mac was moving out of a woman's way, her toddler in the cart was bawling and she looked ready to explode.

"Bro, I can't hear you. I'll be right there," Mac said.

He pushed his cart through the aisles of the market as fast as traffic would allow and returned the few items he had. The station wasn't far from the market, he arrived in less than fifteen minutes.

The male officer at the counter buzzed him through to find Jason at his desk. Mac plopped down on the chair placed at the side of the desk. His friend shared the room with three others.

"Okay. Start your story when the officer arrived at the accident," Mac said.

"The front of Coach's car pinned him in the driver's seat and he was despondent. The firemen used the jaws to pry off his door and then the paramedics took him to the hospital. The officer looked through the Cadillac he was driving and found a large quantity of fentanyl. You'll never guess where they found the drugs."

Mac's mouth fell open. "Are you shitting me? Where?"

"In a box of tubes labeled 'sports cream'. The tubes were filled with the powder. He's being charged with conspiracy to possess with intent to distribute, a felony and if we can tie the drugs to Seth's death, he'll be looking at more charges."

"Now what?" Mac asked.

"He was under the influence when he ran the red light. Once the toxicology report's complete, there will also be a few traffic violations - the least of his problems. We want the person who gave him the drugs. We also want the people who Coach sells the drugs to. Coach is the middle man. We want the top dog."

"How're you going to get that out of him?" Mac questioned.

"Once he's sober, and understands his predicament, the thought of time in a federal prison should motivate him to give up some names."

Desk phones rang in odd intervals at the desks in the room. The room was almost as noisy as the market had been.

"We have an officer stationed outside his room. We aren't sure how 'Big' the big dog's operation is. Coach might be disposable to save the business."

"Wow. Depending on how he was behaving, Coach was at the top and the bottom of my list of potential drug dealers. I never thought it'd turn out to be that big of a business. My assignment's over, right?"

Mac wasn't sure he was ready to walk away from the academy. There was something wrong with Dr. Sawyer's priorities. As much as he hated the way she treated him, he feared she wasn't focused on what was in the kids' best interest.

"Not yet. Until we find out who was working with Coach, the Chief wants you to stay at the school." Jason looked up at an officer who gave a cue for Jason to go with him. "Hang tight, I'll be right back."

Mac sat next to Jason's desk noticing the piles of paperwork needing attention. As he looked around the room, he saw the cork board labeled 'FBI Most Wanted'. There were a few darts here and there on the faces of photos. Even though Osama bin Laden was dead, there was still a cluster of darts dead-center on his forehead. He snickered to himself. It was something they did to unwind after a stressful shift when they were in the sandbox. They threw darts at photos they'd posted of most wanted terrorists and maps of the region they were in.

Dan dropped some binders onto his desk behind Mac and startled him. Mac turned. "Sorry..." Dan's face registered recognition. He extended his hand. "Hey, Mac. Did you hear?"

It was the first time Mac had seen Dan smile. Maybe he wasn't the shy guy he first thought. Mac nodded. "Nailed the fucker."

"Drinks tonight at the Grill. I'm buying," he said. The two men shook hands.

Jason hurried back to his desk. "Dan, let's go. Coach wants to talk."

CHAPTER 57

Coach lay on the thin pad on his so-called bed in his cell. He crossed his arms under his head. He stared at the wires and springs above him. He hadn't been there long, but was already tired of the small space he was in and the smells of urine and feces. From his first day at the county jail, he'd not had a single visitor. He didn't expect his uncle to visit, he was more worried about saving his own ass.

Coach closed his eyes and thought about the boys at the school he counseled when they were in trouble with their parents. His agitation grew. Not one had come to visit him and offer any counsel to him. None of the staff. None of the board members. Not even Ozzy.

He could almost hear his mother scold him for getting mixed up with drugs. "Chucky. What were you thinking? Chucky, you're an idiot." He sighed. His mind whirled with justifications. How the hell could I provide her with a fancy home? One with an elevator?

It was almost sunup, and along with lukewarm coffee brewing in the cafeteria, so was a verbal fight. It was the same thing every morning. A big dude in another cell whistled a tune. The whistling pissed people off and they'd yell at the whistler to shut the fuck up. He listened as his neighbor began his morning tune. The whistler was good at whistling. He liked the whistling and he imagined the whistler smiling before and after every tune. Coach preferred the whistling to the yelling and the cursing.

His neighbors thought they were tough behind locked doors. As soon as the cell doors opened and the 6 foot tall, 280 plus pound whistler walked out of his cell and into the common room, nobody said a word to him.

Coach sat at a table watching the TV with the other idiots.

"Andrews, your attorney's here," the guard barked.

He shuffled along with the guard. Fred Collins waited for him. Coach gave Fred a half smile. He felt like grabbing him and giving him a bear-hug.

They sat across from each other. Fred had a yellow notepad

out and a pen. He asked, "How're you doing Coach?"

Coach leaned forward. "As you'd expect. When am I getting out of here?"

"Soon. They want to offer you a deal if you'll give up who you bought from and sold to," Fred said.

"I can't do that."

"It's either that or federal prison. They have you man, no getting around it." Fred showed no emotion on his face. "You can tell me who they are, and I'll help you figure out how to get out of this mess. What you tell me is privileged." Fred held his pen ready to take notes.

Coach thought about it for a few seconds. He looked around the room they were in. A small slice of sunlight shined in. Everything was cold metal. And it was noisy.

"What did Clarence do with momma?" he asked, his attorney.

"She's been cremated as you said she wished."

"Where's she now?"

"I assume Clarence has the urn."

"What's happening with the house?"

"I'm not sure, I can check on that for you and have an answer next time."

Coach nodded and became quiet. He listened to the metallic sounds on the other side of the door.

"It was Clarence," Coach whispered.

"What was Clarence?" Fred asked.

"I got the drugs from Clarence. He makes it in his basement," Coach said.

"I see." Fred put the pen down on the notepad. "And who did you sell to?"

"Stu and Kevin," Coach whispered.

"Hmmm. That's a problem," he replied.

"Why? Why's that a problem," Coach felt anxious. He felt like he should have kept his mouth shut.

"I have a conflict of interest, and they're minors." Fred was too calm for having just learned his son was a drug dealer. "Do you have evidence against any of them?"

Coach tried to think. *Evidence?*

"You'll get a deal when you give up your uncle, but you won't get much more for giving up the boys. I'll need to research the best way to proceed."

"Meanwhile, bail me out," Coach said, "Use the house. I own

it free and clear."

"I'll see to it," Fred nodded and gave Coach a thumbs up as he left.

CHAPTER 58

The front doorbell chimed. Coach was upstairs in his bedroom dressing after he'd taken a long hot shower. He hurried to finish putting his socks on, but no shoes.

The melody of the chimes rang again. He ran down the stairs and skidded across the foyer like a kid.

Fred Collins was waiting on the stoop.

"Come in." Coach was happy to see his attorney. "I'm glad you're here."

Fred looked polished in his suit and tie. He carried a briefcase like the one Coach used to carry.

"Where can we sit to talk?" Fred asked.

"The living room," Coach replied.

As the two walked to the living room, Coach reminisced. "When momma was alive, I wasn't allowed to use the living room. She said it was for guests who came to visit. Except nobody ever came to visit." Coach pointed and the two men sat on the large sofa.

Fred pulled some papers out of his briefcase and handed them to Coach. "Coach, I can no longer represent you in this matter."

"Why not?" Coach stood up.

"Because you've involved my son. I told you there's a conflict of interest," Fred also stood. "Stu said you approached him and Kevin last year and asked them if they wanted to make some money, and they said no." Fred's face was unreadable.

Coach said nothing.

"I've advised the court that you'll need another attorney," Fred said.

"Wait, no, Fred…come on, man…I need you. You can't do this to me. We've been friends for years. You always said you'd have my back if I ever needed you. I need you now," Coach grumbled.

"That was before you accused my kid of being a drug dealer." Fred turned toward the door. Coach grabbed his arm and flung him around to face him.

"You can't do this to me. You know I'm going to prison

without you as my attorney," he begged.

"It's either you or Stu. Sorry."

Fred let himself out.

Coach stood in the living room. His ears rang and he felt he was going to vomit. He heard his cell phone ring upstairs. It was on the bedside table.

He sprinted up the stairs and scooped the phone up. He didn't recognize the number. "Hello."

"Chuck, it's Clarence."

Coach felt relieved. "Where the hell have you been? Fred just left. He dumped me. I have to find a new attorney. Can you help me?"

"Why would I help you? I heard you turned on me to cut a deal." His uncle's words sliced through him. "Did you really think bragging about your deal to the other guys in jail wouldn't get back to me?"

As soon as Coach had said out loud who he'd been working with, he regretted it.

He should've listened to his gut and not told Fred or anyone else anything. He should've taken what he deserved and left it at that.

Coach slumped and sat on the bed.

"I hope you socked away some money so when you get out of prison, you'll have money to live on. You won't get that pension you've been paying into," his uncle's voice laced with sarcasm. "I put your momma on the mantel in her bedroom. I'm in a country that doesn't have an extradition agreement with the U.S. You better hope we never see each other again, Chuck. I won't forget and I don't forgive." The phone went silent.

Coach sat in the same place for over an hour. He forced himself to get up.

He went to the portrait of his mother on the wall in his bedroom. He had it done before her disease took over. She looked beautiful and vibrant. That's how he wanted to remember her.

The hinged portrait swung away from the wall and Coach entered the code into the keypad on the safe he'd had installed.

He loaded his revolver, closed the safe and returned the painting to its proper place. He stood facing his mother for a long time. Years of memories passed through his mind.

He drug his feet on the walk down the hall to his mother's bedroom.

The last time he'd been in there was the morning after she'd died.

He sat at the table where she ate her breakfast and first wrote out his confession. There was nothing to lose now; he named his uncle and the two students.

Next, he wrote a last will and testament leaving everything he owned to his twin brother, Kent.

If Kent was dead, fifty percent of his estate would pass to Lucy, his mother's personal attendant, and the other fifty percent would go to Blackstone Academy. He signed and dated the letter and his will.

He crawled onto his mother's bed and lay on his side with his knees pulled tight to his chest and began to rock.

Kent popped into his mind. *What if Kent was still alive? What if he did run away from home? Maybe he wasn't an underdog. Maybe he was the stronger twin all along.*

His mind wandered as he rocked himself. Everything would have been fine if Blackstone hadn't hired Mac.

The sound of the shot reverberated off the walls in the large fancy home. There wasn't anyone there to hear it. Nobody to call 911. It would be several days before the cleaning lady would find him on his mother's bed.

CHAPTER 59

Mac walked into the police station and nodded to the officer on duty at the counter. He was dealing with a scruffy looking old woman claiming she'd been robbed. He buzzed the locked door separating the public from the back office where they conducted police business. Mac went down the hallway to the familiar conference room. Jason's voice carried out into the hallway.

When Mac entered the room, Jason and his partner, Dan Ruiz, looked up. They sat at the table drinking coffee and eating donuts. The two men stood and shook hands with Mac. He helped himself to the coffee and pastries provided by an unknown host or hostess. They fell into a friendly banter about football.

Police Chief Contee arrived about ten minutes later. Michael Stromberg arrived last. He shut the door behind him.

The Chief called them together for a debrief meeting. It was the first time they'd all been together.

Chief Contee began, "Well gentlemen, we made a dent in the drug problem at Blackstone. It's unfortunate Coach Andrews took his life. I'm thankful he left a signed confession. Because of that, the judge granted a search warrant on Clarence's home. He'd cleaned the place out, but the dog did find traces of narcotics in the basement."

"Too bad Coach didn't know the district attorney was agreeable to offer a deal, he wouldn't have had to serve too many years in prison," Jason added.

"The mayor will be angry when he learns the manufacturer of the drugs that killed his boy fled the country. The person who distributed the drugs killed himself. And the boys who may have given him the drugs that killed him have lawyered up and aren't saying anything," Michael Stromberg said, "He wants someone to pay for supplying Seth with drugs."

Mac observed Dan Ruiz, who appeared to be writing down everything that everyone said. He hadn't taken his eyes off his notepad since the Chief began speaking. He thought, *He was in shy guy mode again. Quite the opposite from how friendly he was at the*

Grill for drinks the other night.

"That's true," Chief Contee said, "Until we get Clarence back here to face charges, we won't be able to tie this up with a pretty bow."

"What's happening with the boys?" Michael asked.

"With Fred representing both boys and the only evidence against them is Coach's signed confession, not much at this point. The boys are suspended from school. That's about it," Chief Contee said, "We'll continue to interview other kids from the school to see if any of them will admit to buying drugs from Kevin or Stu. If we get something, then we'll charge them with distribution."

Michael shifted his attention to Mac. "Mac, are you willing to continue at the school? When Kevin and Stu return to school, who knows what those boys will be up to next."

Mac replied, "Since we've severed the drug source, it seems unlikely we'll have a drug problem any longer. And to be honest, Dr. Sawyer can't stand me. Working with her hasn't been pleasant."

"I can't go into details, but she has her own problems. Her hostility toward you is in part because the school board has her on a short leash. She may have thought you were there to keep an eye on her."

"I made a commitment to Jason that I'd work at the school for the school year. You may not need a marshal next year. Let's ride it out and decide in June. Fair enough?" Mac said to Michael.

"Fair enough," Michael replied.

The men stood and shook hands. Jason and Mac remained in the room. Jason shut the door.

"What's happening with Kevin," Mac asked.

"Bro, I can't do anything with the veiled comments he made to you after his dad's sentencing. He didn't confess to you," Jason replied.

"He made it sound like he orchestrated everything. His mother asking me to meet for coffee. Her giving me the key to the cuffs in the secret room. Me going to see his grandfather. All because he hoped to be rid of his father and it worked," Mac said.

"All that's circumstantial and the jury found his father guilty," Jason said.

"So, the little sociopath gets to find his next victim?"

"I can't do anything, Mac, I'm sorry," Jason said, "He's on my radar, and yours. You'll be at the school for the second semester, watch him. "If he's a sociopath, he's just getting warmed up."

Thank you for reading Unknown Threat.
While the story is fresh in your mind, leaving an honest review is always appreciated.

If you liked Unknown Threat, you'll also enjoy…

UNKNOWN ALLIANCE

Book 2 in the Marshal Series

UNKNOWN ALLIANCE

Book 2 in the

Marshal Series

This famous quote by Andre Malraux describes several of the characters in Unknown Threat, "Man is not what he thinks he is; he is what he hides."

There's a storm headed for Brookfield—it has more to do with a father's rage than it does the weather. After someone assaults a teenage girl at a neighborhood party, the victim's desperate father asks Mac MacKenna for help. There's a catch—no police.

After eight deployments to the middle east and 20 years in an elite special ops unit in the U.S. Air Force, Sergeant Mac MacKenna returned to his hometown to live a quiet life—until the police chief asked him to pose as a marshal at Brookfield Academy where crime outranked grade point averages.

Mac doesn't know the victim, and he's never met her father, but the air force trained him to aid others at all costs and keep his missions secret.

A Mystery/Thriller based on disturbing reality.

Continue for an excerpt from
Unknown Alliance

Unknown Alliance
Chapter 1

Elaine spat out a mouthful of toothpaste and asked her husband Scott, "What time is it?"

From the bedroom, he said, "Ten minutes before eleven. What time did you tell Brandi to be home?"

"Eleven." She sensed his worry.

With a mischievous look on her face, she ran from the bathroom and dove onto her side of the bed causing the down comforter to puff up between the two of them.

"It's not Brandi who concerns me. It's Simone. She's a bit wild," Scott said.

"The party's at Fred and Vanessa's. The kids won't pull anything there."

"But it's an indoor pool party and a bunch of teenage girls and boys with raging hormones."

A few seconds passed before the security monitor on Scott's side of the bed made two faint dings, alerting them the front door had opened and closed.

Elaine smiled. "See, I knew she'd be home on time."

Scott muted the TV.

They listened as their daughter, and her friend thundered up the staircase.

"Go check on them," he said.

"What do you expect me to find? A boy?" She giggled and snuggled up to her husband.

Scott leaned away to set the security alarm for sleep mode. He glanced back at Elaine. "Just check on them, please."

"Okay. Okay." She swung her bathrobe over her shoulders and slid her feet into fluffy slippers before padding down the hall to their daughter's bedroom.

Elaine leaned against the door to listen. She shook her head. *Men don't understand teenage girls. You have to give them some freedom, or they'll rebel.* She heard water running in the bathroom. Confident they were brushing their teeth, she opened the door.

She froze.

Brandi, sprawled out on her pink comforter, appeared to be naked from the waist down with a towel over her lower torso.

Elaine stormed the bathroom.

Simone jumped when she burst through the door. Dark streaks of mascara washed away by her tears ran down the girl's cheeks.

"What's wrong with...." Elaine stopped. She stared at the sink filled with red sudsy water. The water flowed while Simone hand-washed the pajama bottoms Brandi wore over her swimsuit to the party.

Elaine pushed Simone away from the sink and turned off the water. "What happened? What's wrong with Brandi? Why are her clothes bloody?"

Simone looked at the floor, her shoulders slumped. She didn't respond. She wept.

Elaine hurried to her daughter. She grasped her shoulders and gently shook. "Brandi. Wake up!"

"Huh?" she mumbled without opening her eyes. "Mom?" Her eyes fluttered and then relaxed as she appeared to fall back asleep.

Elaine shook her a little more. She looked up to see Simone sitting on the window seat, gnawing on her fingernails.

"What's wrong with her?" Elaine said in a stern voice.

"I don't know. We were having fun playing Marco-Polo in the pool and listening to music. Brandi told me she didn't feel well. She got out of the pool and sat in a lounge chair watching us."

It took tremendous restraint for Elaine not to yell to Brandi's friend, *"hurry-up, spit it out."*

"After everyone got tired of playing the game, most of us got out of the pool. I sat with Brandi. She said she felt dizzy. Wanted to change back into her clothes and lie down on the back seat of my car."

"And you let her? All by herself? When it's cold outside?"

Simone said between gulps of air, "I... have... a... blanket... on... my... back... seat." She inhaled air a few times before continuing. "She was only out there a half hour before... before...." She sniffled. "When I got in my car, she was covered up and looked like she was asleep. I swear."

"Take a minute to get your act together while I clean and dress her. Then finish telling me what happened to her at the party," Elaine hissed...*she tried to stop thinking of the rumors about the Collins's parties she'd heard over the years.*

The end of year pool party was an annual event at the Collins's home after the holidays. Always on the Saturday before school resumed. The tradition started before they'd all had kids. A New Year's Eve party back then. Back in the day, they were rumored to have been quite provocative. For a week after, the talk of the town was about their get-together.

After the boys came along and the Collins's friends started having children, it turned into an end of the year party. They'd invite their friends and offspring. As the boys got older, they were allowed to ask some of their friends. Only 'hello at the market' type friends with Fred and Vanessa, Scott and Elaine never made it onto the guest list. But Brandi, who had known Stu, their oldest son, since elementary school, was always invited.

A few years ago, when Brandi started showing signs of womanhood, Scott voiced concern to Elaine about their daughter not being mature enough to handle boys coming on to her. He wanted to forbid her from attending the parties. He'd also heard the gossip. Brandi always pleaded to let her go. He found it difficult to say no to his little girl.

Elaine used a warm, wet washcloth to wipe dried blood from her daughter's inner thigh area. Dressing Brandi in pajamas was like trying to put clothes on a sack of sand. Her daughter helped a little. She tried to say a few words, but they came out slurred and unintelligible. No longer concerned about her daughter needing medical treatment, Elaine tucked her into bed as she had done not so many years ago.

She then turned her attention to Simone who continued to chew on her fingernails. "Were you kids drinking alcohol at the party?"

"No. Nobody even offered me anything. We drank soda pop."

"Were adults in the pool area?"

"Mmm-Hmmm. Parents were around all the time. Never just kids." Simone stopped talking to blow her nose. "I think I should go home now."

"I agree. But before you go, I have more questions. What specifically, did Brandi say about feeling dizzy?"

"She said her stomach felt upset and her head spun a little."

"Did she say 'spinning' or did she say 'dizzy?'" Elaine felt there was a considerable difference between the two statements.

"Ummm. I'm not sure. She looked normal, so I didn't think anything was wrong."

Simone and Elaine jumped when Scott opened the door. "Is everything okay in here?"

"I'll be right there, hon," Elaine shooed him away.

Scott retreated and closed the door.

She continued her interrogation. "Exactly how long was Brandi in your car before you decided to leave the party?"

"Maybe...thirty minutes," she said hesitantly as if she were afraid she'd be yelled at again.

"You left her out in your cold car feeling sick for thirty minutes?" Elaine couldn't contain her irritation.

Simone grabbed her jacket and purse and scurried out of the bedroom.

Elaine hustled to tell Scott to disarm the alarm but was too late.

Simone fled down the stairs and out the front door triggering it at the same time Elaine appeared in the doorway to the master bedroom.

Scott jumped. "What the—?" He entered the code to turn off the alarm.

"I'll lock the front door." Elaine turned and darted from the room.

When she reentered the quiet bedroom, Scott stopped pacing along his side of the bed.

"What the hell's going on?"

"Something happened to Brandi at the party." She sat on the bedside with him and shared all the information she knew.

Elaine took Scott to Brandi's bathroom and showed him the sink where her bloody pajama pants soaked.

Scott went to his daughter's bedside. He stood there looking down at her for a long minute before he bolted from the room.

Elaine rushed after him.

He began changing into his jeans.

"What are you doing?"

"I'm going to speak to Fred."

"How will that help Brandi? Fred won't know what happened. He probably doesn't even know anything about it. And he'll assume you're going to call the police. Next, he'll kick into attorney mode. No, please don't go there."

He zipped his jeans and looked at his wife. Tears formed in his eyes. "I have to do something. Someone hurt our little girl. I can't just go to sleep," he said before he slumped onto the side of the bed.

"I want to do something too, but what? We don't know what happened," Elaine said.

"Could it be her period? Maybe we're jumping to conclusions." Scott dropped his head in defeat.

Neither said the 'R' word out loud.

"She had her cycle last week, so it shouldn't be from that. I'll take her to my gynecologist on Monday. She doesn't have school until Tuesday. The doctor should be able to tell me if the blood was natural or from sex."

Scott blurted out, "I had a bad feeling about that party. Damn it! We shouldn't have let her go."

Unknown Alliance
Chapter 2

"Hey, mom, how was your day?" RaeAnn grabbed a soda pop from the refrigerator.

Sloan Bowen leaned against the kitchen island while she tossed dressing on a salad. It had been a busy day at the bank, and her feet throbbed from hours of standing at the teller window.

"A typical Monday. Busy. How was yours?"

"Just another boring day of doing nothing but hanging out." RaeAnn sighed. "I'm looking forward to going back to school tomorrow."

The bar stool made a nails-on-chalkboard scraping sound across the tile floor when she pulled it away from the kitchen island.

Sloan glared at her daughter. "Jesus, Rae, how many times have I asked you to lift the chair a bit before you pull it out?"

RaeAnn sniffed the air. "What's for dinner?"

"Pizza and salad." She lifted the salad tongs to show her daughter what she thought seemed obvious.

"Ummm. Ciera and Haylee want me to go with them to a movie Friday night. Can I?"

"What movie? Who else is going?" Sloan opened the oven to peek in on the pizza.

"An age-appropriate movie. Some guys they know are also going."

Sloan turned around to face her daughter. "Boys? You don't know them? Do they go to Brookfield High?" She waited for answers, wanting to get a read on her daughter's expression to determine if her gut detected honesty or lies.

"Geez, Mom, what's with the interrogation? It's just a frickin movie." RaeAnn rolled her eyes.

"It doesn't matter because Uncle Steven will be here for dinner."

RaeAnn scraped the stool across the tile floor when she scooted it back to stand up.

"Rae!" Sloan assumed her daughter did it on purpose to annoy her.

"Why do I need to be here? He's your brother. I hardly know him." Her hands planted on hips.

"Really?" Sloan frowned. "He's getting out of rehab on Friday, and he's spending one night with us before he checks into the independent living facility."

"What does that have to do with me?" RaeAnn folded her arms across her chest and straightened her stance.

"I'm too tired to argue. The answer is no, you cannot go to the movie."

RaeAnn started to leave the kitchen but turned to face her mother. "Sometimes, I hate you. You never let me do anything."

"Listen here, young lady." Sloan shook the tongs at her. "Say anything you want about me in your head. But, don't let it pass your lips again or you'll be grounded for life."

Her daughter spun on her heel and stomped down the hallway to her bedroom.

Sloan heard her husband say, "Hey princess. What's wrong?"

RaeAnn screeched, "Mom," before she slammed her bedroom door.

Drey shook his head as he entered the kitchen. "Wow, what'd you say to get her in such a huff?"

"She wants to go to some movie Friday night. Ciera and Haylee want her to go with them and some boys she doesn't know. I shouldn't have bothered asking for details because she can't go. Steven will be here. Our little princess got huffy, told me she hated me and stomped off." She shrugged. Her body ached with fatigue. "Some days she hates me, some days she loves me."

"Does she really need to be here and hang out with Steven? It's not like they're close."

Sloan lowered her voice to the level of her exhaustion. "I want her here with us, so Steven feels a part of our family."

"I think you're overcompensating and trying to parent better than your mom did because she let you run wild," he said.

"Overcompensating?" She sighed as she pulled a barstool out from the island and sat. It felt like she'd been standing for days. "I'd appreciate your support. It's important to me."

The timer on the oven sounded.

"Would you please tell Rae dinner's ready."

Drey turned to leave.

"You can be the good cop, but please don't give her permission to go to the movie," she said to her husband's back as he left the kitchen. Sloan leaned toward the hallway and raised her voice. "And remind her there's school tomorrow, so lights out and TV off at ten o'clock."

Unknown Alliance
Chapter 3

After three weeks away from Blackstone Academy for Christmas break, Mac MacKenna—better known as Mac—arrived at work early to get back into the swing of things. Other than his truck, Marlene's car was the only vehicle in the staff parking lot.

He'd known about Superintendent Dr. Sawyer's leave of absence before he'd received the letter from Michael Stromberg, the school board president. Marlene, the superintendent's administrative assistant, had called to tell him.

Surprised the school board had suspended the superintendent, Mac felt relieved at the same time. It was still a mystery why she'd disliked him. Dr. Sawyer always seemed to be in a lousy mood and directed it primarily at Mac as if he were the source of her irritation.

Last summer, after Mac retired from the air force, he returned to Brookfield where he'd grown up. The police chief asked Mac to pose as a school marshal at Blackstone Academy to learn who was dealing drugs. The Academy is a public school generously supported by the affluent Blackstone Estates community. Although the superintendent hadn't been privy to his real role, she'd made his job more difficult by micromanaging his every move.

At the conclusion of the first semester, Michael Stromberg asked Mac to stay on until the end of the school year to ensure the drug dealing didn't recur.

"Morning, Marlene," he said rounding the corner into her office.

"Good morning, Mac."

Mac sat on the chair next to Marlene's desk. "Are you ready for round two?"

"No, haven't even met the new guy. I came early thinking he'd be here. Dr. Sawyer could be bitchy at times, but we worked well together. I'll miss her." She wrapped her hands around her coffee mug.

"Do you know why she's on a leave of absence?" Although he'd asked, he felt reasonably sure it had to do with her extramarital affair.

"When Michael wanted me to type his letter, I quizzed him. Said he couldn't talk about it. I tried guessing, but he wouldn't give me anything." She shrugged. "Do you know why?" She paused. "You do, don't you?" Releasing her coffee mug, she leaned toward him apparently expecting to hear the secret scoop.

"Afraid that's above my pay grade. If you don't know, then I sure wouldn't."

Marlene flashed a winning smile before she turned serious. "Going to be weird without Coach. I've met the new PE teacher. Seems nice enough. He's young—only been teaching four years—and now he'll run our athletic program. I hope he's capable."

"Michael must think so, or the board wouldn't have hired him, right?"

"True."

"See you later. I'm going to dust off my computer and get ready for the kiddos to arrive."

Marlene nodded before she took a swig of her coffee.

Mac unlocked his office door. The glow from the wall of security monitors greeted him when he went inside.

With a quick check of his unopened emails, he saw nothing urgent. Twenty minutes before the school came to life, he locked his office and went to the teacher's lounge to fill his travel mug with coffee.

Finding only a few teachers in the lounge, Mac looked over at the corner where Coach had once aggressively chatted with Rita. He shook his head. *Hard to believe in such a short time Rita moved and Coach no longer worked at the school.* Unsure how the second semester would pan out, he hoped for less drama than the first.

The clock on the wall reminded him it was time to join Roni outside. She worked part-time for the school as a monitor before and after school and some days at lunchtime. To keep peace and order, she and Mac watched the kids arrive in the morning and depart in the afternoon. The first time Mac saw young—Roni, he mistook her for a high school student. Not far off, he learned she took classes at the college, going for a degree in criminal justice.

Mac found her standing at her usual spot in front of the school.

Roni's face lit up when she saw him. She gave him a hug. "Happy New Year."

"Hi, happy New Year to you too. How're you doing?"

"Grrrrreat!" She sounded like the tiger in a cereal commercial from Mac's youth. "I couldn't believe it when I read in our welcome back letter that Dr. Sawyer's on a leave of absence. Do you know why?"

"Nope."

He noticed her short haircut. "No more ponytail?"

Pulling off her beanie hat, her long blond hair tumbled onto her shoulders. She'd had her hair coiled inside the cap.

"My ears were cold. Have you met the new boss?"

"Nope." Mac shrugged. He wouldn't admit it aloud, but it felt good to be back at the school. To have a purpose.

"And Mrs. Ross's on the school board. How will that turn out?" Roni tugged her cap over her ears.

"Let's give her a chance and see."

A few parents parked in the visitor lot and helped the little ones with their backpacks before they walked them across the street. Mrs. Ross pulled into the staff lot. Some might question whether she was considered an employee. She apparently thought her new board member status entitled her to staff privileges.

Anna Beth Ross, her seven-year-old daughter Savannah, and nine-year-old son Teddy trudged straight over to Roni and Mac. Anna Beth's perfume arrived before they did.

Mac smiled when Teddy pulled up his pant legs to show his two different colored socks. One blue with white stripes and the other red with blue stripes. Teddy's mother usually caught him before he made it to the car and had him change into his navy-blue socks that conformed to the uniform guidelines.

In unison, Mac and Roni said, "Good morning, Mrs. Ross, Savannah, Teddy." They looked at each other and laughed.

Roni slugged Mac's arm and whispered, "You owe me a Coke."

Before his mother could respond, Teddy stretched out his arm to shake hands with Mac, and then Roni, before blurting, "Miss Darling, Mr. Mac, what's the difference between a guitar and a fish?"

Roni looked down at him. "Don't know. What's the difference, Teddy?"

"You can't tuna fish." He bent over laughing.

"Okay, Teddy, follow your sister inside," Mrs. Ross said in the friendliest tone Mac had ever heard her use.

Before Christmas break, she forbade him from speaking to her children. Her gruff persona seemed to have softened.

Mrs. Ross returned her attention to Mac and Roni. "I'm sorry. He received a new joke book for Christmas and tells a joke every time an opportunity arises."

"Hey, I like his jokes," Mac said.

Roni nodded in agreement before she walked off to speak with a parent.

Mrs. Ross straightened her shoulders. "Have you met Dr. Zita? I sat in on the interviews."

"No, I haven't."

Mac observed the man he presumed to be the interim superintendent exit the school, greet the children and when their paths crossed pat them on their backs. He wore a tailored suit, and his gray hair was cut high and tight. He thought, *He has money. Maybe ex-military?*

"Dr. Zita," Mrs. Ross waved her hand for him to join her. "I want you to meet School Marshal MacKenna and Roni Darling."

Roni must have heard her name because she stopped talking to parents and scampered to where Mac stood.

Dr. Zita had a firm handshake.

"Please, call me Victor."

Roni nodded to everything Victor said as he rattled off his resume. Years of experience. Changes he'd like to make. Her nodding stopped when he said he'd observed needed improvements.

Mrs. Ross continued to listen with stars in her eyes.

Grateful for the distraction, Mac felt a familiar tug on his pant leg. He looked down and was met with Jillian's gaze. His first-grade pal took a liking to him at the beginning of the previous semester.

"Hi, Mr. Mac. Happy New Year." She smiled, revealing she'd lost a bottom front tooth during the break.

"Hello, Jillian. Happy New Year to you too."

Mac nudged Jillian toward the school entrance. "Have a good day, Jillian."

Victor extended his hand to shake again. When Mac grasped his hand, Victor pulled him close. He whispered, "I understand there was some trouble between you and my predecessor. You stay out of my way. I'll stay out of yours. And we'll get along with no problems."

He released Mac's hand and turned away joining Mrs. Ross, already on her way inside.

"What did he say?" Roni nodded toward Victor.

"Nothing important."

One by one, parents pulled their cars forward rolling to a stop along the curb to drop off kids and departed in an orderly manner. Mac didn't miss the disruption Mr. Jackson's behavior caused to everyone's morning last semester. Always scolding Kevin in front of everyone.

Mr. Jackson's sister-in-law Jane Ramsey—Kevin's legal guardian drove up in her sister Susan's car to drop off her nephew. Kevin blew past Mac as if he were invisible. Mac nodded at Jane, and she reciprocated with a smile.

The perpetually late parents rushed to get their children inside before the tardy bell. It rang as the stragglers sprinted through the front door.

Roni couldn't hang around. She hurried to make her class at the college.

Available now at www.robinlyons.com as well as wherever you purchase or borrow books.

ROBIN'S READER CLUB

Learn more about Mac MacKenna in **MAC: A Prequel Novella**. The ebook is a FREE gift when you join Robin's Reader Club.

Reader Club members are automatically included in FREE curated, membership only bookish giveaways. Because of sweepstakes laws and shipping cost, most giveaways (not all) are only available to USA residents. Robin's family members are not eligible for drawings.

Email addresses are never shared. Robin values your privacy as much as hers.

Join the club on the website at: www.robinlyons.com

AUTHOR'S NOTE

A few years ago, I ran for and was elected to the school board in my hometown. Small town politics was enlightening. Six years into the school board position an employee gunned down a beloved principal in his office during the school day. He didn't survive. The loss felt by the school district and community was tremendous. This traumatic event, my work experience, and my true-crime research provide inspiration for my stories.

The Marshal Series began as my way to raise awareness about crimes occurring at schools. Since more books have been added to the series, the main character, Mac, has evolved and become more active in protecting the community as a whole.

I've had the pleasure to work with many outstanding teachers and school staff. And I've met many awesome parents, and watched amazing children grow and succeed. Nothing I write is in any way meant to cast doubt that public schools provide a quality education. When I write about school students, parents, and/or staff, I write about the 1% who have ill intent.

Thank you for reading my book.

-Robin

ABOUT THE AUTHOR

Robin Lyons lives in Northern California with her husband and family.

Close to thirty years working in public education and the tragic loss of a colleague to workplace violence provided inspiration for the Marshal Series.

Connect with Robin on her website or through social media, she responds as fast as possible to posts, tweets, messages, or email.

WEBSITE: www.RobinLyons.com
BOOKBUB: https://www.bookbub.com/profile/robin-lyons
FACEBOOK:
https://www.facebook.com/robinlyons.author
GOODREADS:
https://www.goodreads.com/robin_lyons
INSTAGRAM:
https://www.instagram.com/robinlyons_author/
PINTEREST: https://www.pinterest.com/robinlyons/
TWITTER: https://twitter.com/2RobinLyons

ALSO, IN THE MARSHAL SERIES.
UNKNOWN EVENT
BOOK 3

This famous quote by Origen captures the essence of Unknown Event, "The power of choosing good and evil is within the reach of all."

Mac MacKenna, retired USAF Pararescue, expected students and staff to return to Blackstone Academy after spring break relaxed and ready to ride out the end of the school year. He didn't expect to find an honor student dead on the first day back to school.

After another death is linked to the academy, the police chief calls on Mac also assist in the investigation.

The school board thought Mac had taken care of the criminal activity at the school, but now with a suspicious death on the campus, the parents are demanding answers from the school board members and the interim superintendent.

Who would murder presumably innocent children for no apparent reason? It's up to Mac and the Brookfield PD to take down a killer before someone else dies.

Evil wears many faces.

A Mystery/Thriller based on disturbing reality.

Available now at www.robinlyons.com as well as wherever you purchase or borrow books.